Called to a crime scene when a terrified woman raises the alarm on a horrifying murder, Detective Hosea Elgin finds the victim's body has been dismembered with professional precision.

Very quickly, two small-time drug dealers are identified as the probable assailants and a manhunt is launched to bring them into custody.

With the two suspects on the run, the consequences of their actions continue to spiral out of control and it becomes clear that while one of them is focused on survival, the other wants only revenge.

As the net begins to tighten on the fugitives, Detective Elgin finds that the case begins to move very close to home and what began as just another murder investigation is developing into something much more personal.

The decisions he makes and the actions he takes may well solve the case and bring the criminals to justice, but in the process he might just tear his family and his church to pieces.

D09970111

# The Butcher's Prayer

This edition first published 2020 by Fahrenheit
Thirteen, an imprint of Fahrenheit Press.

ISBN: 978-1-914475-16-0

10 9 8 7 6 5 4 3 2 1

www.Fahrenheit-Press.com

F 4 E

# The Butcher's Prayer

## By

## Anthony Neil Smith

## Fahrenheit Thirteen

*An Imprint of Fahrenheit Press*

*Also by Anthony Neil Smith and published by Fahrenheit 13*

- *Slow Bear*

- *Trash Pandas*

*This book is dedicated to our three beloved French Bulldogs: Idgie (who inspired Pecan), Jada (our one-eyed rescue), and my bestest buddy of them all, Herman C. Smith. All three were our wonderful friends, and have all now passed on. RIP*

# CHAPTER 1

*June 8th, 1996*

Forgiveness was out of the question. Not after what he'd done.

No matter he'd been filled with the Holy Ghost, spoken in tongues, washed in the sweet blood of the Lamb.

Rodney Goodfellow was fucked.

Four in the morning. He fled the scene in his pickup soon as they saw the girl had escaped. He left Charles behind. Let him find his own way out.

Blood on Rodney's clothes. His tools abandoned in Charles' garage on a vinyl boat cover, where they'd done the work once the meeting went bad.

Rodney's truck was steamy, no A/C. His glasses fogged up. He rolled down the window. The June air on the Mississippi coast rushing by at seventy miles per hour was as cool as it was going to get all day. Most of his sweat was from fear, though.

They were coming for him. Bet the call had already gone out: Rodney's name, description, make and model of the truck. Armed and dangerous? He was neither, but that's what they'd tell all those cops out there, itchy with adrenaline.

Supposed to go different. Supposed to be a simple negotiation.

Charles' fault. Charles had pulled the trigger. Charles had ended the man's life. All Rodney did was…

So, yeah, no forgiveness. God himself was like, "Dude, sick."

Rodney should've never called Charles in the first place. Used to be thick as thieves, through high school and after, smoking dope, meth, and popping pills.

Then Rodney cleaned up his act, joined the church, married a Godly woman – Rachel, his pastor's daughter – and had a couple gorgeous kids. But he'd started to backslide and take her with him.

Rachel had enough. Kicked him out two days ago. Rodney didn't think this was *the end*. He figured they'd get back together, talk it out, make promises, forget the fight ever happened.

Plenty of other couches to surf, but no, it was Charles. He lived in his grandmother's house, left to him in the will. The back yard sloped down to the bayou, but nothing fancy. A seventies ranch-style.

The first night, plenty of beer and weed, talking about back in the day, laughing. Nothing to it. He would wait for Rachel to calm down, call her the next day.

She didn't pick up the phone.

Charles was all, "Sure, as long as you need, bruh. My home for my homie, you feeling me?"

Charles, a redneck if there ever was one, was fascinated by rap and gangsta culture. Racist to the core, but he wanted so bad to fit in with blacks.

Charles also said, "Got Burt driving over tonight. He wants to collect."

Burt was a guy in Houston they'd bought a shit-ton of pills from. They were going to split them up and sell them, settle with the guy later. But both of them had gotten lazy, and Charles was popping too many. Burt wanted the money he was owed and the leftover pills. Charles had been putting him off for a month.

"You got my back?"

Rodney didn't get it. "Sure. Yeah. Always."

"Getting tired of his bullshit, man."

"Are you good for it? I don't have enough for my half."

"Let me worry about that."

Charles' sharp-lipped grin made Rodney uneasy.

2

Rodney went on to work. Turned a side of beef into steaks, roasts, and ground chuck. The smell of blood seeped one day deeper into his skin.

Came back to Charles' place, tried Rachel again. Nothing.

Shit, it was serious this time. A pit in his stomach. He missed the kids awful bad, thought about driving over to the house, apologize face-to-face, but three beers and two hours of *Cops* reruns kept him glued to the couch.

Charles was cranked up, *way* up. Loud, restless, in and out of the room all night. He'd never noticed how Charles acted when he was cranked, because Rodney was cranked along with him. Not this time. Beer would do.

Nighttime. Closing in on eleven o'clock. Outside, a couple of doors slammed. Out the front window, Rodney spied a nice Audi convertible parked behind his own shitty F-150. Burt and a girl walked up the driveway. Guy had brought a girl along. Jesus.

Knock on the door. Ushered in. Then all four of them were standing in Charles' kitchen, the sticky linoleum squeaking when they fidgeted.

Burt, tanned and dressed for a beach party in flip-flops and cargo shorts, said, "What's it going to be? I've let you slide long enough."

Charles, *definitely* flying, did a song and dance. "You guys want a beer?"

"I don't have time for a beer."

"You sure? Wanna smoke with us?"

"Do you have the money?"

Charles patted his shorts and t-shirt up and down. "I don't have it all on me. Come on. How about two hundred? What will two get me?"

A laugh. "Wasting my time. I fucking told you. I drive all this way…goddamn it."

Rodney leaned over, whispered to Charles, "What are you doing?"

The girlfriend was also tanned and ready for a party, but

not here. No neon, no bar with bright fruity drinks, no techno. She was out of her element in super-short cut-offs, a neon yellow tank top, strappy sandals. Bored.

"Believe me, sorry about this. How about next week?" Charles shrugged. *Pretty please.*

"Three grand? You'll find three grand in a week when you haven't been able to do it in a month? That's what you're telling me? Are you going to take out a loan?" Burt nudged his girlfriend. "Win the lottery?"

"I'm good for it, yo. Come on, you guys. Let's all settle down and smoke a little. Let's party." He eyed the girlfriend up and down. "How about you? Up for it?"

"Ew. No." The girlfriend pulled languidly at Burt's arms. "Let's go."

"It's business, baby."

"These guys are gross."

Gross? She called them gross? Sure, Rodney didn't have the coolest hairstyle. No need to change what worked. He'd never swapped his blocky, metal-framed glasses because his prescription was pretty thick and these were comfortable. He was no turn of the century fashion plate, but the joke would be on all these suckers when the Lord returned and raptured the church up to Heaven right after Y2K.

He wanted to smack her backhanded, but wouldn't. He'd never hit a woman. No matter how many times they'd laughed at him, goofed on him, said, "God, no," to his face. He'd slink off, thinking of all the things he might do if he had a spine.

The girl watched him, twisted her lip.

Burt stepped up, cupped Rodney's chin and cheeks in his hand and turned his head towards him. "Hey, you. Got some sort of idea in your head? About my girl?"

"Dude, please."

"No, come out with it. What were you thinking?"

Rodney tried to shake his head out of Burt's grasp. Burt held on tighter. Smiled.

"Nothing. Wasn't nothing."

Burt nodded, let go. "Goddamn right it was nothing."

Should have been the end of it.

Then Charles, goddamn it, Charles had to go and pull a gun.

Laughed about it. "Hey, bitch, how about now? You want to party now? If I hold this to your head, you think it would still be gross to suck my dick? Huh?"

A cheap nine millimeter, easy to buy, easy to get rid of. Popular among the gangbangers who couldn't afford Glocks yet. Rodney wanted no part of it. He wanted to go home, hug the kids.

The girl flinched. "Shit, Burt!"

Rodney was all, "I'm sorry. He didn't mean to—"

"Hey, don't apologize to them." Charles straight-armed the gun, waving it from Burt's face to the girl's. "They should be groveling right now. On your knees."

Burt, palms up. "Let's all calm down here. We don't want anyone getting hurt, right? It's only money. Let's talk about it some more."

"Give me two weeks. I promise, my half in two weeks," Rodney said.

Burt nodded. "Okay, okay, I can live with it. Thank you." Turned his face to Charles. "Now, let's take it easy. Stay cool, and we'll be on our way. I can call you about this later."

Charles took a step forward, planted the gun against Burt's chest, screwed it in. "I *said* on your knees."

A glance at the girl, crouching but still standing.

"Okay, okay." Bert went down on one knee, then the other.

Charles kept the gun on him.

"Alright, I'm down. I'm sorry. I don't *need* the money. We can work it out some other time."

Charles sneered down the sights. "No. I'm tired of this shit."

He fired. Hollowpoints. Three times.

Ringing ears. Pain.

Streams of blood and heart and lungs from the exit wounds.

Charles grabbed the girl, turned her around, and clamped his hand over her mouth before she could start screaming.

Dragged her out of the kitchen, down the hall.

Rodney followed.

Charles' bedroom – an unmade mattress on the floor, piles of dirty clothes. A Nintendo hooked up to a big brick of a TV. The girl struggled, but Charles kept hold of her, lifting her off her feet, headed toward the closet. The door was open. This closet was where he stashed the drugs. He'd put a Master Lock on it. He threw her in and slammed the door before she could start clawing at him. Rammed the lock into place and stood back, winded. The closet muffled her screams, thank God.

Rodney rubbed his hands over his face. "Jesus, what was that? What the hell was that?"

"About had it with this fool. I didn't know he was bringing the bitch with him."

"You planned this?"

Charles sniffed. "Weeks, now, he's been messing with me. Disrespecting me. Had to teach him some manners."

He stalked out of the bedroom, leaving Rodney with the screaming girl beating on the door. "Please? Please?"

Rodney closed his eyes, tuned it out. "Would you calm down already?"

Back in the kitchen, Charles stood over his prey as the body bled all over the linoleum. Dark red, nearly black, spreading across earthy beige and brown. "Look at his stupid face. His stupid scared face."

Rodney stared into Burt's unblinking eyes. Slack mouth.

"When they ask, tell them it was self-defense."

Rodney lifted his chin. "What?"

"The truth, bro. You saw it. He forced me."

Self-defense wasn't going to fly. Neither of them were smart enough to pull it off. And how many of the neighbors heard the shots? This was bad. Real bad.

Charles said, "What are we going to do?"

Rodney whipped his head around. "We? *We?*"

"You're part of this. Don't even think you're innocent, boy."

6

"Are you insane? I didn't shoot anybody! I told him I'd pay him back. All I wanted was to sleep on your couch a couple days."

"So, what are you telling me?"

"Shit, I don't know." Rodney stepped back, away from the spreading blood.

"We get a gun, put it in his hand. Self-defense."

"What about the girl?"

"What about her?"

"Fuck's sake – "

"No, listen. We keep her quiet. Tape her mouth, give her Xanax. Cops won't even know she's here. By the time they figure it out, we'll be long gone anyway."

Long gone? Rodney didn't want to be long gone. Not without Rachel and the kids. "Seriously, this isn't happening. I've got to call Rachel."

He headed for the cordless phone on the kitchen counter, but Charles got in his way.

"We don't call anyone until we've got this set up the way we want. You owed him money. You were here when it happened. You know good and well those pills are half yours. You're screwed as much as me, unless we do it right."

Rodney paced the kitchen. He imagined Rachel's expression when he told her.

She'd understand, right? Of course she would. She'd forgive him. He should haul ass out of here, call Nine One One, throw himself at the mercy of the Moss Point Police Department. That would make him a good man. A *real* good man. One Rachel could be proud of.

Then he imagined the other side of the coin flip. No mercy from the cops. Guilty guilty guilty.

Rachel, a sour expression across a prison table in a sweaty visiting room. Rodney would watch his kids grow up from behind barbed-wire, and later a photo every now and then once Rachel stopped bringing them along. Until she didn't bother coming herself anymore. Until he received the divorce papers in the mail, a little sticky arrow pointing out where to sign. All because he couldn't leave well enough alone.

Talk about wishful thinking. Probably wouldn't survive his first week. They'd call him a rat. He'd be the daily special on the menu at Parchman, the infamous state pen. *Won't last a day* is what some lifer might say, but of course Rodney would last more than a day because the predators liked to play with their kills first.

"What are we going to do? Jesus Christ, what are we going to do?"

Charles lifted Burt's legs. "Help me take him out to the bayou. Let the gators have him."

"Are you serious?" Rodney held his hands to his temples, fighting the throbbing. "Oh, man, oh, man, shit."

"Why not? Get him under the arms. No one will know he was ever here."

"You think the gators will eat him whole?"

Charles dropped the legs. Gun still in his hand. "Then what? You're so smart, what?"

It should've stopped there. Rodney should have called the police. So what if it got him into some trouble? Better than *this*. This was accessory to murder. The girlfriend? Kidnapping. Spiraling out of control. He should've called the cops and said it was all Charles' fault and take what was coming.

But Charles was right. He was already in too deep. Might as well have pulled the trigger himself. On the Law & Order shows, they gave reduced sentences if one person told them everything first. They would *have* to believe him over Charles, right?

Jail meant no wife, no kids, no privacy, no peace. No *teeth*. No place to hide in jail. No place to run.

Then what about Charles? Like he was even going to let Rodney pick up the phone. Like he wasn't jonesing to pull the trigger, watch another man die, even one of his best friends.

Rodney had an idea.

A terrible idea.

Now, the interstate ahead, dark. Rodney knew daylight would creep in soon, and he would be easy pickings for the law. He wondered if there were any highway patrol troopers lying in wait along the shoulder of the road. He was amped. Hard to keep it under the speed limit.

Deep, deep breaths. It didn't work. Nothing could calm him down.

Getting some cash from an ATM would leave a trail. Same with getting gas on a credit card. The gauge said he had half a tank. How far would it stretch? New Orleans to the west, Pensacola to the east.

What would he do once he was there? He didn't know anyone. Born and raised on the Gulf Coast, what was left of his real family was here, but most wouldn't welcome him in. Too many burned bridges.

Rachel?

His cheeks burned. How could he think of dragging her into this? The kids. Not yet.

A flash: Burt's dead face. Eyes wide open.

Another flash: the feel of the fat and muscle between his fingers.

All he wanted to do was get on with his life, try to get Rachel back, get tight with church again. Getting the Holy Ghost had been about as glorious as chasing the dragon. No, it had been better.

But all the stuff after that, about being good and doing all this work for the church, unpaid, sucked. Being good meant eyes were on you all the time. Jesus', yeah, but also everyone from the church, waiting for you to stumble.

A flash: the sound of Burt's shoulder popping out of its socket.

He pounded the steering wheel. "Fuck!"

Tears in his eyes. Burning.

Where could he go?

Reminded him of a hymn: *Where could I go but to the Lord? Seeking a refuge for my soul.*

He hummed along. Broke down into heavy sobs. Eased off

the interstate, but the shoulder was soft and the tires slid into a ditch, knee deep in stagnant water.

There was only one person he could go to now.

It was a risk. Might get turned away?

Rodney had to try.

He checked the center console. There were a few quarters, some dimes and nickels. Enough for a phone call. Not too far a walk to this Circle K he knew was around here.

Yeah.

Rodney tossed his keys to the floorboard as water began to seep into the passenger side. He climbed out and started down the road.

One face in his mind, one voice.

CHAPTER 2

Not yet sun-up, Detective Hosea Elgin pulled to the curb a
few houses down from the house flocked by Moss Point
Police cruisers, a seventies brown-brick ranch-style with a
patchy front yard and a screen door with cardboard where the
screen should've been.

Hosea climbed out of his car and unfurled. Six-feet-five,
lanky. Dressed to the nines in a beige three-button suit, a light
blue shirt, and a snazzy yellow-and-navy-striped tie. His
blonde hair was gelled back, fashionably messy. He was
looking good. He knew it. Might as well dress for the job same
as for Sunday School.

He said a silent prayer, not for the victim so much as
himself, because he'd been told this was a bad one. Hands in
his pockets, he walked up the driveway. Patrol cops had strung
up tape and hung a sheet shielding the inside of the garage, lit
up like a movie set, shadows moving behind it.

The real action was coming from the backyard. Folks in
hazard suits coming and going through an open gate on the
chain-link fence.

Hosea headed over. Nodded at a few cops he knew.
Through the gate, the yard was overgrown but a good size.
Cypress trees grew along the bank of the bayou creating a
thick canopy, flashlight beams flicking around underneath.
Spanish moss hung from the branches. There were crickets
chirruping, frogs croaking, and the chatter of uniformed
police officers doing the dirty work.

He walked down to the bayou, the ground getting softer,
wetter. Some trees barely hung on by their roots as the water
eroded the soil. He wished he hadn't worn his Gucci loafers.

Those things needed to last him a lifetime.

Cops and forensics people stood in the water, up to their knees with fishing nets on long poles. They swatted at the surface to keep small alligators away. Lots of retching. One of the cops waded back into the yard and dumped a pile of something awful on top of another, larger pile of something awful set aside on a tarp. The smell rolling off it was death – Hosea knew it well – but more like a dead thing spoiled out in the sun, a tang to it that made his stomach gurgle. He pulled out a handkerchief and covered his mouth and nose, but it didn't help much.

The victim was literally meat and bones, wet and slimy. Another cop waded in. Another heap of flesh and fat, this time with a bone sticking out of it.

"Hey Preacher." A voice from behind him. His nickname. Of course it was. He usually played it off, but yeah, it stung every time.

Hosea turned. A beefy patrol cop named Lydia Hunter waved him up the hill. "Porter wants you up here."

"Fine with me. You been down there?"

"Worst I've ever seen."

"You said it. I've seen people burned up, seen gunshots, shotgun suicides, drownings, and some sat around dead too long. But this?"

"A full-on butchering. Hell is too good for whoever did this."

Lydia impressed Hosea plenty. She was built like a brickhouse, or a linebacker. Hair pulled back tight. Took no shit from anybody. On weekends, she put on her cowboy hat and boots and moseyed on down to rodeos and honky tonks.

She led him to the garage. Inside, a powerful light made him squint while flashbulbs popped. It was a tight fit around an algae-stained fishing boat. The forensic folks did their thing. As far as Hosea was concerned, they were magicians. The problem was good magic took a long time, and he had murderers to catch. Most of what he did while waiting for lab results was ask a ton of questions to plenty of people, hoping one of them might say the right thing at the right time. You know – police work.

Once his eyes adjusted, there was the decapitated and delimbed torso on the ground. His stomach fluttered. Knives and saws scattered on the garage floor. Reminded him of something, someone. The Sergeant, Porter Broussard, caught Elgin's eye and nodded him outside.

Hosea stepped out, swallowed some fresh air and then leaned over, hands on his knees. Broussard was right behind him.

"Jesus," the Sarge said.

"Ain't that right? Have you ever—"

"Not like this. Never like this."

"How about down there?" Hosea pointed his chin towards the bayou.

"Worst I've ever seen."

Broussard filled him in on the timeline. The girlfriend had escaped, ran to the neighbors, and luckily got someone to open up. They said she was hysterical. With good reason. When the cops arrived, the current tenant of the home was gone. The victim's car was gone, and then there was another guy the girlfriend mentioned. She didn't know his name. She said there had been a truck outside. It was gone, too.

"Our guys got here, cleared the house, found parts of him in the garage, and went searching for the rest of him. I don't think we got it all. The gators and crabs got him first."

"Got a name?"

"According to the girlfriend, he was Burt Layman. They're both from Houston. The girl says he drove over to collect a debt. No idea what it was all about."

"Drove over? That's eight hours at least."

"I'll take her word for it now, but his wallet is gone."

"Venture a guess?"

"I'm guessing it's all the pills and weed we found in the bedroom closet."

Couple of magicians and the photographer exited the garage. Hosea and Broussard stepped inside for a closer look.

13

All quiet except for the buzzing lights. The smell grew thicker. Bits of flesh and gristle all over the blades of knives and saws, the kind a real butcher uses, one at the meat counter. Hosea crossed his arms tight, watched his feet. Careful to avoid blood on the concrete, blood on the tarp. *Really* shouldn't have worn the Gucci loafers.

What was he thinking when he put those on?

Probably thinking about seeing Dawn Hollingsworth later, how he wanted to look good for their lunch date. She was a singer in the church, the first woman he'd had the nerve to ask out in a long while. Now he wondered if he would even get a lunch break.

"Where's your partner?" Broussard asked.

"Day off."

"Lucky her."

Theirs was a small department, only two detectives right now plus a want ad hardly anyone had answered. They needed all the help they could get – casinos moving in down the road in Biloxi, Gulfport, then the drugs and robbing and killing followed right behind, oozing into the surrounding cities.

Moss Point was a sleepy Gulf Coast town clinging to the side of the slightly larger Pascagoula, known for its shipyard, rumored to be on its way out. Mostly black, mostly low-income, mostly out of hope. But it was home for Hosea, had been for most of his life after his dad gave up missionary work in Africa to come here and start his own church. A white church in a black town. Pastor Elgin would rather have people of all races worshipping together, but that wasn't how it worked here, way down South. One of the old man's biggest disappointments, besides his younger son's fall from grace.

"So," Broussard said. "We've got two guys on the run. One of them rents this house – Charles Lott, twenty-four. He's the shooter. The other, we don't have a name for yet. The girl described him as nerdy-looking. He had those metal glasses, you know. The ones serial killers wear."

"She said that?"

"Almost word for word."

"What else?"

"She wasn't in good shape. Go talk to her at the hospital."

Hosea nodded absently. "My brother-in-law wears those glasses."

"I'm sure a lot of people still do."

"He's a butcher at Lee's Groceries." Hosea pointed at the knives and saws.

"Coincidence?"

"Oh, yeah, absolutely." Hosea stared at the body and imagined what it would take to do something so gruesome to a person. Tried to imagine Rodney doing it.

Unnerving.

"Give me a few minutes."

Hosea drifted out. It was bothering him, a real butcher having done this. Rodney might've been a weirdo, might've run with a rough crowd before joining the church. Menial jobs, no ambition. Small-time drug slinging on the side. Then he met Hosea's younger sister Rachel, and the next thing everyone knew, this guy was beside her in church, then getting baptized, then speaking in tongues.

Hosea was there when Rodney proposed to Rachel in front of the congregation at a Valentine's Day dinner. He had flinched, hoping she would say no, then had felt guilty for hoping so.

Rachel didn't say no, and the wedding happened pretty soon after – simple, small – and things were smooth for a long time. Two beautiful children, Hosea's niece and nephew. As far as everyone could tell, Rodney was a great dad. An affectionate husband. It took a couple more years before the signs pointed towards backsliding – Rodney growing out his hair, beer and cigarettes on his breath, cable TV at their house. Rodney began to skip church as much as Hosea did, so his dad said, as did Rachel, which was a shock. He had never expected *anyone* to sweep her out.

It was a familiar story, though. After all, living a Pentecostal lifestyle wasn't easy. It took a lot of sacrifice and clean living. It took being under the microscope all the time.

He pulled his cell phone from his pocket. These new ones were smaller than the last generation, but it still felt like carrying a brick in his pants. Rung Rachel.

"Hello?" Obviously awoken from sleep.

"Hey, it's Hosea. Can I talk to Rodney? I need to talk to him."

Quiet for a moment too long. Then, "Why?"

"Wake him up, please. Hand him the phone."

"Tell me what's going on."

"Is he there?"

"Who told you?"

This wasn't going as well as he'd hoped. "Who told me what?"

"We had a little fight."

"What, Rachel?"

"I kicked him out. Not forever, only a few nights."

"Where is he now?"

"Hosea—"

"*Where?*"

Silence.

"Rachel?"

"Don't tell Dad."

Hosea turned to the bayou, cops still adding to the pile of human debris. "Where is Rodney right now?"

"I don't know. With some friends? I don't know."

"Which friends?"

"I don't know! I never met his friends! I don't know who he knows, that was all before he met me."

Hosea closed his eyes. Nauseated. "You're sure he didn't go to Dad? Or Glen?" Their older brother, their dad's right-hand-man at the church.

"What's going on, Hosea?"

"He hasn't called you?"

"Tell me!"

"I can't. It might be nothing. If you hear from him, call me right then and there."

He hung up. His phone rang again immediately, Rachel

calling back, but he didn't answer. He stared into the garage, the light reminding him of Christ's empty tomb, those Easter paintings where sun is beaming out of the cave. This time the dead guy wouldn't be walking out.

It couldn't be. This was dumb. Rodney was probably at his own dad's house, across the border in Alabama. Some predictable shit.

But they had a real dead man in pieces in the garage. Nothing predictable about that.

Hosea found the Sarge. "The girlfriend, she said there was a truck, right?"

"Right."

"Did she give you any details?"

"Only it was white."

Hosea wrinkled up his face. "Aw, goddamn it."

"What?"

Could he say it? Was it too early? Broussard blinking, waiting for an answer. It sounded ridiculous.

"My brother-in-law drives a white truck. I don't believe this."

Broussard nodded. Didn't say a word.

With the sun now rising above the horizon, there would be more neighbors up and down the street flocking to get a closer gawk. The more time passed, the farther away these murderous fuckers might run.

He dialed his partner, Tara Killebrew, for a rude awakening. Told her to meet him at the hospital.

It was going to be a long day.

# CHAPTER 3

So, what happened was this.

Burt's blood going cold on the linoleum in the kitchen.

Charles making threats. Rodney's balls in a vice.

Rodney said, "What if…"

The picture in his head, thinking about what he did eight hours a day. Hack. Slice. Grind. Over and over. Numb to the fact the side of beef on the hook, on his table, had once been a living, breathing creature.

Peering down at Burt, what was he except another slab of meat? Same as any of us, when you got right down to it.

Charles, hands on his hips. "Yeah?"

"Know how you said throw him in the bayou?"

"You want to?"

"But listen. What if, like, he was all cut up? Little pieces, ones the gators wouldn't have such a hard time with?"

"Sick, man. Some sick shit right there. I ain't doing that."

"You're not thinking, goddamn it. We've got to get rid of him, like he was never here." Leaving the next part unsaid: *Her, too.*

In the heat of the moment, Rodney only thinking of getting back to Rachel and the kids, this was the easiest way. Go up to the store, grab his tools, break Burt down into steaks and chops. Filet the bones. If he didn't think too hard, didn't look at Burt's face. This was doable.

Charles swore he could do it. "This is stupid. You're like the devil."

"*You're* the one that shot him!"

"Yeah, but – "

"No, I'm telling you. It's either we call the cops, and they get the story from the girl, which sure as hell ain't the same as ours, or make this all go away. Fast."

"Aw, homes." Charles buzzing, still way up there. "I won't do it. The cutting, I won't."

"I'm going to need help. You're gonna have to help some."

"Like what?"

Rodney shrugged. The smell of Burt shitting his pants, pissing himself, bleeding out, getting all up in his nose. "I give you a trash bag. We fill it up, you go down and empty it at the water. Can you do that?"

Charles danced in place, a boxer, fists up and ready. Puffing tough guy breaths. "Yeah, okay, yeah, I can do it. Let's go! We can do this! Fuck yeah!"

Rodney grabbed his truck keys. The grocery store where he worked was in Pascagoula. Ten minutes there, ten back. Shouldn't be no one around to notice him, slow him down. Easy peasy.

He headed for the door. Charles said, "Hey, wait."

Rodney stopped, stared straight ahead.

"You better not be bullshitting me. You better not go running off."

Rodney hadn't thought about it until right then. Why not, right? Go home, call the cops, face the music. They'd believe him, right? And Rachel's brother was a cop. Used to be a preacher before he got caught slipping his holy cock into a married woman's holy pussy. Now he was a detective. Had to be a good thing, right? They hadn't gotten along all that warm and cozy, but that shouldn't matter. He was still family, sort of.

Think, though: they'd still get him on the drugs. And Charles would get his say, which might tack on another couple of charges. He couldn't afford bail. Rachel's family sure as fuck couldn't, the brothers sinking what little money they had into their wardrobes, striking an appearance they were more well-off than they actually were.

Rodney gave Glen a pass. He and Glen used to be pretty tight. Glen was cool, for a preacher.

Rodney forgot how long he'd been standing there,

rethinking things, until Charles picked up the ratty little gun from the counter and lifted it in Rodney's direction.

"Jesus, bro!"

"You swear you're coming back? No joke?"

Going to the cops, shit, even if he did have family…taking a chance, man. Throw of the dice.

"I swear. I wouldn't lie to you, man."

Charles was buzzing all over, a moth on a lightbulb. "You'd better not."

"I said I swear."

"Alright, then."

Rodney got his ass out of there.

Quick drive to the store. Lee's Grocers had been there going on forty years, starting to wear its age. Not many parking lot lights left, should've been replaced. Some flickering. Rodney parked around by the loading bay. There was an easy way into the back, they all knew about it. At some point or other, they'd all needed to come in after hours, take a "sample" – a sample bottle of ketchup until pay day, or a sample load of bread, or a pound of ground chuck. A sample tall boy Bud, sample pack of Marlboros. Every once in a while. Any more, it might get noticed.

No one else was there this late. This was past the end of Market Street, where all the high school kids cruised up and down. He could hear some of their horns when he climbed down from his truck. Used to be him. Pile your friends into whoever had their parents' car that weekend, troll down to Highway 90, turn around outside Ed's Drive-In, then all the way back to the seawall, seek out other friends or trouble in the parking lots. Good times, man.

Burt's stupid face.

Made Rodney flinch, check over his shoulder.

Just get this done.

Back there behind the meat counter, he picked up the tools of his trade. Knives, saws, a cleaver, snips and hooks, all in one set. Nice and sharp. Cold in here. The smell of blood, never going away, was hardly masked under the smell of bleach. They scoured the place every morning, then every night.

He set down his knives and placed his hands flat on the cutting table. Thick wood, scarred by decades of blades gouging, slicing, stabbing. Rumor was they'd be getting a stainless steel replacement soon. It wouldn't be the same.

He thought it would've been a lot easier to bring Burt here, like a side of pork. A whole hog. Do what needed to be done, wash the gore down the drain, and stack the meat in the walk-in – ribs, roasts, steaks. Spritz the bleach, wipe it all down. Who would know?

The bones, the head, hands and feet, no need to worry about them right away. Put them in a black trash bag, toss them in the bed of the pick-up, and nobody would ever pay them any mind. Every good old boy had a black trash bag of empty beer cans in their truckbeds.

Rodney shuddered. How did he even imagine such a thing? A rational man didn't do that, sit around dreaming up ways to get rid of a body. This was his first – fuck's sake he hoped his *only*. He hoped for some sort of Godly beam of light, or the soft voice of Jesus, or Holy Ghost fire, what he saw in church all the time, to come down and shout, *Stop! Don't do it, my son!*

But he didn't see, hear or feel a goddamned thing.

This was God's payback for him doing it all for Rachel instead of for his own soul. He had joined her Pentecostal church, spoken in tongues, danced in the spirit – he was *saved*! Anything and everything he could do to show how much Rachel meant to him. Flip his whole life upside down. Kept at it for over two years, married the woman, studied the Bible, attended every service, three times a week, twice on Sundays. He became a *father*, which he'd never expected. Loved it.

Still, there was an itchy feeling in the back of his brain – *If she dumped you, would you stay saved? Would you still live for Me?*

Better to change the subject than dwell on it. Wasn't going to happen anyway – he was planning to stick with Rachel for *life*.

But then, old habits crept into his every day doings. The freshness of church had worn off. Rachel started to backslide alongside him, which was a shame. It was her godliness that attracted him in the first place, a preacher's daughter. It was as if she glowed when she smiled. She didn't need anything extra – cigarettes, drugs, alcohol, casual sex – to make her high. Whatever it was giving her such an energy, he wanted it. He wanted *her*.

He started missing church now and then, then more and more. Beer came back first. Then cigarettes, hard booze, pot, in that order. Beautiful shit, man, he'd forgotten how sweet it was to get fucking high. Rodney convinced Rachel to try smoking weed, and she was into it.

Then she abandoned her modest dresses for short-shorts and tight jeans, shirts revealing her midriff. Thick make-up, bright lipstick. She had never cussed much, but now, Jesus, he wished she'd never started, the filth she came out with. He didn't want to share her with the world. Didn't want men leering at her the same way he'd leered at other women – tramps.

It went on, the two of them taking the easy way out. What most Pentecostals would call a sinful lifestyle, the rest of the world called *normal*. If there was any shame, a couple bottles or a couple puffs helped shove it back into the vault.

Rodney would tell you, sure, he still believed, but goddamn, he was having a lot more fun now.

Then, the night Rachel kicked him out, he came home from work to find her crying and praying on the living room floor, begging her God for forgiveness, the kids wondering what they'd done to break their mommy this way.

Holy shit, he thought, what sort of damage had he done to her? What an asshole.

She didn't let Rodney get a word in. She laid down the law and that was that – Here's what's about to change, buddy, and if you won't change, you're not going to like living with me much anymore.

Which led him to say…

Oh, how he wished he could take it back now.

He called her a Holy Bitch. Said she'd rather suck Jesus' dick than her own husband's.

Climbing into his truck, setting the tools on the seat beside him, Rodney flinched. If only she would pick up the phone, he would grovel. He would take it all back. He would give her the respect she deserved. And *of course* he would promise to go back to church, quit the drinking and pot, be an all-around better man.

If only she would pick up the goddamned phone.

Rodney jumped the curb, tires on the grass, and got out, knives in hand.

Kept his eyes straight ahead up the driveway.

He let himself into the house, closed and locked the door behind him. "Charles?"

No answer.

Good. Rodney guessed he'd spent the time getting ready – moving the body, cleaning up.

But he rounded the corner into the kitchen and almost stepped in the blood, Burt still laying wide-eyed in the middle of the kitchen floor.

Some thumping and grunting from the back bedroom. Then, "*You bitch!*"

*No, shit, no.*

Dropped those knives. Sprinted to the bedroom.

He rounded the corner and slid into the doorway. Charles was pushing the girl onto the bed face down by her neck, trying to take her shorts off with his other hand. She was giving him hell, kicking and squirming.

"Jesus, fuck, Charles!"

Charles looked over his shoulder. Nasty grin. "Get out of here."

"Are you serious?"

"I said go, man, unless you want to do her two on one."

"What?"

"As long as you and I don't touch dicks."

Saying this while his arm is all popped muscles, crushing the girl into the mattress.

Rodney stepped over, gave Charles a shove. "Don't do this."

Charles slapped him away. "Fuck you, man. Bullshit."

"We've got to hurry. Shit, we've got to get done before morning."

Charles tore the girl's shorts down to her ankles. Gave her ass a slap and a "Woo!" like Ric Flair.

Fuck it.

Rodney wrapped his arm around Charles' head, a sleeper hold, which accomplished jackshit except Charles' muscles popped more and his face went red.

The girl scrabbled loose from Charles' grip and tried for the door, but he caught her by the ankle and held her in place. She let out a long wail.

Rodney had to choose.

He let go of Charles, straddled the girl's back, and clamped a hand over her mouth. "Not another word. You stay quiet, everything will be –"

But then Charles was on him, slamming a fist into the back of his head.

"Jesus! What are you doing?"

Still going at it.

Rodney ducked, weaved. "Listen to me!"

"You cockblock me? You want to get in my way?"

"Calm down and fucking listen!"

His head throbbed. Charles backed off and paced. A tiger in a cage.

Rodney climbed off the girl, helped her to her feet, and pinned her arms to her side. He walked her back to the closet. She dug her feet into the carpet and pushed back, pleading. He pushed her back inside and locked the door. This time, her spirit was broken. No shouting. No banging.

Rodney rubbed the back of his head. He got in Charles' face. "Shit, that hurt, man."

"If we're going to kill her anyway, when's the next time

we'd get a chance to fuck a specimen fine as this, not the usual skanks? One of the rich, spoiled girls? Once in a lifetime, bro."

Idiot. He had no clue. "We don't want to leave evidence these two ever knew us. What if parts of her survive, and they find your jizz all up in her?"

"Shit, man."

"You know what we've got to do. Don't make it worse."

Charles wouldn't meet Rodney's eyes. "I could go get a couple of condoms."

"I got my knives. Let's get this done."

He should've never come back to the house.

# CHAPTER 4

Tara was waiting for Hosea inside the ER doors. She was impossibly thin, but a voracious eater. Dark-skinned, straightened hair, must have dressed in a hurry. Shorts, sandals, yesterday's thin button up shirt over a tank-top. As per usual, she was underdressed to his overdressed.

And she was pissed.

"Demetrius was so mad, he wouldn't even talk to me." Her husband. They were supposed to go out with some friends on a boat. "One day away was all I wanted."

It was a good thing he caught her before they left. She refused to carry a cell phone and left her beeper at home on off days.

Hosea let her rattle off a few other complaints. "You're a smart one, aren't you? Can't you handle a dead body without me for the day? Are you that incompetent?"

He said, "This girl watched her boyfriend die. They locked her in a closet while they cut the boyfriend into pieces and threw him in the bayou."

"Oh, God."

"You'll see what's left at the morgue."

She lifted her eyebrows, curled her lips. "I should've told you I was sick today."

"Well, you will be. Come on."

He brought her up to speed. The admitting nurse knew them by sight if not by name, and led them back to a curtained corner, a uniformed cop standing guard. This wasn't their first trip to the ER to talk with victims or perps.

They stepped inside to find the girl – Kris Cole – curled on her side, staring at nothing. She sat up, pulled her knees close to her chin.

She was bruised on her arms and around her neck. One eye was purpled. Skin pale in the harsh lights.

They introduced themselves.

"Did you catch them yet?" Exhausted.

"No, but you rest assured we've got every cop between Mobile and New Orleans out there. The more dogs hunting, the better the scent. Trust us."

She didn't look trusting. Instead, she trembled, her feet rubbing together under the blanket, as if the killer might walk in to finish the job at any moment.

"I'm so tired."

Tara eased over to the bedside and gently wrapped her fingers around Kris Cole's arm. "I know you are, and you should be. You were brave. Thanks to you, they're not going to get away with it."

"Burt? He's dead? He's really dead?"

"I'm afraid so."

She didn't fall apart over the news, but it made her shrink further into herself.

"Was he…a boyfriend? A friend?" He didn't want to add, *Your dealer?*

"We hung out, you know? Nothing serious."

Hosea realized she didn't know Burt had been chopped to pieces. He wondered who would be the one to tell her.

Tara squeezed the girl's arm. "You talk to your parents?"

A nod.

"Good. Are they coming to see you?"

Another nod. Tears tracked down her cheeks.

Hosea's turn. "I know you've been over this already, but we need to ask. People remember more each time. Our brains are great about it. You've got all the details up there."

He tapped his temple.

Kris closed her eyes. "But I'm tired."

"I promise a few more questions and we'll let you get some rest."

Another nod.

"The truck your boyfriend parked behind. You said it was white. Do you remember what make it was?"

"I don't remember."

"Try. Try to remember."

"I don't know. I don't—"

"But *try*." Straining a bit. He couldn't lose it already. Questioning people had been his job for years now. Try too hard, and it might make her shut down. But he was getting impatient. "If you had to take a guess?"

"A…oh, I don't know. Ford?" She made an oval in the air. "Is that Ford, the round one?"

*Jesus.*

"Good, good." Lump in the throat.

Tara took over. "Tell us what happened after you got inside. Try to remember every little detail. Don't leave anything out."

She took them through it. What Burt told her in the car, him dropping by to pick up some money he was owed before they headed to Biloxi to party at a casino. Knocking on the door. Meeting in the kitchen. Tough words. The mean guy, then the other one.

"I called them gross. The crazy one got real mad, but Burt got in his face. The ugly guy stopped the crazy one from raping me. He left the closet unlocked, which is how I got away."

"Describe him one more time. Think hard."

"His hair was boring, parted in the middle. You know, a nerd? He wore those old metal glasses, square, with the bar up top." She rubbed her finger between her eyebrows. "He had a soft voice. Didn't blink a lot."

Was it Rodney? She was ticking the boxes, one after the other.

"How did he stop the mean one from raping you?"

The effort of trying to think back took its toll. Hosea hoped she wouldn't wilt away yet. "He was pushing me onto the bed, trying to…you know. The other one came in and pulled him off, told him to leave me alone. But when I tried to run out of the room, he grabbed me and put me back into the closet. I knew it then. They were planning to…"

She swallowed.

"They were going to kill me, too. I know it."

"No one can get to you here. You're safe."

Kris grabbed Hosea's arm. He couldn't pull away. He didn't want to get any dirt or hospital goo on his suitcoat.

"Please, please, don't let them get me."

"No one's going to get you." Tara patted the girl on the head like she was a cat. "You're safe with us. Completely safe."

The girl let go of Hosea and turned to Tara, locking her arms around her, sobbing loudly.

Hosea excused himself, pulled his phone from his pocket. Checked his sleeve. Nothing obviously dirty on it. He took a seat on a doctor's stool out in the middle of all the action, and dialed his father, wishing he didn't have to.

"Hello?"

"Dad."

"Son. Good morning." So formal with his kids. Drove Hosea up the wall.

"Listen, I'm working right now, but tell me – did Rodney stay with you and Glen last night?" Glen was Hosea's older brother, still living at home because he was the assistant pastor of the church. Also because Dad needed the company after their mom died.

"He didn't stay at the house. Why?"

"What about the church?" There was a bedroom for visiting preachers, or the occasional sad sack who needed someplace to stay for a few days.

"I'd have to ask your brother. I don't think he did, though. What's wrong?"

"Please, if he shows up, let me know. Don't tell him I'm looking for him, though."

"Son," The disappointed tone. "Rachel has already called. What is it you're not saying? She's worried sick."

The man was a guilt tripper. A powerful one.

"I can't—"

"You could, but you don't want to. There's a difference." A long pause from Dad. Then, of course, the lecture. "There's God's law and there's Man's law. You represent Man's law, but this is family. Family is God's law."

God's law was a pain in the ass. "I'll drop by later. I'll tell you when I can." He hung up and took a deep breath.

The girl's story wasn't proof. Still no solid evidence. Rodney was probably sleeping off a hangover on his mother's couch. He'd need to call her. He had only met her once, at a church picnic. A pleasant lady. Loud and funny, with what they called a whiskey-stained voice. She obviously didn't think much of the church her son had joined. Friendly enough to them all, but Hosea caught a few eye rolls, a few whispered asides to Rodney, got him ticked off. She was an open book, and that book wasn't the Bible.

The things Hosea had learned about people since becoming a detective far outnumbered those he thought he knew when he was an evangelist.

He pulled out his wallet. He still kept some photos in there, hadn't cleaned it out in a long time. He wondered if he still had…

Yeah, there it was. A pocket-sized shot of the happy couple on their wedding day. Rachel in a simple dress, Rodney in a cheap Sears suit, not a tux. They had wanted a small, quiet affair on a Sunday afternoon right after the service. With Rachel already a couple of months pregnant, Hosea was surprised Dad agreed to marry them at all. The Rodney in this picture was cleaned up, smiling. Not the same man he was these days.

Hosea stepped through the curtains again. Tara was sitting in the bedside chair, holding Kris' hand.

He handed the photo to Kris. "You might need to give it longer, concentrate. I'm sure he doesn't look the same—"

"No, it's him!" The girl's voice rising. "It's him, it's him!"

The uniformed cop peeked in, asked if everything was alright.

"I don't know," Tara said, her eyebrows crinkled. "Hosea, what are you doing?"

Hosea's stomach turned to stone. "Are you sure it's him?"

"Those glasses. I'll never forget those glasses."

"Jesus."

"Hosea?" Tara took the picture from the girl. "This is your sister, isn't it?"

He cleared his throat. "Excuse me." Slipped through the curtain and stood in the middle of all the ER hubbub. It was too dirty, the cleaning staff unable to keep up with the trauma. A garbage can overflowing. The floor scuzzed with dirt, possibly blood. Then the noise – raised voices on so many levels, the beeping machines, the groans and the crying.

A hand on his shoulder made him flinch. It was Tara.

"What the hell happened?"

Hosea couldn't meet her eyes. "It's him. The guy she described. It's my brother-in-law. My fucking *brother-in-law*."

"Are you kidding me? Tell me you're joking."

"He's a butcher at Lee's. He drives a white Ford truck. He wears those glasses."

"Maybe she's wrong. Maybe it's the glasses throwing her off."

"Maybe."

His cell phone rang in all its sing-song digital glory. He pulled it from his pocket, answered.

It was Broussard. "We found the truck."

"A white F-150?"

"The very one." Quiet a moment. "We ran the plates."

"And?"

"Rodney Goodfellow."

He turned to Tara. Her eyes went wide.

"We're on our way."

CHAPTER 5

They drove separately, giving Hosea time to think, headed towards Vancleave, a small town in the woods north of the coast. Lots of people there with lots of land, big country houses. New construction due to "white flight." A shame, especially when it came from people who said they only made the decision after they prayed about it.

"Better for my kids."

Bullshit.

Hard to believe Rodney was…*this*. A butcher. A killer. Even if he wasn't the one who shot the guy, Jesus, what he did to the body. Thinking back to the scene in Charles Lott's yard, Hosea felt acid rise into his throat. Maybe they could still go easy on Rodney if he turned over on the killer. But right now, with both of them in the wind, things did not smell good.

Hosea called the station, told them to send some cruisers to his sister's house, make sure Rodney hadn't tried to sneak back home.

They were never friends. At church, they had sometimes prayed together - Hosea didn't pray much anymore. They called each other "brother" because all the men of the church called each other brother. Before the wedding, Rodney had been one of the front-pew guys. First on their feet to clap for songs, or shout "Amen" at a good line in a sermon. First to run laps around the church or dance in the spirit.

Hosea had drifted to the middle pews after he gave up preaching. Now he sat in the next-to-last row. He never joined in the adrenaline-fueled worship sessions on Sunday nights, but he was still there, watching. Maybe he had lost his faith, and maybe he questioned everything he had taken for granted as he grew up in church, but he could never imagine leaving church for good.

To Hosea's dad, Rodney had been a success story, a life completely transformed by the Holy Ghost. Pastor Elgin had entrusted Hosea's older brother Glen with keeping Rodney in line during those early weeks and months. Keep him learning about the Bible, keep him fired up in services. A shoulder to cry on, a teacher.

Once Rodney began to slip, though, and Dad saw what was happening to Rachel, the man had lost his shine. Hosea knew his dad felt foolish, watching his youngest child, his only daughter, slip from the hands of God.

Hosea needed to call her back.

Fumbled a little, one-handed dialing while trying to drive.

"It's Hosea."

"Are you going to tell me what's going on here? I've got cops pulled up outside, scaring the kids."

Great. "What do you know?"

"Nothing! Not one thing! What is going on?"

"Have you heard from Rodney yet?"

"My God, is he dead? Is that why you won't tell me?" Her volume rose. "No, no, no, please tell me he's not dead."

"He's not dead. Rachel…it's complicated."

She grew quiet.

"I don't want to do this over the phone."

"Hosea, I'm falling apart. The kids. Please."

He told her. The shooting. The butcher's tools. The body. She broke down. "Help me, Jesus. Help me, Jesus."

"We've got to find him. If he tries to get in touch—"

"Hosea, what am I going to do?"

"If he tries to get in touch, let me know immediately. Let the officers there with you know. Trust me, Rachel. We'll find him, and we'll keep him safe."

"The kids! Their father! Tell me it's a mistake." A ragged breath, then quietly, "I *sleep* with that man."

"We'll find him. And we promise we'll listen to his side of

the story."

"Oh my God."

"I've got to go."

He fumbled with the buttons, ending the call, almost swerving into the other lane. How was anyone supposed to drive while talking on one of these things? Mindboggling.

Rachel might have had the roughest go of the three Elgin kids. All were raised deeply engrained in their parents' Pentecostal faith. Only Glen had made it this far without falling away. But the rules for living a holy life were tougher for the women than it was for men: no make-up, no jewelry, no shorts or pants, only long dresses and skirts. Nothing to expose shoulders or cleavage. Never cut your hair. Modesty, modesty, modesty.

After all, when it came to the Bible, it was the sinful woman luring the easily-tricked Godly man in for some dirty fun.

Then Mom died six years ago. Breast cancer. It ripped them all to shreds, but especially Rachel. A girl and her mother.

It very well could be Mom's death that set up Rachel for backsliding into the waiting arms of the world. Hosea had gone wayward much earlier, but catching Rachel red-eyed in a marijuana haze once still filled him with ache. Not his baby sister.

Live and let live.

Broussard and Lydia were waiting for them, along with two highway patrol cruisers, a Sheriff's car, and a tow truck ready to drag the white F-150 pick-up back to one of their stations for inspection. Multiple agencies meant multiple hoops meant a longer day for everyone.

Even before Hosea climbed out of his car, there was no mistaking Rodney's truck. All the dings, the rust spots, the places where heavy metal band logos had been scraped off the back window, replaced with Christian bumper stickers: *Don't Believe in Jesus? That's okay. He Believes in You*, and *In Case of Rapture, This Car Will Be Unoccupied.*

Hosea got out, waited for Tara, then walked over to the others.

First word out of Broussard's mouth: "Blood."

"How much?"

"It's enough. I'm guessing it's not his own."

The front right tire was stuck in the ditch. Filthy knee-deep water, mosquito heaven.

"Did he leave it on purpose?"

"I don't think he was coming back for it. Keys were on the floorboard."

Tara stuck her head inside through the open window. "It stinks."

Hosea stepped behind her, sniffed. "It always stinks. The odor seeped into the seats. The guy's covered in blood all day long. Cows, pigs, chickens."

"And your sister married him anyway?"

A shrug. Hosea turned his head to the South, tried to remember how far the nearest gas station was. Then to the north, same thing. A few miles? He was already sweating after a few minutes in the direct morning sun, hot air rising from asphalt, the smell of exhaust from eighteen-wheelers on the nearby interstate. It had been a long morning. He would need to dry clean this suit pronto.

"So, what's the drill?"

Broussard said, "Spread out through the woods, the swamps, the bayous. Bring in the dogs. A whole lot of folks already on their way here. Roadblocks. A full sweep."

"He's got a head start."

"That's the fun of it," Lydia said. "Makes it sporting."

"A good old-fashioned manhunt."

"The only way a girl like me can catch a man, right?"

"I'd head into the woods with you if I could, but son of a gun, I'm overdressed for the part." Hoesa held his hands out. *What're ya gonna do?*

"You dick."

A while later, Hosea and Tara pulled into the twenty-four hour gas station he remembered and went inside. They asked the cashier a few questions, then flashed Rodney's wedding picture. Hosea needed a better photo to pass around, one more recent. Tara had gotten an old high school picture of Charles Lott. Not the best, but use what you have.

No, the man hadn't seen them. He hadn't been on the night shift. Hosea asked if they could zip through the security tapes recorded between midnight until the cashier started his shift.

It took too long and didn't give them a damned thing. Neither of the suspects came into the store, and the people who used the outside phones were blurry and near the far edge of the screen. Hosea and Tara couldn't make out any details – man, woman, white, black, thin, fat.

Hosea bought a blue raspberry slushie and walked out to his unmarked LTD, leaned on the trunk. Tara pumped gas into her own LTD, then joined him in the sun. The hot metal burned her thighs.

Hosea gave himself brain freeze.

"What next? Talk to Lott's people?"

"Then Rodney's."

"Someone needs to go talk with the girl in the hospital one more time."

"And Rodney's coworkers in the meat department."

"The whole store."

"Don't forget the morgue." Hosea twisted his lips. Tara mimed gagging.

Another slug of slushie. Careful not to overdo it.

"I've got to tell my Dad."

"Shit." Tara ran her toes along a crack in the concrete. "How's he going to take it?"

"No idea."

He hit the bottom of his slushie cup – sucked it right down, hadn't he? More people showed up to get gas, get coffee, get beer. There was always someone getting beer.

"So…do we *have* to go to the morgue?"

"Might as well get it over with. Let's drop off my car first and go together."

"Give me a sec." Hosea pulled his phone from his pocket. Dialed a number he had only recently memorized.

She picked up.
"Hey, Dawn. About lunch…"

# CHAPTER 6

Charles Lott was "at large." He was "on the run."

He didn't feel either. More like "on the sneak."

Itching to move faster, but moving faster would put a target on his back in neon with bells and whistles.

Once the girl had escaped, there was no time to hunt her down. He should've. He should've headed right over to the neighbors' house and busted in, gun doing his talking for him. He should've shut down the bitch and her rescuers, let Rodney dismember them all, bit by bit.

But Rodney took off immediately. Left Charles literally holding a bone.

So Charles took off, too. Grabbed his gun and booked it. He borrowed Burt's Audi – not like the asshole had any use for it – which he realized was a stupid idea around Biloxi.

Leaving a trail of breadcrumbs. No, he needed to disappear. Why was he driving around in the *target*?

The car stank of the girl's sickly sweet perfume. Made Charles sniff. Man, why'd Rodney have to cockblock him? And what the fuck was Rodney thinking, cutting up the body? The whole thing was crazy. Charles didn't mind killing a bitch who needed it, but that butchering shit went too far.

Let the cops come get him. Charles had been thinking about this for a long time. He wasn't scared of cops. He wasn't scared of the boys in jail, neither. But he wasn't going to go quietly. Might as well take out some more people along the way. If he got a shot at Rodney, even better. Dude was a Jesus Freak anyway.

Charles pulled off the interstate and drove down to the

beach, backtracked to the Isle of Capri casino. He eased the Audi up the parking garage ramp, higher and higher. Dark aisles, then the flash of fluorescents, then dark again. Going to leave it right in the middle, hard to find. The word was "inconspicuous."

He got out, left the keys in the driver's seat in case anyone wanted to take it. Let the cops follow the breadcrumbs to someone else. He had grabbed a clean t-shirt on his way out of the house, and now took off the bloody one he was wearing. Slipped into the fresh one. He still had blood and muck on his hands and arms, but a lot of it had dried and flaked right off.

No money, no wallet, no watch. Wearing only a t-shirt, cargo shorts, and some Adidas Velcro sandals. His gun was down three bullets. Twelve left.

Sounded like fun.

Charles strutted across the parking level, gun shoved into his waistband. Down the stairs and out into the early morning air. It was that weird time of day when it was still night but not last night and not *to*night, and the air felt different on his skin than it had a few hours before. His teeth were tight, ready to crack in two. Brain buzzing. He felt alive. Time to find some new wheels and drive himself out of the danger zone.

A different casino parking garage? Shit, by the time he walked that far, it would be daylight, and besides, he couldn't hotwire a car. Stealing one from a valet was too noisy. Instead, Charles drifted over to an all-hours convenience store.

Lit bright enough to blind you to anything beyond the parking lot, empty at the moment. No one hanging around outside. Charles took up a spot on the side of the building, holding up the wall. Arms crossed, cold but hot, goosebumped but sweating. Sea breeze coming off the coast, salty, mixed with the smell of grease from the Burger King across the street. Had to wait it out.

Because if Charles knew a thing or two about stores like this at an hour like this, it was that someone would be coming soon. Beer or cigarettes or gas. And when they did…

Right on time. He could hear it coming from blocks away. *Thrum. Thrum thrum. Thrum. Thrum thrum.*

It rolled into view. An eighty-something Cutlass Supreme, brown, pimped. Chrome rims, tinted windows rolled halfway down, shaking the earth with bass. Oh yeah. Charles loved that song. Tupac. *California Love.* The car turned into the parking lot, slowed to a stop, parked across three spots.

A twentyish black man climbed out. On the stout side. He left the car running and the bass pumping. Exactly what Charles was hoping for. Otherwise, he might have to beat a brother down.

Soon as the driver walked into the store, Charles flashed to the car, opened the driver's door, and slid inside.

He was about to throw it into reverse when he heard the digital dong of the store's front door, and the driver shouting, "Hey, man! You motherfucker!"

Charles locked the doors.

The driver, all pissed. "What you doing?"

"Nice wheels, bro."

The driver tried the handle. Clunk, clunk, clunk. "Let me in, man!"

"Step off."

"What'd you say?"

"You heard me."

The driver thrust his hand through the open window and reached for Charles' throat, clamped around it. That shit *hurt.* Charles pulled away, reached for the window switch and rolled it up. Driver couldn't get his arm out in time, trapped at the wrist. He let out a yowl.

Now the cashier was in on it, standing on the curb with a shotgun.

"No, man, don't shoot my car!" Then to Charles, "Please, please, please, let me go, please, let me go." Pulled his arm. Pulled hard and kept yowling.

Charles grabbed the driver's wrist and yanked down hard on it. Over and over. "Fuck you! Fuck you! Fuck you!"

The wrist cracked. The window exploded into pebbles,

barely held together by the tint. The driver screamed, pulled out his hand and cradled it. The cashier was too shocked to keep his gun aimed at the car.

Charles pushed open the door, banged the driver, who fell on his ass. Charles whipped out his raggedy-ass pistol. "Easy with the shotgun. I'm faster."

The cashier let it go limp, dangling in his fingers.

"Good."

Charles reared back and kicked the driver in the gut. "Stupid! So stupid! All you had to do was call the cops and they'd let you know where to find this heap once I got tired of it. But no, you had to go and play Rambo!" Another big kick.

The cashier fumbled trying to raise the gun but Charles got his in the air faster.

"I told you."

Shot him in the shoulder. Shot him again in the chest. He went down.

The driver was freaked. Teeth chattering. "No please no please no please…"

"See what you made me do?"

Charles sighed, bent over at the waist, and dug his gun into the driver's temple.

Pulled the trigger.

The chattering stopped. Everything stopped. Charles had more blood on him now, on the gun too.

He stood, spun around. People had to have heard the noise they'd made. Someone would be calling the police. He might as well take the Cutlass anyway, at least for a little while.

Back to the driver's side door, brushed the glass pebbles out, and dropped back into the seat. He turned the stereo a little louder.

Time to cruise.

Rolling down the road with his arm dangling out the busted window gave him time to think. He weaved his way back onto the interstate, heading west to New Orleans.

But what was he going to do there? Couldn't pay for a hotel, couldn't keep this car, couldn't hold his own against N'awlins gangbangers or those Quarter rat kids, sleeping in parks or huddled behind buildings. He didn't need the attention a fight would bring down.

And he only had nine bullets left.

Didn't even think to stop and pick up the shotgun.

He pounded the steering wheel. "Goddamn it! Shit!"

Daylight on the horizon.

Under half-a-tank.

He laughed. A bark at first, but then he rolled with it and the whole tragic thing was funny, in a way. Kill one man, premeditated, it was guaranteed death row. Or at least life in prison. Kill three men, same difference, right?

Why not keep on going? End up behind bars as a *famous* motherfucker. Who was going to mess with him then? He'd be on the news. Appeals would keep him out of the chair for years, decades. Was it even a chair anymore? Or lethal injection? Like being put to sleep by heroin.

This was his time. This was his moment.

Who better to start with than the bitch who ratted him out and the bastard with the brilliant "cut him up" plan?

"Yes! Yeah! The real shit right there."

He didn't bother waiting for an exit or a crossover. He swung the wheel to the left and u-turned through the median ditch, spinning grass and dirt. This was going to be fun.

# CHAPTER 7

Molly played with her dolls and some of her brother's insect action figures. Joshua was too busy with his robots to notice, making *krash kaboom* sounds as he slammed them together, pieces flying, Rachel flinching. It made Molly laugh, so Joshua did it some more. The robots were stars of some overly violent cartoon, probably full of demonic messages. Why oh why did Rachel let Rodney talk her into cable TV?

It wasn't completely his fault. She'd had the TV and VCR well before he came along, but only for "approved" videos from the Christian book shop – Carmen concerts, choirs, some movies about the Rapture and the Mark of the Beast that scared her badly. Rodney was fine with the "family fare" for awhile, but then he started renting some harder movies at Blockbuster, and she fell right into the habit. Which led to basic cable – a little news and weather, some decent sitcoms – which led to expanded cable, HBO and Cinemax, then to a larger screen. Before long the kids were glued to loud ads for candy and cereal while Rachel was hooked on *Melrose Place* and *Rikki Lake*.

She couldn't get her mind off these little things now that Hosea had called and told her what Rodney had done. Examining every facet of their relationship, straining for clues. She'd been mad enough to throw him out, but the fight was fixable, wasn't it? She'd seen intensity from him, but nothing *violent*. A still silence that could be very frightening, but she'd never been worried he would hit her or the kids. Which was the real Rodney – the convert she married, or the smirking man who'd turned his back on the church and introduced her to marijuana and soap operas?

Oh, admit it, Rachel, you wanted some of this yourself. Tired of the goody two-shoes that didn't fit any more. She'd cut the beautiful hair that used to hang halfway down her back, "a woman's glory" as the Bible said, to one hugging her neck. She wore short-shorts now even though it still embarrassed her, letting people gape at that much of her skin. She had to fit in.

Then, make-up. She used to use hardly any – only enough to give her cheeks a little color. Now, all the bright colors, the thick mascara, lipstick like paint. Did it make her feel better about herself? Prettier? Smarter? No, but other women did it. The ladies on *Melrose Place*, even the women at the Baptist and Methodist churches.

Rodney had pushed it, telling her a little bit was no harm, but it didn't stop with a little bit. In fact, after trying the things he'd told her to try, she wondered if he cringed at who she'd become.

No one to blame but herself, though.

The pressure had built until the fight. She kicked him out, needed time to think, time to pray. To sink to the floor beside her bed, sobbing into her mattress so the kids wouldn't hear. She had heard him in the other room, telling Molly and Josh he had to leave, but he loved them very much and would be back before they knew it.

The drinking – more than light beer or a wine box in the fridge. She had a bottle of vodka in the freezer that she mixed with fruit punch or lemonade.

The pot – oh, God, ashamed to think how silly and horny it had made her. Imagine if it hadn't been the two of them together, alone, but out at a party somewhere. Oh God oh God.

She knew…no, she *suspected* he might be selling a little pot or some pills. She never pushed him on it. She didn't want to know.

*He chopped a man to pieces.*

She shuddered. What else was he capable of?

The police had left the house after a thorough search. Rachel felt like a suspect somehow. Two of them were still out on the curb, sitting in a cruiser, would get the neighbors talking. Bad enough already, but what about when the story hit the news?

Oh God, oh God.

He better not try to come back home.

Where would he go?

She smoothed her hands across her lap. Goose-pimpled skin where long skirts used to cover her thighs. The cops had taken her by surprise, arriving so early. She had rushed to throw on yesterday's clothes, call in sick to work at the county tax collector's office (a little white lie) and call her Aunt Eileen, tell her the kids wouldn't be over today. The rest of the morning was a tearful blur. Hosea called and gave her the news. Now she was sitting on the couch, staring into space.

Molly stumbled over, still learning to walk, and brought Rachel a doll. She said it wasn't feeling right.

"Lay your hands on it," Rachel said. "Pray like we do at church."

Molly pressed her fingers against the doll's forehead and shouted, "Be healed! Be healed!"

"She should be all good now."

Molly giggled. "Be healed!" She swung the doll by the arm, marched around the room. "Be healed! Be healed!"

*Krash! Kaboom!*

"Glory! Glory!"

It stirred a headache. Rachel stood and went to her bedroom. *Their* bedroom, Rodney's and hers. It was a small house with only two bedrooms, a living room, one bath and a kitchen. It was too cold in winter, too hot in summer. All of the windows were open, curtains billowing like white flags. They were renting, all they could afford right then. It was claustrophobic, being crowded into these few small rooms with the kids and Rodney all evening, every weekend. Sometimes wonderful, sometimes crushing.

She left the door partially open to better hear the kids, sat on the bed. Her side.

Jesus, this was hard.

She loved him, she loathed him, she worried about him, she prayed for him.

Now she picked up the phone. She should call Hosea, give him any help she could to find him. She didn't know a lot about Rodney's life before they'd met, but she'd picked up some random pieces here and there.

Yes. It would be the right thing to do. It didn't mean she loved him any less.

Or did it?

Rachel had been born in America, but was too young to remember when her family moved to Africa, where she absorbed the music, the languages, the animals, and much more. They moved to Mississippi when she was twelve, and adjusting to the kids here was tough. She dressed funny – the long skirts and dresses, the long hair – but she got along with her classmates early on thanks to her stories of Africa. The wild revival services. The safaris. The food. The tribesmen with spears who could run faster than anyone she'd ever known.

As Rachel grew older, she started keeping secrets from her folks. She couldn't watch TV or listen to the latest boy bands at home, but she heard all about it at school anyway. If the girls offered her a little make-up or a puff on a cigarette, she'd give it a try. But she didn't curse or sneak booze or give blowjobs. Most of her friends didn't mind that her church made her different. She was still cool even if she wasn't allowed to go to slumber parties, or movies, or concerts.

By eleventh grade, Rachel was bored.

She met a boy at one of the youth events. Both of them felt "freedom from sin" meant "chained up." They did the best they could with heavy petting, over the clothes. Then fingers, then mouths, then…

It was the scariest two weeks of her life, waiting to for her period.

When it came, she cried like a baby at the altar and promised God, "Never again!"

She swore off men then. A stumble was all it was. Youthful indiscretion. Jesus understood. She would meet Mister Right when the time was right, anyway, and she would keep her panties on until then.

But…Rodney.

She was twenty-three. He was thirty. He was a new convert, and he locked eyes on her his first day in Sunday School.

Persistent. All of her rejections bounced off him like rubber bullets. Rachel *liked* Rodney fine, but she couldn't see herself dating him.

As the months wore on, he stayed on the front pew every service, still praising God, or at least putting on a good show of it. They became friends. That wasn't going to be enough for him.

He chipped away at her defenses. *Chip, chip, chip.* He let Bible studies stand in for real dates. He was the perfect gentleman, sort of.

She fell for him. Never head over heels, but it was…comfortable.

Then, there she was, once more waiting to see if her period would come. When it didn't, she was happy this time.

There was no way to have known this was the path her life would take. Great at the beginning, a small wedding because her dad was disappointed at her getting pregnant first. Rodney kept up the flame for her and for Christ. Loving father, a doting husband. Rachel could not point to a specific moment when things started to change. Him pressuring her to "loosen up." Little by little. Before she knew it, she was out of church, smoking weed, and watching filth on TV. Her kids *watching* her change like this.

When she couldn't take it anymore, the fight happened.

Rachel squeezed her eyes closed. A bad taste in her mouth. She tried hard not to think about it, his voice, his touch. About how much she loved to be touched the way he did.

"No," she whispered. "No more. In Jesus' name, don't let me remember."

Like she was taught – whatever you ask for in Jesus' name *must* come to pass. No doubt about it. Right?

Opened her eyes. Still felt the same.

The phone, slick in her sweaty palm. She lifted it to her ear. The dial tone had gone to a busy signal. Yes, yes, she was about to call Hosea, tell him what little she knew.

Then she hung up. Recoiled from the phone as if it were a snake. She took in breaths hard and fast through her nose before balling her fists and swallowing the knot of anger in her throat.

Why *not* call?

Husband, father, lover.

*Drug dealer? Pervert? Killer?*

She couldn't do it. Licked her dried lips, picked up the phone and called her Aunt Eileen. Told her she might drop the babies off after all.

She went to the closet and reached into the back for some of her old church dresses. She was on a mission.

Then to the living room, where she plastered on a smile for the kids.

*Krash! Kaboom!*

CHAPTER 8

Hosea and Tara pulled into the trailer park where Charles' mother lived. A sad place that hadn't been cleaned up from the last hurricane. Junk in the yards – abandoned washers, car engines, stained and broken lawn furniture, and grimy children's toys and bikes and pieces of playhouses strewn everywhere. It was right off the main road and smelled like exhaust.

Moss Point and Sheriff's cruisers parked every which way, twirling lights reminding Hosea of the county fair. Bumper cars. Cops of all shapes and sizes searched every square inch of the park. Down on hands and knees, going door to door, or beating the shrubs.

One uniformed cop in a car kept an eye on the mother's place. Eased back in his seat, windows down as Hosea and Tara walked by.

The cop said, "Hot enough for you?"

"Nice breeze out here."

"Bullshit. Don't you get hot in that suit?"

"Don't you in that uniform?"

"At least I got short sleeves. Now, Tara, girl, look at you. She's got the right idea."

She flipped him off. Grinned.

These two, him and Tara. Her still dressed for the boat, him still dressing in his preaching suits. It also summed up their personalities. Good contrast made for good partners. So did separation – after ten hours a day, they were sick of each other until the next morning.

They walked through a gate, knee-high mass-produced

plastic. A postage stamp yard, but handsome and clean. Up some rickety wooden steps. Knocked on the door.

A young girl opened it. One of Charles' sisters or a cousin. Hell, maybe even his own child, if he had one. Hosea didn't know. Things were moving fast and they were behind on the details. A few more kids were hanging around inside – two girls and a boy – with hair stuck to their foreheads by sweat, flushed cheeks, dirty feet. They played video games. There were trails of smudged dirt on the carpet between the door, kitchen, and couch.

Charles' mother, Meredith, sat at a small table in the kitchen next to her boyfriend, smoking menthols. Unlike the living room, the kitchen was virtually spotless. A drainer full of clean dishes, freshly-wiped counters, the smell of bleach. She took pride in this room, spent all her time in here. The boyfriend stared at the floor, drank from a sweaty glass of cola with lots of ice.

No room to sit down, so Hosea and Tara leaned on the kitchen counters and told them what they knew. It didn't go well.

Meredith shut her eyes. "No, he wouldn't do that. He would never."

Hosea knew Tara was holding back, *He sure as hell did*.

"We need to talk to him and get his side of the story. It's better if we get to him before he hurts himself." Hosea hated this part, pretending to sympathize with the family of a killer. Charles' rap sheet was chock-full of violent outbursts, beatings, public drunk, and drug possession. Murder had been lurking, waiting for its time to shine.

"Bullshit. You think I don't watch *Cops*?" Meredith brought her cigarette to her lips with shaky hands. Hosea wondered how old she was.

When Hosea had been a traveling evangelist, town to town all over the southeast, he had thought every person, no matter what sins they'd done in life, was worth the effort. Several years as a detective had changed his mind. Some people would never shake the demon off their backs. They didn't want to.

They fed it whatever it asked for.

He summed up the boyfriend: Greasy skin, unbathed. Messy hair. *Bet there's rum in that Coke. Not even noon.*

Meredith sniffed back tears. "I ain't seen him for a month."

Lies.

Pointless, too. Easy to disprove. Why bother? *Of course* she had seen him in the past month. *Of course* he would've called her in the early hours with a sad story about how he hadn't done nothing.

One of the kids out in the living room screamed bloody murder and ran into the kitchen, holding up her arm to the boyfriend. "Daddy! She bit me! Look at her teeth marks!"

The boyfriend slumped. "Helen, just…go bite her back. I don't know. Take it outside. We're busy."

The girl ran out of the kitchen, already shouting, "Daddy said I can bite you back!"

"Don't bite her back!" Meredith slapped at him across the table. "Jesus, Daniel."

Tara let out a deep breath and knelt before the woman. Eye to eye. These two were already uncomfortable from having one of "the blacks" in their home sweet home, Hosea could tell. Tara knew it, too, and loved poking the bear.

"We're going to catch him. We'll be all over you and Danny here and all your relatives until he's in jail. We're very patient. We're panthers when we hunt. He won't get away, and we'll say, his momma sure didn't help us. Maybe she was even *aiding* him, helping him along. And then what will you think the next time we have to come out here and drag you kicking and screaming from your hovel?"

She punctuated it with a growl and curled fingers, Catwoman-style. Hosea thought Daniel the Boyfriend had sneaked a peek at Tara's tits while she was down there.

Meredith blew a plume of smoke all over Tara. "I. Ain't. Seen. Him."

Tara plucked the cig from her, ground it out in her sawed-off beer can ashtray. "But you've talked to him?"

"No."

"I don't believe you."

"Believe what you want." Meredith turned away. "I don't scare easy."

"Who said anything about easy? We love a challenge. But…" Tara wagged her finger, then glided out into the living room and corralled the kids. "It's my turn on the PlayStation. Who wants to beat me?"

Meredith was all about to get up and fight, but didn't. Hosea leaned his aching neck back and sighed. On the ceiling above Meredith's head, a yellow stain, darker in the middle. "Any friends you can point me towards? Other family members? Any special places he hung out?"

"Said I don't know, means I don't know. She can't speak to me like that, can she?"

"She can speak to you however she damn well pleases."

Charles' mother bristled.

Hosea flicked his eyes towards Daniel. "You want to betray any confidences?"

"Barely know the boy."

Hosea believed him. Daniel had probably gotten together with Marilyn as a last resort and couldn't stand staying or leaving. He'd probably never said more than ten words to Charles. Probably never looked him in the eye. Embarrassed to.

"Okay." Hosea pushed off the counter. Headed for the door. "Okay."

Outside, while Tara was finishing off a round of shoot-em-up with the kids, Hosea crouched and peered through the latticework surrounding the bottom of the trailer to see if Charles was under there in the mud and spiders. Shined his flashlight around. Nothing but more broken toys – Hell must be full of the damn things – and busted bricks and a couple of hissing cats.

Even if Mommy was telling the truth, Hosea had a feeling Charles would try to get in touch with her at some point. That's what sons in trouble do. *Mamma, just killed a man*. But when? It would be a waiting game, one the cops would win because they were more patient than a man with a guilty conscience.

He heard the door open. Looked up. Daniel stepped down, holding onto his rum and Coke for dear life, and said, "Wait a minute."

Hosea stood. Waited.

"We didn't mean to be impolite. You know it's hard on her, too."

"Yeah, I suppose."

"But I'm telling you the truth. I don't think he's called. And I got no idea where he would be." Sip. With his other hand, Daniel fished out a cigarette from the pack in his back pocket. Put it between his lips. Pulled out a lighter and lit it.

"Anything you could tell me, though."

"All I can say is that boy ain't one to run. He's too stupid. Too headstrong. When he is here, it's like he owns the place. Treats his momma shitty. She'd kill me if I told you, though. He's still her favorite. Her oldest." Daniel shook his head. "She doesn't deserve that sort of behavior."

Hosea took out his wallet, pulled a card from it. He wrote his cell phone number on the back and handed it to Daniel. "How about you let me know if he shows up or calls?"

Daniel glanced over his shoulder at the trailer, then slid the card into his back pocket with the cigs. "She'd kill me if—"

"Then don't let her find out."

Some shouting from the trailer. The two women inside yelling over each other, neither going to back down.

But soon enough, Tara shoved the screen door open so hard, Hosean thought it might come off the hinges.

"You black-ass bitch!" Meredith, shouting from the door. Barely containing herself from saying the other word on her mind. If only Tara wasn't a cop.

Tara was about to turn on her heel and teach the woman a lesson, but Hosea shouted, "Time to go!" Made her stop and think about it. Hosea had her back in a few rumbles before, and would any time she needed him. With this many cops on the scene, they'd all swear Tara was in the right, too. Blue came before any other color.

Always?

Hosea didn't want to test it right now.

"Got an appointment."

Tara stopped her roll, stared down the lady at the door. "This ain't finished, you hear?"

She let the door slam and bounced down the stairs.

Breathing hard, hands on her hips, she stopped by Hosea and Daniel, pointed to his cigarette. "One of those, please."

Daniel pulled out his pack of Marlboro's. She shrugged. Not her favorite brand.

"That'll do."

Next stop, the morgue.

The head, hard and plastic under the glare of the lights, could've been mistaken for a prop in a horror movie if Hosea didn't already know the truth. The face, calm. Of course he'd already been dead by the time Rodney had sawed through his neck.

The torso, mottled. Flesh shredded by bullets. Skin pulling away from muscle where he'd cut off the limbs.

Tara took short careful breaths through her nose, exhaled with pursed lips. Hosea held his handkerchief over his nose and mouth, but it didn't work, same as at the crime scene. He should've known by now it was useless.

The ME stood with her arms crossed, glasses on the tip of her nose. She hadn't cut into the torso yet. It looked more like a terrible Greek sculpture than a real person on the stainless steel table.

The horror of it was nothing compared to the table beside it.

Bones scraped free of meat. Piles of skin and muscle leaking bayou water and bodily fluids into the drain.

"Been doing this job for twelve years," the ME said. "Worst thing I've ever seen."

Tara cleared her throat. "They didn't leave anything to the

imagination."

Hosea kept his lips closed, went *Mm-hm*. The smell was bad enough, but he didn't want the taste of this freak show on his tongue.

"We know who did what. We kinda know where to start looking for them. So, what else you can tell us about…" Hosea waved his hand over the meat pile. "*This?*"

The ME stepped around the table, peering down on the slop. She picked up a long bone, either an arm or leg. "They used some extremely sharp tools. The bones are shaved very close. The butcher knew what he was doing. The saw wounds are clean and fast."

"He used the saws on beef and pork, most of the time. Ribs."

Tara whistled low. "The exact same tools. If this turns me into a vegan, I'm going to kill both of them with my bare hands."

"Imagine if they'd succeeded and he'd taken those knives back to work? You ever buy meat there?"

"I'm going to be sick. What kind of person – ?"

"My brother-in-law, apparently. The father of my niece and nephew. Guy who used to sit on the front row of my dad's church every service."

The ME said, "Shall we?" and motioned towards the torso.

"Do we have to?"

They got on with the autopsy.

Later, Tara smoked another cigarette while Hosea sucked on an Altoids.

Hosea said, "Our work is cut out for us. Literally."

Tara curled her lips. "Shut up."

# CHAPTER 9

A duck blind, sitting unused since the end of last season, on the edge of the bayou. Rickety, as if someone had nailed together whatever wood they could find in a hurry, obscured by dead branches and camouflaged netting. Slats of wood lining the front and back, vertically. A tin roof held up with two-by-fours, a platform between two big trees.

For now, it was Rodney's home.

The man who brought him here by boat promised no one would find him, not until the start of duck hunting anyway, but that was a long time off. No way he'd be stuck here until then. The man left Rodney with a plastic grocery bag with some cold sandwiches, some leftover roast potatoes in a Tupperware, some water in a plastic thermos, and three cans of Diet Coke. Told Rodney he'd be back in the next night with more.

It was a kindness he didn't deserve.

But, shit, this wasn't about *deserve*. This was about desperation.

This man was the one person Rodney knew would help without even asking what was wrong. He was willing to hide Rodney, keep him fed, wait until the heat died down before helping him leave the Gulf Coast, right under all those cops' noses.

Rodney hunkered down, couldn't sleep. Mosquitoes. Thoughts of snakes and gators, imagined boat engines and voices. He ate a full day's worth of food in six hours.

*What have I done?*

Flashes of the girl flailing to get out from under Charles.

Flashes of Charles pulling the trigger. Smiling about it.
*Think about it. Compared to what Charles did…*

No, this was bad. What he'd done was as bad as killing the man.

Flashes of Burt. His dead eyes and dead sneer.

Before he'd started carving, Rodney had closed his eyes, took a deep breath. Listened. Maybe the long quiet voice of God would intervene, stay his hand as he'd done with Abraham, who came close to killing his own son as a sacrifice. This was different, the man already dead, but still.

No voice. No nothing.

He wanted rid of the head first. Make the rest of the body seem less human. Getting through the neck without being sick was the first major hurdle. Charles couldn't take it, already spewing on the tarp halfway through. The blood was like syrup.

Charles reached down, grabbed the skull by the hair, and pulled it along the concrete garage floor, gagging. He found a plastic grocery bag filled with nails or sandpaper or some shit. Dumped it and flung the head inside.

Hands. Snipped off the fingers.

Sawed through elbows.

The arms. Rodney had to pop them out of the socket. The sound sent Charles out to the backyard. Shit, he wasn't helping at all. It was *his* body, though, *his* kill. Whatever. Rodney didn't need him. But every thrust of the saw made him feel hotter, clammier, as if this was a preview of his place in Hell.

Knees. The knees were hard.

More trouble with the thighs where they connected to the hipbone. He ended up smashing the pelvis until it was a bag of shards in order to saw through.

Next, the fillet knife. Shearing flesh, fat, and muscle off the bones.

While he was doing it, Rodney reminded himself it was only meat.

Now, out on the water, it was much, much worse. On his

hands and knees, he threw up into the deep. Felt like sheer fire, smelled like rot. He caught his breath and flopped back. Watched fish pop at the mess that had come out of him, hoping for food, finding jack shit.

It was a night unlike any other. No sleep, no rest, the sick feeling in his gut never going away.

By morning, soaked in sweat and dew as the sun rose, his hideaway felt more like a coffin.

When your friend comes today, tell him you're ready to turn yourself in. Tell the cops Charles was the killer. You were only there accidentally. Tell them Charles was the one to say, "Go get your knives." Who would they more likely believe? Maybe they won't even put you in jail.

Buzzing winged insects, bumblebees and wasps and mosquitoes, whirring crickets, driving him insane. He rocked back and forth. Didn't dare stand or take a peek around. It was a great hiding spot. Every time another mosquito or horsefly bit him on the face, he reminded himself how great of a hiding spot this was.

Rodney wondered if Charles had found his own place to lie low. Might be stupid enough to try hiding under his mom's trailer. He could already be in custody, singing a totally different tune: It was all Rodney's fault. Rodney shot Burt. Rodney attacked the girl. Rodney cut up the body.

*They'll believe whoever talks first. Don't matter who actually killed him. As long as someone goes down for it.*

Rodney *saved* Burt's girl. Shouldn't his good deed count?

*You were ready to cut her up and toss her into the water, same as her boyfriend.*

Cartilage and fat, blood and bone.

No one would believe him. He didn't even believe himself.

He heard a boat. Small engine. Maybe his savior had come back early. Maybe the cops had started searching the water for both he and Charles. No way to tell at that moment. The engine grew louder, closer.

Along the front of the blind the slats were nailed up sloppily, with uneven gaps between them every now and then.

One was wide enough for Rodney to peer out with one eye. He saw a slice of the bayou, but no boat. He could still hear it coming, though. A high, whiny engine.

His knees were killing him, wobbling badly.

The boat came into view. A beat-up skiff, nearly the same as the one in Charles' garage. Two men, one at the back steering the engine, and one at the front. Neither wore life jackets, both wore ball caps. One had a sleeveless t-shirt split down the sides. A big cooler between them. The engine coughed before coming to a stop. They both bent down, came up with fishing poles. The one in back opened the cooler, pulled out a couple cans of beer, tossed one up front. The guy at the front almost lost it in the water. They laughed.

They *just happened* to pick this spot to fish. Right in his line of sight. Great. They cast their lines and sipped their beers and, well, they fished. Truth was fishing was less about fish than most people thought. A man might even find himself annoyed at a fish on the line. Interrupted his beer drinking.

He imagined the two good ol' boys fishing behind Charles' house last night, what they would've caught. All those fish now with a taste for human flesh.

He held it together. Kept his breathing calm. Couldn't let them know he was there. That would be bad.

Or would it?

*No.*

Think about it. Call them over, say you're stuck out here, need some help.

*No.*

Push them overboard, take their boat. Or, they've got a knife somewhere on that boat. Can't fish without a knife. Gut them both. More gator food.

*No.*

He held his breath, hoping to clamp down on his panic. It bottled up, like shaking a Miller Lite. No good.

He let it out in a long, slow stream.

Checked to see if the fishermen heard.

Didn't seem it.

How long? Would they drift along with the current? Would they anchor here?

Eye between the slats. Every muscle aching.

Should he take their boat or wait them out?

Kill them or sit tight?

Hm?

# CHAPTER 10

The manhunt was on all along the coast. Hosea was one tiny gear in a huge machine. It was damnable work for which he was paid meekly. It was still "his" case, but a case this big didn't belong to any one person.

So, middle of the afternoon on the first day, Hosea sneaked off to his dad's house to give him the news – if he hadn't heard it from Rachel already.

Hosea pulled up to the parsonage. Glen's car was there, a Nissan that had racked up a lot of miles between Bible college in Jackson and home, but still clean as new. Jesus, he didn't want to deal with Glen today. He parked behind Dad's Lincoln Town Car and got out.

Dad had made Glen his assistant pastor the moment he graduated, his own way of saying, "not long now." He wasn't really old – only sixty – but the mental demands of pastoring a church had worn him down. He was considering the next step, perhaps moving up the ranks as an administrator in the denomination, supervise missionaries or sit on the board. Move close to church headquarters in Columbia, Missouri. Whatever it was, he could see it in his dad's face, hear it in his voice. The man was hurting and needed to get away.

The house appeared small from outside, but it had three bedrooms and two baths, a nice dining room. The front lawn bordering the church parking lot was big, clear of trees. The church kids played volleyball there. The lot itself was a big asphalt L at the back of the sanctuary. It was a decent-sized church with two buildings – the new sanctuary, and the old church, which housed the fellowship hall and Sunday School classrooms for the kids. There was also a youth pastor's apartment, empty at the moment, and an evangelist's quarters for visiting preachers, also empty right then.

At least Hosea thought they were.

In the house, Hosea called for his dad, but there was no answer. Didn't bother calling for Glen. He checked the bedrooms. If they were on their knees or flat on their faces, deep in prayer, they might as well have been in a coma. No one else was coming between them and the Lord.

He sat at the kitchen table. Once he moved out, Hosea's half of the boys' room had been taken over by all things Glen as quickly as possible. As if Hosea had been erased from the house – except for the parrot calling out his name now and then. Rachel's room had been turned into a makeshift library.

Hosea thought it was weird, Glen still living in their old bedroom. Why did a nearly thirty-five-year-old man not at least ask for the youth leader's place, give himself a *little* privacy. But he argued how Dad needed someone around. If not, he'd be here alone too often, and he was already pretty melancholy. Thus, Glen never left home, hadn't married or even dated much, and didn't seem to mind.

Hosea didn't like his older brother one bit, and Glen didn't care much for Hosea either. It had been that way since they were kids – vicious knock-down drag-outs – but Hosea preferred the beatings they had given each other to the cold, phony "love" Glen radiated these days, starting back when he went to Bible college. As far as Glen was concerned, there was no more hate in his heart for Hosea at all. A holy automaton. Hosea had given up trying to get through his armor to have any sort of relationship.

Being back here reminded Hosea of his dad's disappointment when he admitted what had happened to bring his preaching career screeching off the cliff like an Old West train. A stupid mistake. He absolutely knew better, but here he was, a cop instead of a minister.

He peered down at his Hugo Boss suit, now sweated-through, and wiggled his toes in his Gucci loafers. Back when he was evangelizing – traveling across seven states – and still living at home, he took the money from his offerings and saved up for the best clothes. He had this Hugo, an Armani, and a double-breasted pin-striped Brooks Brothers. The Gucci loafers took six months of savings, several weeks of five-night revivals. He'd also picked up some Bruno Magli boots. Had to look the part. He belonged in the pulpit.

Pentecostal preachers ran the gamut, same as the churches – old-time religion out in the boonies, pastors with one suit to their name, all the way to big city slickers in designer duds who say their congregations demanded it. Hosea remembered a preacher criticized for his expensive suit coming back with, "You think Jesus wants me wearing rags, or does he want me wearing a beautiful and handmade suit that'll last thirty-years? He appreciates quality! Holy Ghost logic right there."

Hosea would've turned out like one of those if he'd kept at it. Some of his best friends, now drifted out of his life, had been fellow young evangelists who would sit around diners swapping stories and rumors – which churches were stingy, which were generous. Which ones were nuts, which were down-to-earth. Which ones had all the pretty women, which had the most pregnant teenagers. Meanest pastor. Best singers. Funniest spirit dancers. Nicest guest rooms. Best home-cooked meals, and on and on.

They took the Jesus part of it seriously, oh yes indeed. Still, they were sober frat boys. Most of them had an eye on pastoring their own churches someday, which took finding a wife and starting a family first. Pastor's kids were thought of as shoo-ins back home. The rest would need to battle it out for one of the thousands of Pentecostal churches attended by hundreds-of-thousands of people across the country, especially in the Deep South. Another rumor they passed around was which pastors were at death's door, no children to pass the church on to, leaving a vacancy.

But Hosea never wanted to be a pastor. He'd done what he loved, wearing fancy clothes and driving a very well-kept used Cadillac. He was traveling all over, seeing new places, saving souls, earning a rep as a clever and fiery preacher, while dating a string of the hottest church girls.

Until her.

Still hurt to think of her name.

Cherish. "Cher" for short.

How he wished he'd been less cocky. Wished he'd been able to resist. No, that wasn't fair to her – he wished *she'd* been able to resist *him*. It was all his fault. A married woman with no kids, regretting the decision she'd made to marry a "worldly" man. They met at a revival in Tennessee. She played keyboards, she loved to dance in the Spirit. They thought they had a spiritual connection.

Spiritual turned sexual over the course of two weeks.

After the revival, he drove from the coast to Memphis and back every weekend for a month, until Cher's husband found out and told Cher's pastor, who called Hosea's dad.

Humpty Dumpty had a great fall.

Why was he thinking about his mistakes right then? He had bigger fish to fry with Rodney and his buddy on the run. No time to sulk.

If Hosea hadn't slept with Cher, would he still be out there on the road today, rather than wearing his ridiculous suit in the summer heat in Mississippi investigating one of the worst things he's ever seen, knowing his own brother-in-law was capable of such madness? He wouldn't have had to worry about stepping in blood and sinew with his Gucci loafers.

He wouldn't have had to sell the Caddy.

Why become a cop, then?

Well, it was the closest thing he could think of as exciting as preaching.

Community college, police academy, several years on patrol, then he decided to become a detective. He was now thirty-three years old, single, and, in Biblical terms, still wandering the desert. "Worldly." That catch-all euphemism for "sinner." Sure, he enjoyed a few beers now and then. Grooved to hard driving rock-n-roll. Watched cable TV, R-rated movies. Admired women showing off too much skin.

Did these seemingly natural and innocent feelings make him as bad a sinner as the killers, the rapists, the dealers and the thieves? He still believed…*something*. Something about Jesus and loving people and forgiveness. Something about this had to be right, after all he'd seen, what he'd felt as he preached, all those people he'd prayed for. If it added up to nothing, what a waste.

Was there more for him in life than this? Was there a family in his future? Would he ever lay himself down before the whole church to tell them he was sorry and wanted forgiveness in order to return to preaching? Would he even want to anymore?

Enough. He pushed himself back from the table. Stood and passed by his mother's African Gray parrot, still calling her name after six years gone. It still repeated Mom's little phrases or sang songs she'd sung.

He left the house and walked across the yard to the church. Through the glass doors into the foyer. Quiet and cold, the lights out. In the sanctuary, the afternoon sun filtered through the simply colored stained-glass windows, raining blue-green onto the pews. The sanctuary was long, with three sections of white pews, an inviting mint green carpet, and a wedding cake platform leading to the pulpit. Organ and Leslie cabinet on one side, keyboards, bass and drums on the other. Choir loft behind the main platform, leading to a large glassless window at the baptismal tank so everyone could witness a new soul dunked in the name of Jesus.

His dad's office was in the opposite back corner. Hosea headed that way before the Pastor's voice reached him.

"Hosea. I already know."

Hosea stopped, barely made out his dad sitting on the steps by the men's altar up front. It wasn't like him. When he was in the sanctuary alone, he was usually praying loudly, walking among the aisles, his sonorous voice echoing off the walls. Hard to miss him.

"Rachel?"

"Yes."

Hosea made his way up front, sat on the altar – a basic narrow padded bench for kneeling. The women prayed on the left side, men on the right. Pastor Elgin, sitting on the steps, stared at his son, subtly shaking his head.

"She shouldn't have told you."

"You should have told me."

"That's not how my job works."

The pastor sighed. "I told you earlier, that's man's law talking."

"And I'm saying to you now that's not the way it works." Hosea stood, hands in his pockets. Paced a little. "But now you know. Don't tell anybody else until I say you can."

Hosea's dad looked as if he was running on no sleep. He had turned insomnia into some sort of religious burden, believing God forced him to stay awake to pray for more people. Hosea used to wake up at two in the morning because Dad was pacing their home, asking, *What else would you have me do, Lord?*

"I should have tried harder. I should've known."

"Rodney made his own choices."

"I know, but if I had gone to visit him more. If I'd prayed with him more."

"Yeah, okay."

"What?"

"I don't know how you're making this about you right now. Rachel is hurting pretty hard."

Pastor Elgin pinched the bridge of his nose. "Son, now is not the time."

"It never is."

"What will you do when you find him?"

"Book him, listen to what he has to say, show him the evidence."

His dad nodded. "Can I talk with him? Once you catch him?"

"When the time is right. Are you going to go see Rachel?"

As if he hadn't heard, "Treat him right. Give him a chance. This is family we're talking about. Give him a chance to repent."

"That's your job. I'm not counseling him. Cops get the bad guys—"

"He's not a bad guy."

"Come on. He *chopped a man to pieces.* It was over a drug deal. He got your daughter smoking pot. Need I go on?"

"His soul is more important than how much time he spends in jail."

"He hasn't been on your front row in a long time."

"Same as you."

Hosea stopped pacing. "Anyway, I came to tell you, like you wanted. I did it. I need to get back to work."

"Fine."

Hosea started down the aisle, the faster the better.

Pastor Elgin shouted behind him, "Will you be here Sunday?"

Closed his eyes. "Probably. Depends on if we've caught them."

"All right."

He kept walking.

In the foyer, almost to the door.

"Hosea."

Oh shit. Hosea turned. Glen stepped from the prayer room. He'd been in earshot all along.

Of course his brother was dressed to the nines, even more than Hosea. Sharp-creased dress slacks, dry-cleaned, as was the freshly starched and ironed Zegna shirt. Leather wing-tips. He didn't make much as assistant pastor, but he also had no car note, rent, or utilities. His other part-time job at a local bank was enough for everything he wanted.

Most likely they hated each other because they were too much alike.

"Guess you heard." Hosea said.

"Heard what?"

"Whatever."

Glen crossed his arms. "Whose team are you on, then?"

"What team? What are you talking about?"

"You're the detective. You figure it out."

Hosea furrowed his brow. "I don't have time for this."

"I know you were talking about Rodney. What did he do?"

No need to soften the blow. "He chopped up a dead man into little pieces and threw them into the bayou."

Glen kept his eyes straight. No blinking, no flinching. "God have mercy."

*For whom?* "It was over a drug deal."

Glen stepped closer. "A terrible thing. He had a lot of potential."

Not much potential. At best, Rodney was the type of guy who could knock on doors Saturday mornings, invite random people to church, and hand them a brochure. He wasn't a brain trust. But Hosea had never thought being a dumbass made him a bad guy.

"If he calls you, let me know."

"If I don't, what then?"

"Are you serious?"

"Curious. Do I go to jail, too? Can you force me to testify against him? Ready to cuff me?" He held out his wrists. Grinning. "You'd love locking me up, wouldn't you?"

"I'll see you later."

"I bet Rachel wouldn't call you if he showed up back at the house. Love works in mysterious ways. Why aren't you off consoling her instead of taunting Dad?"

An amateur psychologist now. Some preachers played counselor, too, regardless of their credentials. Glen liked the power, the authority, that came with pastoring a relatively small flock – only about a hundred souls. The Baptist church across town was over five hundred. He got off on helping people, whether they needed it or not.

"Rodney hasn't called you, has he? I mean, why would he?"

"Because confession is good for the soul."

Hosea wrinkled his brow and took slow steps towards his brother. He was a few inches shorter than Glen. Hated having to look up to him. "He confessed to you?"

Glen's grin broke into a smile. A dark laugh. "Yanking your

chain, baby bro. You are too serious."

Hosea turned away, headed for the door.

"You go get him, Mr. Detective. Go with God."

He fumed all the way across the yard. Kept thinking of comebacks he should've said. But Glen was a little faster. Always.

Before getting in his car, he took a hard once-over at Glen's Nissan, looking for clues to Rodney having been a passenger.

Like what? A smell? A bloody shoeprint? Get real, Hosea. Besides, Glen wouldn't want anyone getting the interior dirty.

He changed his mind and drove away.

# CHAPTER 11

You can't go home again.

Charles cruised by his momma's trailer park and sure enough, pigs here, pigs there, pigs everywhere.

But did any of them notice him? Right under their noses? Ha.

Elbow hanging out the busted window. Bass thumping.

Home was out of the question. He should've known it would be.

Where to next?

Charles thought about the beatdown he'd given Burt's girlfriend. Did he ever catch her name? He'd expect she went to the hospital after the beating he doled out. But he couldn't walk in asking for a bruised-but-still-fine-piece-of-ass. Sounded suspicious.

Man, it was *hot* outside. AC wasn't working as well with the window busted out. He rolled down the other three and enjoyed the breeze. The hospital wasn't too far away. Couldn't hurt to check.

*Rollin'.*

He parked down by the pond in front of the hospital, got out and crossed the bridge to the front entrance. Inside the sliding doors, the security guard gave Charles an up-and-down, went back to his newspaper. Easy peasy. Charles remembered from visiting his grandma once how they had a list of names and rooms for visitors to check. If he saw the chick's name, it might jog his memory.

*Started with a C? Chastity or Chris or Christine or Christa or Chrissy or Chris or Carla, no, it was Chris, had to be Chris.*

Slid his finger down the page.

"Can I help you?" The woman behind the desk, skeptical but still smiling.

"I got it. Thanks."

"If you tell me—"

"Serious, I got it."

He picked out all the Chris-like names. Even one with a K. Five. Memorized their room numbers.

"It's not visiting hours."

Charles lifted his eyes to her. "But I'm family."

"Whose family?"

"Chris' cousin." He pointed to the K name. Kris. "We grew up on the same street."

The woman rolled her eyes. "Elevator's around the corner."

Charles knew what she was thinking. He was no cousin. He was a boyfriend the girl's parents didn't want around, but what could she do, right? Not her job to tell Romeo, "Fuck off."

He skipped the elevator, went up the stairs instead. Itchy itchy. Didn't want to stop moving or his skin would crawl. He felt dizzy but a good kind of dizzy.

The first two Chrises were busts – a man in room one, a kid in room two. Doors were part open. He didn't even have to sneak in. Another one was too old, wrong hair color. Another one wasn't in the room. He stepped inside, looked for details this was the one, but figured there was too much crap – blankets, flowers, stack of magazines, for this to be someone who only arrived this morning.

It was too warm in here.

A middle-aged guy with a mustache and t-shirt from one of the coast casinos walked in, stopped short. "What are you doing in here?"

"Wrong room."

The guy had to have seen the blood on his hands. Eyes roving.

Charles brushed past him. "Excuse me."

"Hey, wait—"

"Got to catch my cousin before she goes into surgery."

Out of the danger zone, into the hallway. Headed for the stairs. Heart *ba-boom ba-boom*. He laughed.

Last one, two floors above, was this Kris person.

Might as well. He was already here.

The fourth floor was bright and cool. Very different from the second. His sweat dried quickly. Quieter up here, the faint sounds of televisions, random conversations. He rounded the corner and – whoa, whoa! – a cop standing guard outside a door. Charles pulled back, made a little circle. Then flat against the wall. A nurse coming the other way surprised him and caused him to walk back the way he came, passing her. She didn't stop him, didn't say a word. Lucky.

A fucking cop, right in his fucking way. She was the one. Kris was it. So so close.

What was he going to do? Choke her, or shoot a big air bubble into her IV, or stomp her until his foot sank into her guts?

Itchy itchy.

He couldn't let this stop him. He had to get into her hospital room. So close, so close. The guard would need to use the bathroom at some point. He could do it then.

Not if he uses the one in her room.

What about if he gets a call?

And how are you going to arrange such a thing?

Gritted his teeth. Pounded his forehead with his palms.

This wasn't going to work.

Charles headed back down the stairs. More sweat. He wanted another bump soon. Give his skin a break. He couldn't get to the girl, but he had her name now. *Kris Cole.* Ol' Kris Cole was a merry ol' soul. He laughed and laughed.

He'd look her up later. He could go to the library, find all the Kris Coles in the Houston phonebook and invite them to a party. Okay, not a party. But go find them one by one and have a party *with each one* until he found her and finished what Rodney had stopped him from doing the first time.

Rodney. Where'd Rodney run to? Goddamned Rodney.

Outside into the sun. Across the bridge to the car. He had to get rid of this one soon.

*Oh where oh where has my Rodney gone,*
*Oh where oh where could he be?*

CHAPTER 12

Where could he be?

Rachel dropped the kids at her aunt's house and started driving. But where to? She needed to feel busy. *Doing* something about Ridney. Sitting at home would make her sick. She put on one of her most modest church dresses, only the slightest hint of make-up, and some comfortable tennis shoes. She went out to the police cruiser on the street and told them she had some errands to run, then left before they had time to call for a tail.

Round and round the town. Trying to imagine some of her husband's old haunts. Had he ever talked about any? Other than the places she'd been with him once or twice, she didn't think Rodney had told her much about his life before the church. The necessary stuff, sure – family, a few friends, his job, but nothing about his drunken nights, his flying-high days, his crash landings.

She'd been with him to the honky-tonk in Pascagoula. Mr. Thunder's place. It was her first bar, and wasn't nearly as scary as she'd expected. They were supposed to be dark, dangerous places, full of men wallowing in sin and sin alone. But what she had actually seen was plenty of average, everyday folks enjoying their time together, listening to the jukebox, downing some beers, a couple of whiskies. Good people.

When she left, though, Rachel felt as if a shadow was following her home. Not a demon, no, even though she'd been taught there were demons everywhere, trying to bind us. She thought of this shadow as her dad's shame, how he could *sense* she'd gone drinking. Dad had never touched a drop. He'd grown up in the faith, and his father would've beaten him severely had he ever tried. Dad had his head on straight. That didn't make it any easier for the children.

Would Rodney hide in one of the dive bars in downtown Moss Point? The places with dark windows, neon signs, Rachel thought looked closed. She knew there were people in there. She'd seen them coming in and out. But if she'd hadn't, she'd think they were condemned.

There was a cinderblock place, must have been a convenience store once. The sign out front had been busted out. Now there was a plastic banner hanging on the wall: *Summer's Dream Daiquiris. Beer & Liquor. Smoking Allowed.* Only two cars outside. It had a drive-through window. A drive through for booze? That had to be illegal.

She parked. She lifted the carefully chosen photo from the seat beside her. Had to be recent, but also had to show Rodney at his worst. Sweaty, flushed, wild-eyed. It had taken her forty minutes to find one from a vacation to Pensacola Beach a year ago. Her first time in a bikini. Rodney, already drinking again. Just light beer, but it added up over the day. Rodney stared straight at the camera with a thin-lipped Mona Lisa grin.

Rachel checked herself in the rearview mirror and brushed her hair back over her ears. She had hoped to pull it back tight, but there wasn't enough for a tail yet. Shameful. She swore never to cut it anymore. And no earrings. She'd gotten used to them. Those would be a hard habit to break.

She was ready. Shaking, but ready.

Inside, the smoke dried out her throat instantly. She coughed, and every head in the place turned. Five in all. Through the fog, she saw a young woman bartender, a middle-aged man on one of only three barstools, two people playing pool, and a shadowy person in the back corner talking on a payphone.

Concrete floor, wooden bar someone must have built in a home garage. A handful of frozen drink machines behind it, and two taps for beer. The liquor selection must have been under the bar, but there were a few bottles scattered beside the frozen machines – schnapps, cheap vodka, bourbon – and a box of red wine. The jukebox was unplugged.

The bartender was a bubbly barely-legal in a tight t-shirt, long brown hair. "What can I get you?"

"Water." It came out hoarsely. "Ice water, please?"

"Are you sure?"

Rachel nodded.

The girl scooped ice into a cup and spritzed the water into it. Handed it across. "Sorry, but it's a dollar."

She handed it over. The man on the barstool was leaning on his elbows, hunched shoulders, watching her while his cigarette burned dangerously close to his fingers.

The girl said, "Your dress is pretty."

"Thank you."

"Are you sure you only want a water?" A sweet girl, not at all the haggard bartender she had expected. This girl acted as if her all male customers, leering, were not a big deal at all. Rachel admired her, but was scared for her regardless.

Cleared her throat. "I'm waiting for someone."

"Fine."

The man lifted his head and finger at the bartender. "I'll buy her next drink."

"Oh, no, you don't have to. I'm sure my husband will be here soon."

"Ease up, Paul," the bartender said. Then to Rachel, "Let me know if you change your mind."

"Wait. I haven't already missed him, have I? Was there anybody here earlier?"

Paul chortled, tried to cover it up by clearing his throat. He crushed out what little was left of the cigarette.

The girl stood back, hands on her hips. "You'd have to be more specific."

Rachel pulled out the photo. It had gotten a little bent in her purse. She smoothed it out on the bar and handed it across to the girl, who didn't take it.

The bartender took a step back. "I do *not* want to get involved in whatever is happening now."

"Please."

Paul turned on his stool. "What did he do?"

"I need to find him."

"He's not meeting you here?"

The bartender waved her arms out in front of her. "Nope. I'm out. I think you should leave."

The bend on the photo was getting to Rachel. Had to be the reason they wouldn't look at it. Why they didn't believe her. She placed it on the bar and rubbed her palm across it, long strokes. "Please, please. It's important. I need to find him."

Paul sighed, lifted himself from the slouch and motioned for Rachel to give him the photo. He took a long moment. Flicked his eyes back towards her. Then back at the photo.

"I know this guy. I'm pretty sure I know this guy. Ali, sweetie, take a look."

"Fine." The bartender took the photo, blinked a few times, and handed it back. "Doesn't ring a bell."

"I think I've seen him at the grocery store. Down at Lee's?"

Rachel stepped closer. "You know him? From here?"

"No, I don't think he's ever come here."

"Rodney. His name is Rodney."

Ali shook her head. "Not on my shift anyway."

The man eased the photo into Rachel's upturned palm. "I'm sorry."

Rachel stared at the pool table. *Clack*. The green felt, worn in the middle. *Clack*. Plastic cups of beer sweating on the rails. What was she doing? What was she thinking?"

"I hope you find him."

Ali pulled Rachel's dollar from her pocket, slid it across the bar. "The water is on me."

Rachel nodded, unable to answer, and left the dollar. She pushed through the door, blinded by sunlight. She tripped into the side of her car, let out a cry, then gritted her teeth and thought, *Jesus, help me.*

Maybe Jesus didn't want her to find Rodney.

She shivered. Got back into the car. Hands at ten and two,

she stared straight ahead and thought about how many more bars she would visit before she had to get back to her kids. It made her feel tired. It made her feel angry.

In the rearview mirror, in the parking lot across the street, was a police cruiser, two cops in the front seat staring her down. They'd caught up with her after all.

It didn't matter. Even if she led them straight to Rodney, she still needed to know. Needed to find him.

She started the car.

Next.

# CHAPTER 13

"Got this from Biloxi police." The young cop named Farragut shook a video tape. "I hear it's the feel good hit of the summer."

Hosea was slightly leery of most things electronic, due to growing up hearing his dad claim TV is evil, video games are evil, and even these innocent-looking cell phones, evil. "Designed to track you, know where you are at all times!"

Hosea thought, we're in the phone book. We get mail. We *want* people to find us.

The worst was Dad saying how pretty soon, people would start getting microchips inserted into their right hands or foreheads. The Mark of the Beast. The End of the World.

Enough to make anyone flinch a little when their cell phone rings.

Farragut replaced the previous tape in the VCR with the new one. Pretty soon, Captain Sarasota was standing behind them, watching over their shoulders. The screen lit up, black and white, jumpy. It showed the front of a convenience store, the right corner flaring from the lights, but very clearly showing an eighties Cutlass Supreme driving up to the store.

"This happened very early this morning, and Biloxi rushed it over once they got the story from the cashier, barely alive. He died at the hospital. And the owner of the car was a real mess."

"Slow down. What exactly is this?" Tara asked.

"We think Charles Lott. They found the Audi belonging to the original victim in a casino parking garage about a mile away."

They watched as a tough-assed white guy swept into the frame, slid into the car, and almost took off before the driver ran outside and confronted him.

The frames jumped, a few seconds at a time, in silence.

The driver got his hand stuck in the window. The thief was barely visible through the windshield. The driver was in distress. Yelling, they could all tell. Then the driver's window exploded. Everyone in the room hissed, turned away. Then the thief was standing on the pavement, stomping the shit out of the driver.

The thief looked up at someone. Must be the cashier, out of frame. The thief lifted his gun. *Blam. Blam.* No sound. Only two flashes of light on the silent tape, but each one made Hosea flinch.

The thief held his hands out. *Look what you made me do.* Then he stepped over to the injured driver. Leaned over, gun barrel to the temple. Another flash.

The thief got back in the car, drove away.

Everyone was quiet. Farragut paused the tape, leaving a blurry image of two more victims bleeding out.

The Captain crossed his arms. "Any word on him since then?"

"They didn't say."

He sighed. "I'll call Biloxi. The rest of you, work it. Work every angle. We'll meet up in a bit."

Hosea started past him on the way out, but the Captain put a hand on his shoulder. "Come on."

They stepped out of earshot, off to the side. The Captain, as usual, smirked instead of smiled. A Southern male through and through – hunted, fished, loved Mississippi State football – with salt and pepper hair, his good looks wrinkling fine. He had been a damned good detective himself before the promotion. Rumors were he would be running for county sheriff soon.

"Hosea, you've been on it all day?"

"Yes sir."

"You need a break. You and Tara both. Go get yourself a po-boy and come back in two hours."

"Now? Sorry, sir, but I can handle it."

"You get much sleep last night?"

"I'll sleep after we catch them."

The Captain was shaking his head before Hosea finished the sentence. "What's this I hear about your brother-in-law?"

"Okay."

"Okay what?" There was no need to ask. The man already knew. He wanted to see how straightforward Hosea would be with him.

"Rodney Goodfellow is married to my sister."

"And that doesn't set off some warning lights for you? Conflict of interest?"

Hosea slipped his hands into his pockets. "I want him caught."

"Yeah, I know, but...Preacher, you should know better."

It stung. The Captain hadn't called him that before. Hosea didn't realize he knew about it. Especially bad because Captain Sarasota was a died-in-the-wool Baptist and known to teach a Sunday School lesson every now and then.

"I'm not a preacher anymore."

"But you're still a brother-in-law. Listen, take a break and come back fresh. I can't let you go out chasing him, but you can work it from the office."

"Oh, come on."

"If we get a hit on Lott, great, he's nothing to you. Have at him. But I can't risk you and the butcher finding Jesus at the wrong time, praying the sin away or whatever."

"I said I'm not—"

"Go home, alright?"

The Captain walked away, called for Tara. It was too late for the boat trip, but at least she could see Demetrius for a couple hours.

Hosea felt awfully bone-tired and thankful he'd been called on it. He waved across the room to Tara and then tossed a few nods around on his way out the door.

Home sweet home was the top floor of a house on a road crowded by live oak trees, twisting and fighting above them, while Spanish moss created a creepy hanging garden. The home was owned by Margaret, a widow in her sixties glad to be rid of her deadweight husband. Now she had friends, hobbies, vacations – a full menu she'd denied herself while married to a hard-drinking son of a bitch. Anyway, she turned her second floor into an apartment and specifically wanted a single youngish man staying around. Hosea mowed the lawn and did some errands, paid way less rent than he should.

Up the side stairs to his door, already hearing his dog scratching inside, eager to pee. Hosea let out the little tan French bulldog, Pecan, and she bounced her way downstairs to the yard, ran around in circles, then flopped onto her back and rolled around. Hosea watched and waited. He didn't want to shout for her – it might alert Margaret he was home, and the last thing he wanted was a talk with Margaret right now. She was louder than a concert and as long as a drum solo. He was hoping to stay out of her way one more night, because tomorrow she was flying out to Arizona to see her grandkids.

Pecan did her business and slowly climbed the stairs. Always faster going down than up. Taking on the old girl was a mission of mercy. Some friends from Hosea's preaching days couldn't afford to keep up with her medicine for severe allergies, but he had a little extra cash and no one to spend it on but himself. Besides, he was lonely.

Inside, he could tell Dawn Hollingsworth had been here to feed Pecan. He'd asked her to help out, mainly as an excuse to give her a key. Not like he expected Dawn to move in or anything. After all, she was a serious church singer, still living with her folks two years after graduating college. At least it was nice to know he could depend on her to feed and water the puppy, get to know her better. Once she was in love with the dog, well, who's to say?

Hosea laughed to himself. They weren't far along yet and he knew he'd never get into her panties before marriage, not a chance.

Don't even think about it.

What the hell was he doing, dating a church girl? She was

almost ten years younger, one hundred percent committed to God, impossibly cute and smart and...

If she was fishing for a husband, then no. Hosea wasn't her cup of tea. Not for a long time, or never. A confirmed bachelor. Didn't they used to call guys like him that? If it was anybody else but Dawn, who took him by surprise, Hosea wouldn't even try dating again.

When he'd gone to bed last night, all he thought about was lunch with her. A second date after last weekend's dinner and a walk on the beach. Easy, casual. But now he couldn't think about that without thinking of pieces of a man scattered all over the bayou, put there by his brother-in-law.

His mail had been shoved under the door by Margaret. He kicked it out of the way. His place was small, considering the size of the house. The woman kept a few rooms upstairs for storage, hoarding, whatever. Hosea was left with a kitchenette/living room combo, the smallest bathroom he'd ever seen but still had a shower in it, and a bedroom so small he could barely get a twin mattress in, not enough room for a bedside table. No closet. He improvised a metal bar nailed into the corner for his suits and shirts.

He flopped onto the bed. Pecan scratched his legs because she was too small to jump up on her own.

"Not now."

She kept scratching.

He thought about Rodney and Rachel. How the man's lovelorn pursuit of her now felt like creepy stalking. His conversion versus her life as a preacher's kid. Marriage as arm wrestling. Someone was going to have to give eventually, and no matter how strong he'd been told the Holy Ghost was at beating back temptation, temptation had a mighty fine track record.

Probably because most of the shit Pentecostals said was bad wasn't all that bad. A lifetime of testing, testing, testing. Testing what? Oh, faith? Faith wasn't the problem. Feeling like you were a zoo exhibit was the problem. A freak.

Hosea let out a deep breath, felt the day's weight on his

back. Pecan stopped scratching, ran out, and came back in with a stuffed alligator she'd nearly ripped to shreds. She shook it hard between her teeth a few times before settling down and licking it.

Feeling himself drifting to sleep as the sun hung low in the sky, Hosea pushed himself up and took his suit off. Sniffed it, scanned it for sweat rings and dirt. This one needed the dry cleaner, stat. Kicked off the loafers. Steamy, muddy around the edges. Damn.

The voice in his head scolded him: *Family emergency and you're still worried about your clothes, your love life, yourself above others.*

What was he supposed to do? Captain Sarasota's orders.

*Go find Rachel. Talk to her.*

That was his dad's job.

The thought came too fast. Shamed him. No, he wasn't as close to his family as they all were to each other, but this time the voice was compulsory.

Hosea went to wash his face. Bags under his eyes. He needed a shower, too, but was in too much of a rush. He peeled off his t-shirt, boxers and soaked through socks, tossed them into the clothes basket, already overflowing, and walked over to the kitchen cabinets. Chocolate-covered peanut butter granola? Good enough for now. Made him think about the few times he'd found Margaret in a diabetic stupor and had to help her out – make her drink super sweet tea, or one time call for the ambulance. She'd taught him how to give her an insulin injection in case of an emergency.

After a couple of those granola bars, he tossed on jeans and a Hilfiger polo, some scuffed up Reeboks, and decided to take Pecan along. The kids loved her. He stopped at the doorway. A part of him wanted nothing more than to stay, watch TV, and doze off on his ridiculously small yellow and brown plaid loveseat he'd found at Goodwill.

But not while Rodney was on the run. Not tonight.

Almost to the car, Hosea heard his name called from the front porch. He couldn't ignore her. Pasted a smile on, turned and walked over to Margaret, in a rocking chair, an older gentleman friend in the next seat. She made introductions – Hosea thought his name was Richard or Wicker or Wilem – and then asked, "Water my house plants?"

"I will."

"If you miss a day, it might as well be a lifetime to them."

He'd missed lots of days before and she had never noticed. "I'll soak them down. I hope you have a good trip."

"I tell you, these kids, I love them but I can leave them, too." She laughed. "One reason I won't move in with my son and his family. Being Grandma is nice in short doses. Right, Willem?"

Or Wicker. Or Richard.

Pecan had settled beside the man's chair, and he brushed his fingertips across her back. Good. If she liked him, he must be good people, but Hosea knew they would never see him again, whatever his name was. Margaret went through old men fast as a game of solitaire.

"I've got to go. Work to do."

Margaret tutted him. "You ought to settle down. Life's not all about work."

He walked to the car. His phone rang. He opened the door and helped Pecan inside before answering.

The news was not good.

# CHAPTER 14

Cops on the curb. Only one cruiser. That's all the wife of a notorious fugitive got from her neighborhood pigs? They could be napping at the wheel. They could be laughing about O.J. Simpson, how the LA cops framed him good but those fucking lawyers still got that black son-of-a-bitch off.

Them blacks, Charles imagined the pigs saying. They're taking over.

Good, Charles thought. They got better food, better music. Long as they leave white women alone, buy what I'm selling, s'all good.

He was watching them from the woods behind Rodney's house, late afternoon. Out here in the boonies, the houses were scattered, the lots were big and there were no fences. Two cops sitting on a curb might as well be a couple of sleeping cats.

Charles had dumped the Cutlass and picked up a Chevy pick-up truck. A rattle-trap. A rust bucket. Damned thing was brown with *beige* racing stripes. He was pretty sure it was an employee's car, way out in the Walmart parking lot. The door lock gave way after a few hard pulls, and there was a spare key above the visor. No one would report it stolen until the end of shift. He had no idea where Rodney lived when he wasn't couch surfing, but a quick look inside the only intact phonebook hanging from the payphones outside the store gave him what he needed to know.

Plenty of time. He was hoping the whole family would be there, even Rodney hiding out in his daughter's closet, or under the bed, a true coward after all. He could put all of them out of their miseries at once. As far as he could tell, no one was there at all. No vehicle besides the cop cruiser. He'd work with that.

A flathead screwdriver, a handful of tries on the backdoor lock, and he was in. Except not, because there was a big ass *something* blocking this door. He gave it a shove. Moved a few inches. He put his whole weight into it and kept it moving until he was inside. A door-tall stack of boxes. Guess there was no more room for storage in a house this small. He closed the door, left the boxes ajar and crouched down below window level. The kitchen was open to the living room. Kids' toys all over the floor. Passed-down furniture, but a new TV. Picture frames crowding one wall, lots of family shots, the kids. Hardwood floor covered by cheap rugs.

Hands and knees to avoid the large front window. Charles scuttled along the short hallway breaking off into two bedrooms and a bath. Once inside the more adult-looking bedroom, he stood. Some clothes tossed around, mostly women's. Unmade bed. Chest of drawers, an oval mirror on a stand.

Charles sat on the bed. The whole house was claustrophobic. He imagined prison must feel like this. How could a family of four stand it?

Oh where, oh where has Rodney gone?

"Hey, buddy, you in here?"

He got down on all fours. No one under the bed. Checked the closet. Nope. Kids' room? Nothing.

"Hey, man, it's me. Your old buddy Charles. We did it, man, we got away."

No sounds. No movement. He wasn't here.

Charles tried to imagine being married with kids. It had changed Rodney. The church had even more, but Rodney wouldn't have bothered with the church if not for Rachel. Charles had never met her. Rodney had cut his ties for a long while there, but then started coming back around. Charles had teased him. A Jesus high could only last so long, same as any other drug.

Thinking about the ways this would end – death or prison

– Charles wondered if he'd be the type to turn to God in jail.

Shit no. All he remembered from going to church with his granny when he was young was being bored out of his skull. Coloring pictures of hippie Jesus and smiling people in robes all the time. When he tried to play with the other kids, always a bit too rough, he was put into time-outs by hags who didn't even know him.

No, church was whack.

If they did catch him alive, then prison for him was going to be the hard road. He'd do what all the white boys did and go Aryan, in spite of him not wanting to. Didn't matter. It was about survival. Tattoo an SS symbol on his neck. There would be no parole for Charles. No Presidential pardon. He'd never go back to the real world. Had to watch it pass by from a cage.

Death or jail.

Death or jail.

Standing in the kids' room, surrounded by bright colors, plastic toys, and cartoon characters, Charles didn't feel invincible anymore. The meth high was deflating, his nerves causing his hands to shake and his bladder to fill. He'd never thought much about dying before because he had a lot of living to do. Taking people out, fuck, what a trip. He'd watched three men die in short order. He liked how powerful it was. Knew what it felt like to be a cop for once, walking around with a license to kill. James Fucking Bond.

But now, how'd his plan sound now, his hopped-up dream of infamy?

He didn't have to answer the question. Someone unlocked the front door.

She came in alone. Had to have been, or Charles would've already heard the kids. Kids don't ever shut up, do they? She closed the door and sighed.

Then her shoes hit the floor – one two – and each barefoot step made a little squeak on the floorboards.

He had hidden himself in Rachel's closet. As good a place as any. Listened to her walk around. Kitchen, living room. Sat down. He wondered how long she would stay put. He might have to try sneaking in there, hoping the cops might be heading the other way.

Soon enough the squeaking continued, and then she was in the bedroom. Charles tried to get a good look at her. If he hadn't known already, he wouldn't have pegged her for one of those Pentecostals, those women he'd seen with the big beehive hairdos and long dresses. This one had the dress, yeah, but a haircut. He tried to imagine her with a beehive. Hard to keep from laughing. Must've left some of her beliefs on her hair stylist's floor.

Rachel stared into the mirror, wrinkled her nose, checked her face. Probably for zits. She started to unbutton the dress, but then stopped. Furrowed her brow. Had she spotted him? She turned to the closet with a gasp.

He pushed the closet door open with his gun and walked right up to her until he was in her face. If not for the gun, she'd be screaming. Every muscle in her face tight.

"So, you're Miss Jesus, the one who saved Rodney."

Nothing from her.

He lifted his free hand, placed it on her cheek.

She whispered, "Please."

"Don't scream. Don't shout. Don't sing a little song. Stay still and tell me where Rodney is."

"Please. I don't know."

He brushed her hair over her ear with his gun barrel. Admired her face. Plain, washed clean, and yeah, a couple zits. But she had a cute squashed nose. A prominent chin. Not perfect, but him and Rodney would never get "perfect" anyway. Perfect was far out of their league.

The girl who had escaped – "Kris," remember for later – she was a lot hotter, younger, showing more skin, had thick mascara round her eyes, the way all slutty girls do. She was half-drunk and hanging out with a drug dealer. Chick like her was more Charles' speed.

But hey, this one...

"Listen," Close enough to kiss her. "I think you know where he is, and I don't think you want to get hurt."

She cleared her throat. Quietly said, "I don't know. I was just trying to find him. I have no idea."

"Seriously? He ain't called you?"

"Not a word."

Charles stared into her eyes while she blinked, tried looking away. "You know what we did, right?"

A nervous nod.

"How'd you find out?"

"The police. The police, outside, the police."

"Not a middle-of-the-night call from your baby?"

Tears now. Involuntary. He could tell she hated herself for crying in front of him. "The police told me. Please, I need to go get my kids. I won't tell anybody you were here."

Charles lowered the gun – nine bullets left, he remembered. None to waste. He stuck it into her gut. "What we need to do is, you're going with me to search for Rodney. You know him a lot better than me. Don't tell me you have no idea. He's somewhere. Me and him need to talk. Badly."

"My kids."

"Goddamn your kids! They're a lot safer where they are than they are with you and me. We're going out the way I came in. You won't make a sound or you'll die so fast you won't even remember dying."

He made her crawl through the living room, into the kitchen, and then they stood, walked out the backdoor. Charles left it open. She was never coming back to it, he figured. Why lock up? The phone started ringing as they descended the steps. Rachel turned around. Charles grabbed her arm, pulled her hard. Pointed straight ahead of her. They walked.

The cops never noticed a thing…until Hosea came blazing up the street a little while later with extra cruisers following.

They'd had their radio volumes down too low to hear the calls earlier. Too busy talking about O.J. to do their jobs.

# CHAPTER 15

Rodney had been preached at plenty about Hell – the burning, screaming, eternal darkness – but he couldn't imagine a worse Hell than this duck blind in the bayou, hiding like a coward.

Bugs, noise, fetid odors, and swishing in the water inches below him. Gators. Had to be. All he could do was whisper prayers, the sort that go *If only you'll let me live, if only you'll save me from prison and the death penalty…*

Far as Rodney could tell, God wasn't listening. No matter what the preacher said on Sundays about an ever-loving, all-forgiving Jesus, Rodney felt his prayers bouncing back. Missed lay-ups on Heaven's half-court.

The elements were fucking with him. The heat made him sweat, then the sweat evaporated and made him cold. Crickets rubbed their legs together by the thousands. Birds called and cawed, angry or in danger, what was the difference?

When his friend came around with more water and food, Rodney begged, "Get me out of here. I can't take it."

"Shush, now. I can't yet."

"Yes you can! I can hide in the boat. I can hide in your car."

The friend, Glen Elgin, crouched and shook his head.

Rodney, on his knees, grabbed the man by the shirt, both hands. "Glen, I'm going to die out here. You've got to help me."

Rodney let go of the shirt – an expensive one, of course – and Glen fell back on his ass, eyes wide. Dirty smudges all over his chest. The preacher cleared his throat, got some composure back.

"Rodney…you've got to be patient. Every cop on the coast is after you." Trying to wipe dirt off his shirt but only spreading it wider, deeper. "This is the best place for you now."

Rodney stared at the plastic bag. More cheap food, only water to drink, but he was parched. He picked up the refilled Gatorade bottle Glen had brought along, drank half of it in one long pull.

"Save it! I won't be back until tomorrow."

Rodney grimaced. The water was cold. "No, man, no, I need to get out of here."

"One more day?"

"You don't know what it's like."

"We've got to be careful. The only reason I'm helping you is to give you time to make it right with God."

Rodney thought for a moment he should get in the boat anyway. Glen couldn't stop him if that's what Rodney really wanted. Get in, duck down, and tell the preacher to figure this out.

Where did he get the fancy boat? Who did he borrow it from, and what did he tell them? Certainly not the truth.

Glen said, "You should turn yourself in. Tell them what you told me."

Like Rodney hadn't already thought of that a hundred times over. "Not yet."

"Think of your kids, man. Think of Rachel."

Rodney stood up. To hell with anyone watching. "You don't think I am? Jesus, Glen, this ain't easy! I need to work some things out in my head. In my *soul*, alright?"

"I can help you. You can't run forever."

"I'm not asking for forever. You said you wouldn't tell. You swore."

Glen nodded. "You're right, I did. But as your friend, I've got to say, this is bad, man. How do you think this is going to end?"

Some friend, Rodney thought. Glen obviously thought he was better than Rodney, condescending. At first, Rodney didn't think much about it. He was "new in the Lord," and he had a lot to learn. Glen went slowly, took him through the

Bible, called him a lot, asking him to go grab a burger and talk about how to grow as a Christian – or what he could do for the church. Clean it up? Run errands? Become an usher on Sunday? Sit on the front row? Put in a lot of hours in the prayer room?

Busy, busy.

Glen was a good guy, but he eventually drifted his attention to other newbies. They got together less often, less still after Rodney married Rachel, even though Glen was Best Man. Good guy, though, and good uncle. But phony. As Rodney began to slide away from the church, Glen tried hard to get him back. More burgers and talks, but this time, it was an act. Rodney was nothing but a butt in a pew, his feelings an afterthought.

Glen shook him out of his thinking with, "We could call Hosea, turn yourself in to him, if it would make you feel better."

The other Elgin brother. The cop. Rodney had kept his distance, thinking Hosea didn't like him much anyway. Sure, *he* was one to judge, having an affair with a married woman while preaching about *sin, sin, sin*! Typical.

Rodney bowed his head. "One more day. Let me think."

"Fine. Tomorrow night. We make a decision?"

Rodney nodded.

"Good, that's smart."

Rodney winced, didn't let Glen see.

The preacher got up, wiped his hands across his trousers. The damp wood had given him wet blotches on the back of his pants. Glen was probably already thinking of putting a towel down on his car seat.

Rodney watched him go, his chest on edge. Each breath pushing him closer to jumping onto the boat anyway. But it receded into the water, silently, until far out in the middle. Glen started the engine, turned, and eased off between trees with bloated roots that looked like they were drowning.

He listened to the engine fade, peeked in the bag Glen left. A pack of bologna. Some Snickers bars. Saltines.

Saltines? What an asshole.

Hours went by. Rodney watched brown pelicans come and go, catching fish in their beaks. Watched the sky change colors. Rethought every decision he'd ever made from sixteen, when he first started drinking, getting high, until the night before, going to get his butcher's tools from the store. Every single moment.

Wooing Rachel.

The fight with Rachel.

The days both his children were born.

First steps.

Sawing off Burt's head.

*No.*

Shuddered at the thought. Another prayer: *Sorry, so sorry.*

Frogs croaked. A chorus of grim reapers.

Soon joined by horses galloping. An army of them.

Impossible. Was it real? Imagined?

He crawled to his peephole, saw only open water. But the sound was growing louder, angrier.

Boats. Not one or two, but a lot.

Shit!

The engines weren't wide open. A steady thrumming growing closer, all around him.

It was a nightmare. An army of bass boats, fanned out from shore to shore, all with at least one cop onboard, holding long poles. They poked along the shore, the bayou, the huge cypress trees and curtains of Spanish moss. Some had binoculars. He lost count of the boats – nine? Ten? – but realized they were definitely coming his way.

It was over.

Rodney shrank away from the peephole, almost fell between the floor and the back wall of the blind. Rickety. Felt as if it might give way. He looked down. Gave the bottom board a push. It moved.

The boats were getting closer. He heard someone say "Somebody's duck blind right there."

"Yeah, check it out."

One of the boats turned his way.

Rodney could fit. If he pushed the board back, he could slip into the water between the floor plank and the back wall.

The boat was getting closer.

No time to think about gators, snakes, garfish. He held the plank as he climbed into position, dropped into the cold brown water as quietly as possibly. Almost to his shoulders before seeing the *bag*! The food, the water bottle. He launched up, stretched as far as he could.

The boat, almost there. They cut the engines. Clear as day: "Sure is a shitty blind."

"Guess it works for them."

"No idea who it belongs to, huh?"

Got the bag with the tip of his middle fingers. Hooked it, swung it over, and under he went. He let go, pushing himself under the plank, finding it with his hand, keeping him steady. He didn't open his eyes underwater, so he'd need to depend on sounds. Hoped to God there wasn't a water moccasin hunting him. Curious fish swam close, he could *feel* them.

Voices, but he couldn't understand what they were saying. Then a couple of heavy clunks – boot soles on the floor plank. Rodney wondered if he'd left any footprints up there.

Another few seconds.

He risked opening his eyes. He hadn't had to hold his breath this long since he was a kid goofing off in the public pool with his friends. About to burst. He couldn't let some out. They'd see the bubbles. Fucking *hurt*.

Then another noise. Tapping. Off to his left. It was the goddamned pole. Sliding it up and down the plank, poking under. He was right out of reach. Then the pole slid up. Rodney realized they were about to poke it down his side.

He kicked his feet, heavy in shoes, to move to the other side. Missed the tip of the pole jabbing downwards, cocked at an angle underneath, sliding up and down the plank.

More voices. Laughter.

Rodney held tight to the water bottle and bag of food. His

eyes burned. What was that off to the right? Something moving. Something big. No, his eyes playing tricks on him.

More bootsteps from above, the vibrations running through his hand.

*I'm going to die.*

It wasn't worth dying for, was it? Should he give up now? Lungs straining, burning, pleading, *Breathe! Breathe!*

Then the boots stepped off the plank. The boat engine revved.

*Breathe!*

Wait, wait.

The engine noise receded.

Hold on.

Receded more.

To a whisper.

Rodney scrambled back to the other side of the plank and burst through the water, spewing out bad air and sucking in fresh. He slung the bag and bottle back onto the plank and rested both his elbows on its side.

Dizzy, seeing black spots, he tried to get his bearings. Hoping the cops didn't hear him. How long had it taken? Hours? Probably only a few minutes. Weak. He was bone-tired. The food, probably okay except the saltines, crushed under his arm. Saltines dried him out anyway.

Were they suspicious? Would they be back with divers? He didn't think so. They would've tried harder, would've stayed longer. No, Rodney had to be in the clear. They would not be back.

But he was wet, clammy. Filthy. The stink of fish and saltwater mixing with his own sweat. Stuck here until Glen came back. The blind felt more like a coffin than it had earlier, if not for the sun high above.

But safe.

Safe wasn't enough. His nerves jangled. He couldn't stay here anymore.

So, what, then? Wait for Glen's next visit and force him to take him along, hide him some place else?

No, Rodney had to go *now*. There had to be other safe places. Safer, even. He wanted to be proactive, not at the mercy of someone else. He'd had enough.

Okay, he'd told Glen he would turn himself in the next day. He'd told Glen they could pray together. He would repent, cleanse himself, and face the law in peace.

He'd lied.

There had to be a better choice out there somewhere.

The engines had faded to a faint echo, blending with the buzz of insects. Rodney took a chance and stood tall, first time in over twenty-four hours. His back was killing him. He stretched it out.

No boat.

Fuck it. He was already wet. Might as well go swimming.

CHAPTER 16

Chaos outside Rachel's house. Light and sound from the cruisers, neighbors crowded around. Cops' radio noise. Cops coming and going.

Hosea had gotten a call from his Aunt Eileen asking about Rachel. She had left her kids there that morning, said she was going on to work, but work said she'd never shown up, and there was no answer on the house line. Not like her at all.

Now he was here with back-up. The two cops assigned told him they hadn't seen or heard a thing before or after she'd come home. They'd watched her go inside. Hosea didn't bother asking why their radio was turned down so low they couldn't answer if called, or when they last actually physically checked on her. He'd get someone else to yell at them for it later.

He rolled down his window a little for Pecan and she barked at all the uniformed cops passing by.

One of the cops had spotted the open back door of the house, called for help. Lydia, Broussard, and a couple others went through there, unlocked the front door from inside.

They met Hosea out by Rachel's car. "No one here."

A small relief. Hosea had imagined his sister dead on the kitchen floor.

Lydia clicked her gun back into its holster.

Broussard said, "No sign of struggle other than the back door pried open. A bunch of toys scattered all over."

"Well…" Lydia, sheepish. "She left her purse. No woman is going to leave her purse if she can help it."

Hosea's stomach lurched. He put a hand to his stomach.

"Jesus."

"Should've had more people here."

"Should've."

"How the hell did he get this far without being noticed?"

"Rodney *lives* here. He knows the place better than we do. He must've sneaked in and waited for her."

Hosea drifted towards the house, Lydia and Broussard in tow. "He pried into the back door?"

"Crowbar or hammer, yeah."

Hosea knelt at the wooden steps up to the front door. He hadn't needed to do this before, but Rachel had told him about it. He felt along the edge of the second step until he felt a piece of wood give. Worked it out. There, on a hooked nail, was the spare key to the front door.

Broussard crossed his arms. "Yeah, but…" He nodded towards the cruiser on guard duty.

"True. And he left his keys in the truck, didn't he?"

"Get someone to check if he took his house keys off the ring."

Broussard got on his radio.

Hosea went inside.

His niece and nephew were safe, but seeing their toys on the living room floor nearly did him in. He imagined them playing with Pecan. He would have to stop by his aunt's house later.

What was he thinking? Hosea had work to do.

A quick walkthrough of the small house didn't help. Of course not. Neither would the tweezer-and-microscope brigade.

Where had she been if not at work?

He found Broussard, asked if he knew about it.

The report came in she'd been out visiting a bunch of bars. One after the other, a few minutes in each one, all around town. They'd kept a tail on her. Then she drove home.

Rachel wouldn't leave her kids with Eileen without a better story. She would've at least called to say, *Can you keep them overnight? I don't want them involved in all this.* The idea she would disappear without a word – her own choice – boggled his mind. This was all about Rodney. His hold on her.

Or was she forced?

The bedrooms. Tangled sheets and blankets. Yesterday's clothes scattered. He stood beside her bed – *their* bed – and put his hands in his pockets. Don't corrupt the crime scene – *his sister's bedroom was a crime scene*. His stomach growled. He checked to see if things were out of place. But how would he know? The men in his family had never gotten to know Rachel as well as they should. She was Mom's. They'd had their own secrets.

Broussard walked into the room as softly as anyone could, the floorboards and all. "Hosea, the Captain wants to talk to you."

He wasn't on the phone. He was actually on scene, out front. Hosea was somewhat surprised. Sarasota wasn't a field man anymore and didn't miss it. He was great in a conference room, though. He'd taken off his tie.

"Anything?"

"Didn't expect anything."

"He slipped right past us?"

"We should get some photos out for both of them. They can't have gone far. I mean, I talked to Dubois and Kingston in the stakeout car. She'd only been home twenty minutes when I rolled up."

"Twenty minutes could mean halfway to Mobile, Biloxi."

"Shit, I know."

"Don't worry, we've got it under control."

"What do you mean 'Don't worry'? It's the only thing I can do."

Out of the corner of his eye, Hosea saw Tara roll to a stop across the street, get out and cross. Wearing jeans and a tucked in MPPD polo now. Work boots. She made her way over, stood next to them, didn't say a word. Hands in her back jeans pockets.

Hosea knew what it meant. When the crime was this close to a cop, that cop's mind might get clouded. Might make it hard to decide when a decision needs to be made lightning fast. Doesn't matter Hosea's record. His commendations. Number of cases cracked. Can't expect a man to draw down on his family if necessary.

"I can do this. I have to do this."

Sarasota shook his head. "Charles Lott is still out there. Keep after him."

"I can do both."

Tara put her hand high on Hosea's arm, gave it a rub. "I've got this. I'll call with updates. You get your head in a better place."

Hosea ran his hand through his hair. Habit. It would mess up the gel, but he didn't care. It was what he did when upset, impatient, frustrated. "Please. I can't tell my dad this. I already had to tell him about Rodney."

"We'll get someone else to."

"No, no, that makes it worse." Hand through his hair again, again, again.

Tara backed up. "There are worse things than letting Hosea shadow us, sir."

"Well, dang it, I've only got two of you. I need you both on different parts of this thing before it gets away from us. Still no sign of Lott, no sign of Rodney, except for this. So, do what I say. Period."

They both mumbled "yessir" but it didn't matter because Sarasota was already headed back to his car.

Tara looked at Hosea. "Don't worry. Go be with your dad."

"Easy for you to say."

"Whatever. Get off my crime scene, will you?"

She walked off.

Hosea sighed, started for his car. Pecan was standing in the driver's seat, her front paws hooked over the rim of the window.

# CHAPTER 17

Didn't matter he had another person in the truck now, Charles still played his music loud and rapped along. Fuck this Jesus bitch. She had followed without much of a fight, mumbling prayers under her breath. She told Charles if he turned himself in, he might still find mercy from the Lord.

"Shit, I don't want mercy. Means I'm not in control."

"But you aren't now either."

"I'm more in control than God is. This man they say we killed, if God didn't want him dead, why didn't he step in with some thunder and lightning to stop us?"

"That's not how it works."

"Exactly. Shut up, will you?"

But he wanted to keep talking because he was coming down, and fear was lurking in the back of his head. His heart was going too fast. Nighttime was coming and he couldn't imagine sleeping yet.

"You said you hit all the bars?"

"Not *all* the bars, I don't know all the bars. I hardly know any bars! I…never mind."

"No, not never mind. You're supposed to help me here."

Rachel spread her fingers across her forehead. "I don't know! I don't know where to go. Whoever he used to be, he didn't tell me much. I mean, who are you to him? I have no idea."

"Just bros. Hanging out. Smoke a little, drink a little, know what I'm saying?"

She let out a hot breath.

"You took him off the map, you know. He got in church, it was one hundred percent. I didn't see him for almost a year after that. I don't know about you guys fighting, but still, even last night? He was a different person. You changed him."

Rachel turned. "Then why didn't he call the police? Why didn't he stop you?"

"He would've tried, I'd have killed him. You believe me?"

She closed her eyes. "In Jesus' name—"

"Don't. Don't pull none of your holy magic tricks. Tell me where Rodney might go."

"Jesus, Jesus, Jesus, Jesus. Does that make you nervous? Jesus, Jesus, Jesus."

Charles flinched. Should slap his name out of her mouth. No, what would his mamma say?

A long stretch of silence, then he said, "I'm not going to hurt you."

"Oh, I *know*." More pissy than afraid.

No fear, no anxiety. Jesus was her superpower. Girl could use roughing up. Had a nice shape to her, worth a good, brutal fuck. But she kinda scared him a bit. Could be the ice fucking with his senses, but she almost had an *aura* or some shit all around her. He blinked his eyes. Even brighter this time.

He wanted Rodney more than he wanted to get busy with his wife. On second thought, he didn't like her nose.

"Listen, give me a clue. Where might he be? Come on, let's go, think, think, think, missy."

She held up her palm, upturned. "I don't – I could check his dad's house, I guess."

"Okay, that's a mighty fine idea. You and him, everything good there?"

"I guess. We don't talk much. Only met him a few times."

"But he wouldn't think it weird, right? You show up at his house?"

"I…guess not?"

Cool.

Charles slid by his momma's place one more time. Still a cruiser in place, all dark, and there had to be others, hidden. He didn't slow down, didn't stop. Nice and smooth. Still trying to figure out how to get in touch with Mom, see what the cops were feeding her.

"Let's go." Charles thumped the steering wheel. "Daddy's house."

Grand Bay, Alabama, was right over the state line, carved out of woods, full of people who preferred the woods anyway. Large lots of land, old wooden houses, the grass high in the ditches and fields. Few lighted roads out on the edge of town.

Charles thought about how he'd known Rodney for years but never met his dad or his mom or even asked if he had sisters or brothers. Rachel said Rodney's mom moved out when he was in middle school, but he chose to stay with his dad and she didn't care. Rodney had been to Charles' grandma's house plenty. His mom lived there between divorces and boyfriends, until she settled in the trailer. Shame, Charles thought. What would happen to Grandma's house now?

The house was narrow, tall, red-brick. A steep roof and a loft room upfront. Gravel driveway, detached garage. The porch light was on, and some windows shone from inside. In the yard, a cracked birdbath, a pile of bricks, some two-by-fours. They parked behind Mr. Goodfellow's Dodge Durango, got out.

Charles was uneasy. Only now wondering, what if the cops had this place shadowed, too? They would be all over his ass by now, right? Or, what would he do if Rodney was here? Then what?

*Nine more bullets.*

What if he wasn't?

*Who cares?*

Carnage for the sheer fuck of it.

He followed Rachel up the porch steps to the front door. She rang the bell.

"You try to tell him I'm here, or you scream, you're all dying. Don't even think about it." Charles held the gun in one hand, loose like he'd hooked his finger into a key ring. Wasn't trying to hide it or nothing.

He heard some thumping, some footsteps from inside. But still, no one opened the door. Shadow behind the curtains.

Rachel rang again.

More waiting.

Rodney and the girl, Kris Cole. Rodney and Kris. Loose ends. Rodney and Kris. The only eyewitnesses. But if there were no eyewitnesses, there'd be no case. If Rodney was here, nine more bullets. But he needed to have some left over for Kris Cole. Man, he was racking up an impressive body count in his head.

The door opened a crack.

The sliver of a man's face. Weathered. One tired eye. "Rachel?"

"Vincent. Hi."

The eye flicked past her to Charles. "You okay?"

"Is Rodney here? I haven't been able to find him."

Eye still on Charles. "Who's he?"

"He's a friend. A friend of Rodney's. Helping me is all."

"Mm-hm." Quiet a moment. Vincent's eye back on Rachel. "I haven't heard from him."

"Please, I don't know where else to go."

"Are you sure you're okay?"

Charles laughed. "She said so, didn't you listen?"

"Just a second."

Vincent closed the door. A few more footsteps. Charles felt his insides getting hot. Boiling. "I told you not to—"

"I didn't! What did you want me to say?"

"I don't know." She turned and knocked on the door this time. "Vincent? Hello?"

The sheriff's car hiding in the shadows across the street came to life, headlights and flashing blues and a double-tap on the siren. It skidded to a stop on the tail of Charles' stolen truck.

Charles didn't hesitate. Turned and fired through the windshield. Couldn't tell if he hit anyone.

He snarled at Rachel. "Bitch, look what you did!"

Lifted the gun to her face.

Vincent swung the door wide open, pushed Rachel aside, and raised the barrel of a deer rifle.

Charles caught it quick and shot twice before Vincent knew what hit him. Rifle dropped. Charles backed up. Vincent lunged for him, shouting.

Another shot, dead center. The man was gone.

Rachel, though. She'd picked up the rifle. She was swinging it.

*Boom!*

Thirty-aught-six exploded, past Charles' head, blew out the living room window. She released the bolt and shoved another one home, ready to fire.

Charles scrambled off the front porch, back to the truck. The deputy on the passenger's side had his door open, ducked behind it, firing *bam bam bam*, putting holes in the truck.

On the porch, Rachel took better aim. Charles opened the door and dropped into the driver's seat, low, cranking the engine.

*Boom!*

The top of the truck ripped, the bullet sliced through. Charles hit reverse and slammed into the front of the cop car. Slammed again, this time pushing it right back into the middle of the road. He rolled down his window, searched for the deputy. Charles saw he'd killed the driver, slumped over the steering wheel. The other deputy was caught between the door and the frame, screaming. His arm and leg stuck in steel jaws.

Charles lifted his pistol, fired point blank at the deputy. Wasted his last bullet.

He got the fuck out of there.

Another *boom* behind him, echoing in the night air.

He was sure Vincent Goodfellow was dead, but now Rachel, despite her Jesus shield, was owed a bullet, too.

Goddamn. Charles laughed and laughed. What a day.

# CHAPTER 18

Hosea sat next to Rachel on the front porch of the Goodfellow place, a blanket around her, Hosea's arm around the blanket. The body of Vincent Goodfellow lay cooling under a white tarp. The carnage of the sheriff's cruiser hard to absorb. The Fire Rescue boys were trying to pry out the deputy's body with the jaws of life. Grand Bay cops, Alabama troopers, plus Hosea, Tara, and the Captain.

She was a ghost, shaking. The police had already talked to her about how she ended up here, about Charles, about her abduction. All those questions. She put her hands over her ears and shouted for her brother.

"Vincent knew there was a problem right away."

"The police had told him everything. It was a waiting game, but they thought – we all thought – it would be you and Rodney showing up."

"He didn't even know Charles."

"But he knew you, and he knew the guy with you looked like the guy that's wanted."

She nodded. Staring off into space.

"Rodney didn't *hate* his dad, but they weren't close either. Said he drank a lot. He seemed nice when I met him."

"Of course he did."

She dropped her face into her hands, the exhaustion catching up to her. "Oh, God. I don't want to be here anymore. Why is this happening?"

He gave his sister a squeeze. "Glad we taught you how to shoot in Africa."

"Charles was no hyena."

"I don't know what he is. He escaped two deputies, a man

with a hunting rifle, and then you. This guy…" Hosea hopped off the porch, stood in front of her. "Let me get you home. You can answer the rest of their questions tomorrow. I'll stay over."

"Drop me by Eileen's. I'll sleep there, the kids are there. I'm a mess. I need someone to talk me down."

"You sure?"

"Uncle Joel has his guns. We'll be fine."

"This guy won't be coming back for you. Not after what you did."

Hosea walked off to where some of the police were talking, cleared it with Tara and Sarasota, with the Grand Bay guys and EMTs, then they headed over to his car.

"Are you telling me the truth, though? Nobody would blame you."

"What?"

"Rodney hasn't tried to get in touch with you? Not once, all day?"

She told Hosea about going out to find Rodney, coming up empty, and how Charles surprised her at home. "I didn't even check the answering machine."

"We did. There was nothing."

"I can't believe…why did he? Why? I wish he would tell me why."

"Rachel—"

"Why wouldn't I be his first call? Maybe he really is dead."

"I don't think so."

"Then where is he? Why hasn't he turned up?"

They got into the car. Away from the crowd, Rachel let a heaving sob overtake her. Head bowed, her hand a claw on her scalp.

"Hosea, what am I going to do?"

"The right thing."

She wiped away tears. "Sure, I'm tough. Look at me."

"I don't know how you did it. This guy kidnapped you, threatened you, but in the end, he didn't hurt you and you got away. You're ten feet tall and bulletproof."

"I said 'Jesus' a lot. Freaked him out."

"How about that?"

"I know, right?" She closed her eyes and took a deep breath. "I was so…so…scared, Hosea, I wasn't strong at all. I was…*mad*. You know? I didn't have time to be anything but mad at him."

He dropped her off at their Aunt's house before deciding it would be the station instead of home. Hosea knew he wasn't going to get much sleep. He had failed his sister. The whole goddamn police force had failed her. This was going to haunt him for a long, long time.

Another victim, though. Vincent Goodfellow died trying to protect his daughter-in-law, who he barely knew. How many more would die before this was all over?

The Captain was right. This was too much for him.

Pecan crawled up from the backseat when Rachel left, curled into her warm spot and fell asleep.

Instead of heading straight over, he found himself driving past Charles Lott's house. Still taped, still some police there working, the big light in the garage shadowing them through the tarp. He parked, got out. Walked up to his colleagues, shot the shit a few minutes, then moved inside.

Evidence – marked, bagged and tagged. He wondered if there was anything left to find.

What he was looking for, though, was Rodney's stuff. He'd been there a couple of nights, according to Rachel.

He found it in the second bedroom, a sports duffel, New Orleans Saints. The contents had already been laid out on the unmade bed.

A wad of clothes.

A couple of plastic lighters and a glass pipe. *Aw, Rodney.*

A Bible with his name engraved on front, as new as the day he received it for a wedding gift several years before. Hosea remembered how Glen made a big deal of it. He wondered if Rodney had even cracked the spine.

Hosea was one to talk. His Bible was dusty enough to write

"Read me" across it. Which Dawn had done when she came over to feed Pecan.

Deodorant, toothbrush, half-a-tube of hair gel.

Baggie of weed.

Nothing to scream guilty, nothing to shout innocent. Nothing to give Hosea some hope.

He sat on the bed, puzzling it out.

The girl in the hospital said Rodney wasn't the shooter. So whose idea was it for him to get his knives and do *that* to the body? It might make a difference.

They had to bring him in first. No way to know otherwise.

Was somebody helping him stay hidden?

If it was up to Hosea, would he do the same thing?

He needed coffee. He needed to stop feeling the panic over Charles Lott getting to Rachel so easily, and then slipping away. This guy was a supervillain.

He stood and yawned. He shoved Rodney's things back into the duffel bag.

Outside, Pecan was still sleeping in the passenger seat. Poor girl. Dragging her all around town, all hours of the night. But wherever Hosea went, Pecan wanted to be. No worries there.

The dog had a simple life. No God to worry about, family long gone. Lots of rest, no ambitions.

Must be nice.

# CHAPTER 19

Next morning, Rodney was gone.

Glen Elgin stood in the duck blind, more appropriately dressed this time. Old jeans and a long-sleeved T-shirt. Sneakers he hadn't worn since he was twenty.

Didn't matter. Rodney was gone. The food and water bottle were left behind, but no sign of Rodney.

Maybe he was hiding nearby, but Glen didn't dare shout his name. He whispered it, hissed it, but there was no response.

Captured? Dead? Or on the run?

Glen stepped back into Brother Kingsbury's boat, which the old man couldn't use without help anymore, and was glad to let Glen take it for a while, "As long as you bring me back some of what you catch."

Glen couldn't remember the last time he'd been fishing. Was it with the man he called "Grandpa Emerho" from the church in Nigeria? He hadn't enjoyed it as much as Hosea had. His younger brother liked getting his hands dirty back then, enjoyed holding the slimy fish Emerho yanked from the river. Glen didn't want to touch it, didn't want the red clay on his clothes, hated the smell of it.

Hosea eventually followed his brother's lead in being a fine dressed man, but Hosea carried a wilder streak inside him.

Where was he now? Chasing the same man Glen was willing to get dirty for.

When Rodney called Glen and blubbered through what had happened, Glen didn't think twice. He picked up Rodney and hid him in the back of his car until it was a decent time to call and ask for the boat. He'd also heard the old man talk about duck hunting, asked if he had a special place he went.

Lucky, praise God.

Glen looked at it this way: God first, the needs of the church second, and his family right behind. Regardless of what Rodney had done, he was family, and he deserved help when he asked for it. Might lead him back to the Lord that way.

Now it was a mess.

Where could he have gone?

Glen puttered along the shore, scanning for any sign of Rodney, or what was left of him. He hated thinking it would be a lot easier if a gator had gotten Rodney. Any normal person in the same position might think it. But Glen wasn't *any person*. He was a man of God. Preacher of the Word. Prophesier.

He prayed the whole time –mumbling, really – for some sort of miracle. Questioned himself, too. He'd thought after a night out here to think about things, Rodney would be ready to turn himself in, but yesterday he still wasn't giving up, and Glen grew afraid this would all get found out. Aiding and abetting. And Hosea would start to suspect if he knew about the boat.

Mile after mile of water, vines, moss, tree trunks.

He slowed the engine to nothing, let the boat drift, and then threw up over the side. The sound cascaded across the bayou. Bile, burning. A punishment. He tried hard to keep it from splashing on his shirt.

After Glen was done, he started the boat, turned around, and got out of there as quickly as he could. He had a sermon to write.

Glen dropped off the boat with Brother Kingsbury and went home. His dad's car was gone, must have been out visiting older members of the church, or dropping in on people at the hospital. Or whatever it was he did in his spare time. Maybe the man just wanted a cheeseburger.

He walked inside, heard the parrot squawk, "My boy's

home!" It was what his mom had said when either of her sons came through the door.

Now alone in the house, out of everyone's sight, his legs turned to jelly and the tension turned to pain. Chest pain? A heart attack? No, no, nothing serious. Panic? Was this a panic attack?

He should have never answered his phone that night. But this was his calling. The caller I.D. box didn't help – payphone – so it was his *duty* as a minister to answer, with no idea who was on the other end. There was a good chance Jesus persuaded someone to call. Brushing it off for a few extra hours sleep was not part of the contract.

Dad had asked who it was as Glen slipped into his clothes.

He had to lie. It felt pretty sorry. "Someone I met last week. Needs me to pray with him."

It had happened to both of them many times before, calls at all times of the day and night – friends, congregants, strangers, family. Inconvenience didn't matter. The man of God went where he was needed, when he was needed. Glen thought about Jonah, refusing God's direction, ending up in the belly of a giant fish until he gave in. Or Job, tested by God, having everything taken from him, but still loyal to the Lord.

Of course, Job had complained a little. Okay, a lot. Some "woe is me," as anyone might expect, until God slapped back – "Who are you to question me?" – before blessing Job with more than he had originally lost.

It took some getting used to, being on call for the Lord, but it was what Glen had signed up for. The hard work first, then the rewards in Heaven. It was worth it to feel the anointing while he preached, the Holy Ghost coursing through his veins when he prayed for others. The *power* he felt. It made up for the low offerings, the needy people, and the other frustrations of pastoring.

No, *assistant* pastoring. The grunt work.

All in due time. Glen knew his dad was close to handing over the church to him.

He also knew he wasn't the first choice. If Hosea hadn't

flamed out after the affair, it would be a different story. Glen had to face the facts: Hosea had been the better preacher. He was a natural.

Glen was smart and steady, and he knew how to inflect his voice with authority. People liked him well enough, people trusted him, but in the way they thought of a stern teacher from school. Hosea had the charisma Glen lacked.

Glen went to the kitchen and poured a glass of sweet tea. Looked at the art and knick-knacks Mom had chosen to hang on the walls and display on the counters, most of it from Africa. Glen wondered how they were able to bring back a boatload of paintings, masks and musical instruments. Must have filled several suitcases. As the oldest, he remembered the frantic preparation to move, a lot of tears from their parishioners, his friends giving him a chilly goodbye, as if he were betraying them. The long airplane rides. Waiting in airports, trying to keep his younger brother and sister out of trouble. Giving up his own room at a large house to move into *this*, sharing a room with Hosea until they both graduated high school.

Everyone in Mississippi was wonderful to his family at first. Then there was a split in the congregation where at least ten families left to start their own church. It was all about his dad desiring to bring more black families into the fold. Oh, they would never put it in those words. They said "bucking traditions" or "not following God's plan."

No matter what they said, it was plain old racism.

The Elgins weathered it. All these years later, no more splits, plenty of new faces, white, black, and brown. The place felt like home.

Glen wished Hosea would leave forever. He made a huge mistake and should've been ridiculed for it. Shunned. But Dad went out of his way to make sure his younger son had a soft place to fall. He wasn't angry at the sin, he was heartbroken for the sinner. Glen pushed for more severe penance, more lasting. But Dad wasn't having it.

When this church became Glen's, he would run things

differently. There were going to be lots of changes.

As long as no one found out about Rodney.

There was a knock on the door, followed by it opening. Then why knock?

"Dad? Glen?"

Glen didn't answer. He took another long sip of tea.

The parrot: "My boy's home!"

Hosea found him after a minute. His brother, the cop, wearing nicely starched khakis, an immaculate print shirt with the sleeves rolled to his elbows, and a blue knit tie. A pistol on his hip.

How dare he.

Glen had no problems with guns, but Hosea wearing one in the house?

Hosea thumbed over his shoulder. "Were you hauling a boat earlier?"

Late into the night, Glen sat down at his desk to work on his sermon for Sunday morning, Dad letting him take the pulpit. He was drawn to the story of Barabbas, the criminal released instead of Christ. But was it too on-the-nose with Rodney and all? Wouldn't the congregation expect that? It would be strange not to comment at all. Rodney had been one of them. The story about what happened to Rachel was starting to spread. This couldn't be ignored.

Go farther back in time, the dawn of man. Cain and Abel. The mark we all carry, the ability to kill another human being.

No, no, no. Accusatory. Not the right tone.

What should we learn from all this?

What should Glen learn?

He didn't know the man who was killed. He certainly didn't know the killer. But Rodney...there was a bad taste in his mouth as Rodney told him, shaking the whole time, what had happened. What Rodney had done, it wasn't *real* in Glen's mind.

Hosea had been on the scene. Hosea was first to realize Rodney was involved. He saw the body, what was left of it.

He'd described it to Glen: "Mush. Bloody mush."

Hard to picture, not the same way he could picture the stripes on Jesus' back, which he'd also never seen.

It was getting close to one in the morning. Dad had come home after Hosea left and was already in bed, an exhausting couple of days for him. He was usually a night owl, up until three or four. When he got home that evening, he said he'd been to see Rachel at his sister Eileen's house. But what Glen heard him say was, *why haven't you?*

He wrote by only the light from monitor screen, which meant a lot of typos. He sat back, hands in his lap.

An image of his sister emerged, weeping. Reminded him of one of the women at the tomb, mourning Jesus. Not only missing a person, but a meaning for her life. Having to depend on a faith that's barely lit, the very idea of it ridiculous, but it was all she had to hold on to.

Glen nodded. It was good. It felt right.

He worked on the sermon for the better part of an hour, helping him to squelch the voice in his head telling him he failed Rodney. He failed the law. He failed his father.

Failure.

Wasn't the Apostle Paul a failure at first? Actually preaching *against* Jesus until his road to Damascus moment?

*You ain't Paul. You're not getting away with it that easy.*

Heartburn. Hand to his chest, rubbing. Swallowing the acid. Grimacing.

*Tap tap tap.*

He looked up. What was that? A squirrel on the roof? A dripping faucet?

Then louder. Insistent.

From his window.

Glen slid from his chair and crept to his window, hoping his dad didn't hear it, too. Stepping over Southern Gospel cassettes and library books scattered around his bedside. Hard to see out there over the reflection of his monitor.

*TAP TAP TAP TAP.*

He brushed back the curtains. Thought he saw movement.

116

He cupped his hands around his eyes and peered through the glass.

A face, a *horrible* face, startled him. Glen stumbled backwards.

Blinked.

Then realized – *tap tap tap tap tap tap* – it was Rodney, looking exactly like Jonah freed from the whale.

## CHAPTER 20

It had taken most of the day to get out of the bayou. Rodney was lost right out of the gate. Had to figure out east and west, north and south. The sun high overhead, hard to track it without fucking up his eyes. Flashing dots. Dark spots. Nothing to point the way.

He leapt from bloated root to bloated root among the trees, hoping to find a chain of them to solid land. But he struck out. Went back the way he came. Weaker each time he jumped.

He had to chance the water.

The shock of it woke him. His shoes filled with water and threatened to drag him down. He kicked them off. Swam like hell with the current – south, definitely south – unable to shake the feeling there were gators on his ass.

Terrified.

Probably garfish down there, too, with long rows of buzzsaw teeth.

Onward. One stroke at a time. His limbs burning, mouth filling with brackish water, Rodney had to turn and blow it out before he choked on it.

Everything around him – the trees and vines and water plants – looked the same. One big circle, never going anywhere.

Was that a pair of reptilian eyes above the water, watching him?

What was that brushing his leg?

Mind on the goal. Mind on the goal.

There, off to the right. A fishing shack, held together with scavenged wood and old car parts. A short rickety pier jutted out into the water.

He climbed the ladder at the end of the pier and flopped onto his back. Heaved in air, coughed up as much water as he could. Even his bones ached. He squeezed his eyes shut against the glare of the sun.

"Excuse me?"

The shout startled Rodney upright. Outside the shack, on two woven folding chairs, sat a middle-aged woman in a tank-top and visor, brown hair strands flying, and her daughter, probably about eleven, dirty-looking. Wide-eyed.

The mother leaned forward, ready to push off the chair. To grab a rifle?

"What the hell?"

Rodney didn't even wait. He jumped right back into the water and kept swimming.

He eventually found a boat launch, empty, and crawled ashore, even more tired than he was back on the pier. He couldn't say how long it took him to get here. An hour? All day? The sun was definitely much lower in the sky. He had to hurry but had nothing left to give. Climbing out of the water on hands and knees onto the concrete ramp in wet socks, soaked through everywhere else, every inch a mile. Sharp rocks, slimy mud, broken bottle glass. Rodney trudged ahead, only wanting a place to lie down.

Across the gravel parking lot was a large dumpster and two port-a-potties. The wind blew, and the odors mingled. Ah, Christ, it was bad.

It might also keep people away. Rodney headed for the dumpster. He lifted the lid, his fingers nearly blistering from the heat. Wasps buzzed all around. It was filled with the foulest of all garbage – smelled like fish, shit, and old beer.

Reminded him of all Burt's pieces. Chum for gators.

He couldn't, could he? In this heat? In the dark? On top of, God forbid, pure filth?

But there was no other way, not at the moment.

No one actually checked first when they threw something away. He hoped.

Rodney, trying hard not to throw up, climbed into the searing-heat of the dumpster. Settled the lid back down, tried to lie still.

The wasps stung him a few times, and no matter how hard he tried to ignore it, the smell was unbelievably bad, He gagged up what little food he'd had, fighting to keep the noise down. Sweating like he was in a jungle somewhere. He wondered if it was hot enough to broil him alive. Another preview of hell.

Even as he heard trucks hauling boats come and go, no one bothered him. He heard a couple of guys use the port-a-potty. One guy skipped the potty altogether and pissed on the side of the dumpster, the odor rising into the already foul air.

The sun sank lower until the thin streaks of light coming in through the rust holes vanished. Rodney was drained. Sleep came to him immediately in spite of the trash and the hornets. A deep sleep. Only the sound of a car horn jolted him awake. He chanced a look outside. Only a couple of pick-up trucks, empty boat trailers. He was clear.

He climbed out of the dumpster, the metal still hot but easier to touch, but the burns on his hands and feet from earlier still stung. He started through the grove of trees running parallel to the road, trying to keep out of sight. He kept the socks on – even soaked through, they were better than nothing. He hadn't dried out in that oven of a dumpster, sweat replacing the bayou water.

Where to?

He could hide, but how long before someone found him? He was in no shape for another cage after the duck blind and dumpster.

It had to be Glen. Glen had helped him before, and he would again.

For now, he needed to keep himself hidden until nightfall, when he could move more easily. He needed to figure out where he was. He needed some shoes.

Rodney didn't find shoes, though, and the ground was brutal.

Had to watch every step to avoid glass, tin cans, sharp rocks. Tearing his socks to pieces. He took them off. His feet trembled.

He had landed in Pascagoula, not too far from Moss Point, but far enough without wheels. He made his way across the city slowly, avoiding traffic, other people out walking. Hiding in shadows or behind buildings, in the trees. Sweating, hungry, nauseated. Afraid.

The sun set around eight-thirty, and it took a long while for the sky to go from orange to purple to night. Rodney fell asleep under a pine tree at one point. Woke up with his back sticking to the bark, sap on his hands and feet.

He found a donation box behind a thrift store and was able to shove his feet into a pair of sneakers two sizes too small. He dug through for more. Found a pair of shorts a little too big for him, a t-shirt from a charity fun-run that smelled as if it had spent years in an attic, but it was better than the shirt and jeans he'd been wearing for days. Chaffing all over, especially between his thighs. The relief was glorious, even if the shoes were pinching the hell out of his toes.

He found an overflowing garbage can next door to the thrift shop – behind a diner – and hid his wet clothes between a couple of bulging bags.

Exhaustion overtook him, but he had to keep moving. From behind the diner, he saw people walking down the street – a couple of black guys and then a white dude with a mullet, all kids. Then another white woman in tight jeans carrying a couple of plastic grocery bags. Rodney didn't want to risk any of them recognizing him – hard to imagine, Rodney's face on TV. Instead, he slipped through backyards, alleyways, and more shadows until he was crouching outside Glen's bedroom window.

*Tap, tap, tap.*

# CHAPTER 21

Hosea could've sworn he'd seen his brother's car…towing a boat.

It was a nice one, too. A top-notch bass boat that had been lovingly cared for. And from the trails of water on the asphalt, easy to guess it had recently been in the water.

At the intersection of Main and Jefferson, the light turned red on Hosea's side, green on Glen's, if it was him.

Hard to tell for sure, being five cars back from the light, but this was weird enough to warrant a gander. He flashed his blinker and moved over into the left-turn lane to follow.

His first thought was to catch up and signal Glen over, ask him point blank. But he changed his mind, following to see where he was going. He tried to keep a decent distance. With the trailer hooked on, it was still difficult to tell who was driving, but if it was Glen, he would know Hosea's car. Getting spotted would ruin all the fun.

Past the dollar store, over the railroad tracks. A mix of thriving small businesses – the po-boy place in an old KFC, standing strong for decades, and vinyl-sided roofing and plumbing and other blue-collar companies, rebuilt after the last hurricane, nice and clean compared to their surroundings. Several more miles along, the driver with the boat pulled off down a residential street into a subdivision Hosea was pretty sure he'd been to once before. Lots of times. His memory was hazy.

It came to him in a minute: Brother John Kingsbury. An old-time church member, one of the first to sit in the pews when Dad opened the church. He'd worked at the shipyard since he was twenty-one, retired a decade ago, and was whiling away his golden years at his and his wife's small home tucked away at the end of one of these roads. Hosea had been here before as a boy, playing with Kingsbury's grandkids when they visited every summer. Went fishing in the exact boat he was following. The man had kept it in mint condition. Hosea hadn't seen it since he was fourteen.

The car and boat turned down Kingsbury's road, and Hosea stopped at the corner where he could still see the house. The driver backed in the boat, sloppy job of it, beside an older Buick, on the grass. A little crooked.

Then, Glen stepped out of the car.

Confirmed.

He headed to the front door of the house, leaving his driver's door open. Hosea U-turned and headed away, not wanting to be seen.

He was on his way to meet the cops who had found Charles' abandoned truck in some strip mall parking lot in Mobile, pierced by bullets from the sheriff's deputies and Mr. Goodfellow's rifle, thanks to Rachel. A Walmart employee reported her Chevy S-10 pick-up stolen, but it had taken hours because she was on the night shift and had no clue.

Worse, the car he'd stolen to replace it, as far as the cops could piece together from a carjacking call, was a red Pontiac Grand Am, one of *the* most popular cars on the road. There were six others alone in the parking lot Charles jacked it from.

Hosea knew Glen wasn't a fisherman. He had been when they were younger, because it was a rite of passage on the Coast. You spent a lot of the summer fishing and crabbing. It was fun, and boys then were expected to know how to bait a hook, take the fish off, and get it ready for super. Still, once Glen and Hosea became teenagers and discovered girls, they got all dressed up and tossed the dirty days of fishing overboard.

Why did Glen need a boat?

In the grand scheme of things, it wasn't on the same level

as chasing murderers, but Hosea couldn't drop it. Did Glen even know how to drive a boat? Hosea had never seen him do it, never heard him talk about it. It had never come up. He thought he knew everything about his brother. They'd had no place to hide. Same room, same high school, same group of friends from church, same *girls* from church.

Hosea turned the car around, called Tara and told her he'd be a little late. Then he drove to the parsonage.

He parked next to Glen's Nissan, since Dad's car was gone. He took a closer look at the tail-end, the back tires. Knelt beside them. Were they wet? Was there anything to suggest it had been able to back a boat into a slip? Water on the tires, a little mud splashed onto the bumper. Curious.

Hosea stood, brushed off his knees, and walked to the front door. He knocked and went right on in.

"Dad? Glen?"

Nothing. The parrot, singing bits and pieces of Southern Gospel songs, interspersed with "Amen" and "The Lord is good," other phrases it had picked up from the radio, Dad, Glen, and especially from Mom. "My boy's home!"

No sound inside. Hosea closed the door, walked through the living room, a reminder of Africa, the best time of his parents' lives. At Hosea's apartment, he had buried most of his African toys and souvenirs in the back of the closet. Not because of the people over there, wonderful people. But the way missionaries tried to turn their church members into Americans was creepy. Changed the way they dressed. Tried to change some of their customs. While Hosea's dad and mom had embraced some of the music, the instruments, some of the clothing, they declared a lot of other things *of the devil*. Hosea winced when he remembered some of the best people turning their backs on their families because the preacher told them not to mingle with *worldly people*.

Hosea was carrying his pistol, damn it. Forgot. It bothered his Dad. Reverend Elgin might have been the only man in the church who hated the gun culture down South. No matter what others in the denomination thought, he could never wrap his mind around Jesus' message of peace tying in with the Second Amendment.

He rounded the corner into the kitchen. Glen was leaning on the counter, as if waiting for him. No "Hey" or "Hello" for them. No smiles. Glen looked funny in a long-sleeved t-shirt, old jeans, and dirty sneakers. A real off day for him.

Hosea said, "Were you hauling a boat?"

"What?"

"A boat. I swore I saw you a little while ago hauling a boat."

A long pause.

"Yeah, yeah, it was Brother Kingsbury's. He let me borrow it."

"Why?"

Glen shrugged. "He told me he's getting to old to use it anymore, and planned on giving it to Clay." His oldest grandson. "I asked if I could give it a spin."

"You want a boat, is that it?"

"What's it to you?"

"Seems weird."

"I've always wanted a boat."

Hosea let a pause hang in the air a moment, giving Glen a chance to take it back. "You never wanted a boat. You held on extra tight when we used to go fishing."

"Things change. I took it out, I kinda liked it, but I don't know if I want one. It was for fun. You saw me and followed me all the way home over this?"

"I was going to drop in on Dad. He's out?"

"I guess."

Hosea nodded, put his hands on his hips. Glen's eyes moved toward the gun. Hosea guessed he'd tell Dad about this breach of manners.

"Glen, Rachel wants you to come see her. She's pretty rattled."

"I've been busy. I'm preaching Sunday morning."

Hosea tried to hide his grin, but failed. Listening to a Glen sermon was like listening to a book-on-tape. He hated those. "On what?"

"Oh, not sure yet." Glen hemmed and hawed. "Waiting on the Lord."

He took another long sip of tea, kept his eyes on Hosea the whole time. Condensation dripped onto Glen's shirt. Hosea could tell he was itching to get out of those cheap clothes.

"How's the murder going?"

"Murders. It's more than one now."

"Have mercy."

"It's hard. I didn't think they'd last this long on the run."

"This Charles Lott guy, after what he did to Rachel—"

"Lucky. God, she was lucky."

"More than luck. Dad says she kept talking about Jesus. He kept her safe."

"Well, there you go."

"Call on His name and He'll be there. I hope it means she'll come back to us."

There was a good chance, at least for a while. Best case, she'd be a mother of two with a husband in jail for a long time. She couldn't make it work on her own. Worst case, Rodney would somehow get himself killed…how would she react? Blame God? Blame the cops?

"Rodney needs to stop this. He needs to turn himself in."

"There are two sides to…I mean three sides to every…we should wait until he wants to confess."

"What was he thinking?"

"Not in his right mind."

Hosea raised his eyebrows. "Insane, you mean?"

"What else explains it?"

"He drove himself to the store, got his butcher tools, and brought them back. He laid them out carefully. He carved the man like beef."

"Exactly. That's insane."

Hosea closed his eyes. "I know he's family, but come on. We know he didn't shoot anybody, but the butchering, that was all Rodney."

"I hope he gets a fair shot. I do." Glen set his tea on the counter. "You can promise he'll get one?"

"Of course." Hosea was careful not to swear in front of Glen, but if he could right now there'd be some "goddamns" and "fuck yous" coming out. Like saying the cops were dirty, or *Hosea* was dirty. "We know the rules."

"What a relief."

Hosea was done, Glen trying to bait him. He'd grown tired of that a long time ago. Not to mention Glen thinking he had "moral authority" over Hosea already. He'd thought every argument they had was a foregone conclusion – that Hosea needed to be taught a lesson.

Fuck this.

Hosea said, "See you later," then turned and walked out the way he'd come in.

Thinking, Glen wanted to try a boat? Bullshit.

# CHAPTER 22

In the shower, Rachel looked along her leg up on the lip of the tub. Blood flowed where she had nicked herself with the razor she borrowed from her aunt. Looked at her blood, thin and pink in the torrent of water. Her hand was shaking. She tried to make it go still, but she couldn't. It angered her. Look what he has done to you.

Why was she shaving her legs anyway? Terrible timing.

She was kind of a suspect now. Nobody wanted to believe she was kidnapped or shot at. The whole thing sounded pretty suspicious.

They didn't trust her? With everything on the line?

Her kids.

Her marriage.

Her faith.

Her life.

Imagine if Charles had killed her. Imagine her funeral. Whenever she'd thought of her funeral, it was natural Dad would be the one overwhelmed by grief, yet still able to deliver a fiery sermon. The church choir would sound better than they ever had before. A worship service would break out, everyone shouting and dancing around her casket.

Of course she had fantasized about her funeral. Who hadn't?

A knock on the bathroom door. "Rachel? Can Joshua have chocolate milk?"

"Yes! Only a little!"

She lifted the blades to her face. Three of them. Shaking. She wasn't finished with her legs but she couldn't keep still.

The sensation moved up her arms, across her shoulders, until her teeth were chattering.

She threw the razor down. It floated over the drain, tilted in, got stuck.

Deep breath. What she should do is keep shaving her legs, a little off her bush, for the next time she saw Rodney. He couldn't run forever, could he? She needed to be ready, whenever it might happen. He might find his way back to her. An outlaw coming home for one more kiss. She couldn't help but think about it.

Still, the next time she saw him, it would probably be at the jail, probably with glass between them.

She picked up the razor, got back to it.

What if he did try to run forever? Never called. Never wrote. Did she mean nothing to him? Had she ever?

Two kids, a house, a life together.

Face it: he's not a killer. He did what he thought was best to not get caught.

The body was a piece of meat, not a person.

Simple.

Like the communion wafer is the body of Christ, a symbol.

That didn't make any sense.

When her father had come to see her and the kids, hugged her for such a long time, which was unlike him, he didn't offer a lot of advice. He told her, "I'm praying for Rodney, too. None of us know his mind right now." He told her, "It breaks my heart." He rubbed his temples. He sat on the floor with the kids and played, which he'd hardly ever done. All this had flipped a switch in the man.

Rachel had asked him, "What do I do? Do I still love him?"

"Of course you still love him. I can't tell you what to do, though."

"Do I support him?"

Reverend Elgin had sighed. "A marriage is a mystery. It doesn't matter what I say. I'm not the one you should be asking."

She had thought to herself, *Who is this man?*

Her father was a man who made declarations. He fire-breathed capital T TRUTH from the pulpit. He claimed to see the spiritual world, the angels and demons fighting for and against us. He believed Jesus would return in his lifetime.

Who was the man tinkering with toys on the carpet? Who was this soft-spoken beacon of love?

Rachel had been Mom's child. The boys learned from Dad, the girl learned from her mother. It was the way of things. It made sense. Mom seemed to grow jealous of Rachel as she grew from child to teen to young lady. The strange part, Mom was jealous of the *mistakes*, almost as if she was living vicariously through her daughter, regretting all the fun she'd missed out on. When Mom had gotten sick, Rachel hoped they could make up for lost time, but it didn't happen. They were close, sure, but not close enough. It wasn't until after Mom died when Rachel learned what the parrot had learned to say when her name was mentioned: "Bless that girl," with a sigh.

She finished in the shower and put on her bathrobe, wrapped a towel around her hair. What she expected was to find Joshua bouncing around from too much chocolate milk with Molly crying about everything being unfair while her aunt played the exasperated grandma, though way too young for it.

Rachel couldn't have survived her mother's death without Eileen's help. She was a large woman, tall and round, and powerful. She had a booming voice – even her whispers were loud.

She expected to find her Uncle Joel in his recliner in the living room, the radio on some conservative talk show, reading a magazine about hunting or guns. While his wife was loud, Joel was quiet. Never a shouter in church, barely said a word at home, but you might catch him humming some country songs under his breath every now and then.

Joel was a hunter and gun collector. In his closet were several rifles, a couple of shotguns, and his prized handguns – a forty-five pistol, a forty-four revolver, and a twenty-two he taught his son and only child, Travis, to shoot with. Travis was in college now. Mississippi State.

Not to mention the Glock he kept in his bedside drawer, no matter how often Eileen told him to move it when the kids were in the house. His answer: "If I tell them to stay out of our bedroom, they'll stay out of our bedroom."

Old-fashioned to the core.

Rachel felt at home here. She felt *safe*.

She expected relief. A soft place to fall after facing death.

What she found instead was a missed message from Glen on her aunt's answering machine.

"Call when you can. I'm sorry about what happened."

If her relationship with Mom was an awkward tragedy, then her relationship with Glen was a wall of ice, miles tall and wide. He had never wanted younger siblings, had only wanted to lord over them when given the chance – no babysitters, just the iron rule of Glen. From day one, he had his sights set on following Dad's footsteps, no matter how much he seemed to forget about the love and joy parts of the Bible in favor of laying down the law. He was the oldest but never left home, except for those few precious years of Bible College. She and Hosea grew closer without Glen around, she and Dad had gotten to know each other better.

When Mom envied her most.

Then Glen graduated, was made assistant pastor, and became a shell of a person. All act, nothing real. The way Dad set him on new converts was scary indeed. Turned them into Holy Ghost robots. Or worse, Christian soldiers, marching off to knock on doors of strangers and hand out pamphlets. Maybe Rodney had rubbed her the wrong way at first, but she sure as hell felt sorry for him being dragged around. Glen's puppet.

Eileen poked her head around the corner. "Are you going to call him back?"

"Later."

A giggle from her aunt. "Surprised he said that much to you."

When Hosea had dropped in earlier, he made her laugh. He

let the kids play with Pecan in the backyard. He asked if they wanted to go to Pizza Hut.

How were *they* the outcasts, and Glen the preacher? Made absolutely no sense, did it?

She thought about Rodney.

A butcher's saw in his hand.

The discounted meat he brought home from work.

Making love to her in their bed, before the kids had come along, the heat of it.

Making her hot now.

She closed her eyes and pushed him away in her mind and wondered if she would ever marvel at his face above hers again.

Then she shouted to Eileen, "Fine, give Molly a little chocolate milk, too."

Better to let them bounce off the walls and sleep it off hard than keep her awake half the night asking for water and "Where's Daddy?"

*I wish I knew.*

# CHAPTER 23

The most alive Charles has ever felt: killing people.

The second most alive Charles has ever felt: almost getting killed.

*Woo!*

Whoever owned this Pontiac had shit taste in music – Celine Dion, Garth Brooks, fucking Meat Loaf. He found the rap station instead, let the beat thrum through his bones. Window down, elbow hanging out, daring someone to notice him.

A purse in the back floorboard. Sixty-three bucks. Couple of Visas. The car belonged to a Sheila – license in her wallet. Daddy must've bought it for her as a high school graduation present, and Charles bet her parents were *so proud* of their C-student daughter now.

She had some decent shades, though. He put them on, feeling a little Bono-ish, and cruised.

Another drive by his mom's place. Still wondering how to get a message to her. If he could have his way, he'd bust on up in there and shoot his mom's boyfriend, save her a life of misery with an unemployable asshole.

Now Charles had the car, pretty clean, pretty nice ride. Guess the girl's daddy would have to buy her a new one now.

He went through an Arby's drive-thru, got himself some roast beef and curly fries. Stopped at the gas station, got himself a Red Dog tallboy, popped it open as soon as he dropped back into the driver's seat. Fuck the cameras, fuck the clerks, he had no worries except finding Rodney now. He owed him *and* his wife a bullet.

What was he thinking going after her? Led him right into a

shitstorm. He needed to think several moves ahead, like in chess. He'd never played chess, but he knew those smart fuckers could plan way ahead. Wished he could.

Thought back to his mom. No fair the way the cops were keeping them apart. There had to be a way to get a message to her. If he went in guns blazing, there might not be a chance to see her as a free man no more. Ain't no one going to take that away from him.

But who could help him out? Someone not being watched by the police. Any of his cousins? Risky. He had plenty of them, but how many would turn him in for reward money?

Most of them. Shit.

And he sure as fuck couldn't trust the guy Mom was sort of shacking up with. Daniel. He'd been around a couple of years now, and Charles could give a shit. Barely talked to the man, not even for Christmas dinner or Fourth of July. A burnout on disability.

Who was left?

He thought of his mom's youngest stepsister, lagging twelve years behind the rest of the aunts and uncles. They'd gotten along, right? She babysat when Charles was a ragged nine-year-old, trying to tear up everything he could get his hands on. When Charles was a teenager, she bought him and his friends beer and cigarettes. Flirted. Teased.

He hadn't seen her much the past few years. So happened you reached an age where whatever family glue had held the cousins and aunts and uncles and step-whatevers began to weaken and people pulled apart.

She'd know him, though. She still talked to his mom a lot. Worth the risk.

He revved the engine. Time to drop in on Aunt Gilda.

Gilda opened the door of her townhouse in a sleeveless t-shirt and yoga pants, hair up and messy, cigarette dangling from her lips. Charles thought he saw a grin. "You're famous now."

"Lies. I didn't do it."

The complex was all broken concrete and patchy grass. Hot

as balls out on the pavement. The vinyl siding was curling, split. Windows warped.

Gilda leaned against the doorframe. Propped up one leg to block him from coming inside. A long foot, dark blue nail polish. Not for the first time did Charles think, *I'd hit that*.

"What do you want? You can't stay here."

"You going to call the cops?"

"Your momma would kill me. But this ain't smart either. What if a neighbor sees you?"

"Tell them it's not me. I don't know. You don't seem scared."

"Should I be?"

He followed the stripe on the side of her yoga pants right up to her hips. No panty line. Not the time, not the time.

She snapped her fingers. "Are you listening? I got kids here."

He blinked. "I want you to call my mom for me. I want you to tell her to meet me." He told her where and when. Told her how it would go down.

"Fine, fine, I can do that. But nothing else."

"Cool, cool."

A slow gaze up and down his body. Muscled now, but he'd been a thin-as-piss teen. She was thinking about it, wasn't she? "I saw what you were drooling at. Don't think about it. Now get out of here."

She slammed the door.

Charles spit out, "Bitch."

It was a long day of driving around the edges of the city, up north in the woods, two-lane roads in the middle of nowhere. Daring cops to stop him, pushing the stolen Pontiac up to eighty, ninety, nearly wiping out on the curves. Laughing about it. Seriously, he was having a ball.

His whole life, Charles was a dud bomb. Plenty of potential, snuffed out by society. Big bad society. White trash was all he was, and he played it up. Why not? No one told him at fourteen that acting out would follow him into his twenties, keep him on the outskirts of respectability.

Shit, wasn't no one teaching him about respectability except his teachers, and only to tell him he wasn't due any.

Right?

Wasn't he owed a chance? Wasn't every human being ever born – since they didn't have any say in it – due some dignity? A chance at better?

My, my, my. He got it. He was on the same wavelength as the brothas, knowing what it meant to be held down by the man. He understood the mind of the black man better than they knew themselves. So why wouldn't they give him a break either? Call him a "wigger" and treat him worse than white people did. What was up with that?

Ain't no one got any respect for Charles?

When he'd gripped the gun, straight line to Burt's heart, the look in his wide, frightened eyes, *that* was the feeling he wanted. Try not respecting *that*, motherfucker.

The hours passed. Time got close to meet his mom. He drove over to D'Iberville, a not-much-there town north of Biloxi. He thought they could meet at this chicken place there and have a real meal before he had to go.

Cruised the main drag a few times. Pulled into the parking lot.

Waited.

Should be any minute now.

CHAPTER 24

Hosea's cell phone rang. Tara lifted her eyes up from her file, landline phone pressed to her ear. They'd both been working leads at the office with no luck. Splitting a bag of Krystal sliders, overdosing on Coca-Cola. Somewhere out there were cops beating the bushes, combing the beaches, motoring in and out of bays and streams throughout the bayous. But not the detectives. So much of their jobs were about waiting for people to tell them which other people they should be talking to, then writing reports about it.

Hosea stood from his desk and dug in his pocket for the phone. Probably Dad or Rachel. But the number on the screen was unfamiliar. Local, though.

"Hosea here."

"Hey, I talked to you yesterday? Daniel?"

Flashed back – Charles' mom's mister. "Yeah?"

"Can we meet? I can't talk here."

Outside a Chevron station, waves of heat rising from the concrete, they parked at the edge of the lot. Hosea sat on the hood of his car and waited while Tara went inside for a Slush Puppy. Didn't take long. Daniel came walking up in jeans and a long sleeve Western shirt, old cowboy boots. Sweating right through it all. One of his girls was with him, the older. He handed her a few dollars and told her to get some candy.

Hosea slid off the car. "Hot enough for you?"

"You get used to it."

"Don't I know it. I used to live in Africa. It put this to shame."

"Really, you did?"

"Yeah, I'm a preacher's kid, missions. Anyway, what've you

137

got?"

Daniel shook his head. "She'll kill me if she knew, but...I don't know."

"I'm not going to say a word."

"She'll still know."

Hosea shrugged. "It's a risk you take, sure. But listen, you've already told me there's something to say. If you've changed your mind, I can take you in."

"Now wait a minute—"

Tara was heading back with the girl beside her, both with Slush Puppies, the girl with a box of Nerds.

"Look who I found inside. How you doing, Daniel?"

"Fine, fine." Shoulders slumped.

"Mm hm." Hosea crossed his arms.

"I'm pretty sure he got Meredith's sister, um, stepsister, to call her. He wanted to see her."

"She told you?"

"No, I was just listening close. I turned the TV down. She didn't notice."

"You did good. I know it's hard on you." Tara ran her fingers through the girl's hair. "What's your name, honey?"

"Gypsy Rose."

"What a pretty name. So pretty!" Tara turned back to her dad. "You've done a good job with them."

Daniel nodded. "Thank you."

"Seriously, think about it," Hosea took over. "What if we can't catch him soon? Do you want him coming back for you? Or for your girls?"

"You're not being fair. I'm trying to help you here."

"So, what's it going to be?"

Daniel gazed off above the gas pumps, the trees, the clouds, and let out a deep breath.

He told them where and when, as far as he knew.

It didn't give them a lot of time.

A ring of unmarked cars surrounded the Church's Fried Chicken joint, cops out of uniform making up most of the customers. They were used to taking down crack houses, not a boy and his mom. Still, they hoped the overwhelming force in a public place would keep the drama to a minimum. No telling what Charles might be packing.

Hosea and Tara waited across the street in her LTD. This wasn't Moss Point, not their streets. They were glorified watchers. They figured out quickly just how many red Pontiacs were on the road.

Twenty minutes late.

Hosea checked the dashboard clock every few seconds. "Jesus."

"Don't worry."

"So, so, close."

Tara laughed at him. "I've never seen you this anxious."

"I can't see inside. The glare." He scratched his face. "We need him. We get him, it helps Rodney."

"Oh yeah, Rodney needs help. Big time."

"No, I mean, you know what I mean."

"Charles Lott is going to pin it all on Rodney, you know."

"He can try, but we'll trip him up. Tie his story in knots."

Quiet for a second.

Tara hummed a little, not a tune Hosea knew. Some radio chatter, another red Pontiac. Not him.

"He might have a new car by now," Tara radioed back.

"He doesn't need one. He picked the perfect blend in. Only thing better would be a Toyota Camry."

Hosea. Clock. "Twenty-*four* minutes late."

Radio: "Wait, I think this is it. Standby."

A car coming down the road, flashing a turn signal towards the parking lot. It was a roughed-up Buick Century. Same car they saw outside Meredith's trailer. It pulled in, parked next to the building. There was a woman, in a Saints cap and sunglasses, shorts and flip-flops. She got out of the car, alone, went inside but didn't head for the line. She took one of the booths in the back.

Radio: "Can anyone confirm it's the mom?"

Tara and Hosea frowned at each other. Hosea took the

handset. "Don't think so. Hair's not dark enough."

Tara said, "She's too young."

"I can't tell. Can anyone tell?"

More chatter.

Radio: "Negative. Could be. We can't say with accuracy"

"Where'd she come from? Which car?"

Before they got an answer, another car pulled into the lot. Not a red Pontiac, but a Dodge Neon, electric blue. But the guy behind the wheel…

Voices from all over.

"What about him?"

"Hooded sweatshirt? In June?"

"I see a mustache."

"Can't tell for sure, though."

They all went quiet, watched and waited. The guy parked kind of far off in the lot. Watching left and right as he got out of the car and walked to the restaurant. Hands buried deep in stretchy pockets.

Once the guy stepped inside, they lost him to the glare.

Radio kept up: "Yep, he's found her."

"Is it him?"

"Still can't…he's going straight to her booth."

"This can't be a coincidence."

"Go! Go! Go!"

Hosea instinctually reached for the handle, ready to sprint across and be part of the bust, but Tara grabbed him by the shoulder. "Wait."

Through the glare they could barely see the cops swarming the booth, pulling the guy out and throwing him to the floor. But then things went slack.

Radio: "Negative, negative. It's not them. But the woman…"

Some more chatter back and forth.

Quiet.

Then: "It's her stepsister. We got played."

Hosea let out a howl, punched the roof of the car.

Tara cranked up, knew what the next stop would be before

Hosea said it.

To the radio: "We're on our way to grab the informant. Fucker lied to me."

Gave them the wrong city, throwing them off so Charles could meet his mother in peace. How did she get out of her trailer with all those cops watching?

The stepsister. Came over, borrowed the car, hid Mom in the back, dropped her off somewhere. Right under their noses.

"Damn it."

Tara said, "Not close enough."

Only lead they'd had. Garbage.

Daniel wasn't at the trailer. They put out his description. No idea if he would be in a car, with someone else, or walking. It was tedious, the waiting.

When he finally showed up, walking home drunk in the middle of the night, Hosea had the cops bring him in and cuff him to a chair by their desks rather than the tank. Daniel turned out to be a quiet drunk. Hosea wondered if the man even knew where he was.

They let him sit there almost an hour before bothering to say hello to him, offer him some coffee. He could barely hold the cup. He was dressed the same as they'd seen him earlier, except sweated through, stinking of smoke and fresh beer.

Hosea sat down in front of him, Tara taking a seat on her desk right behind him. There was a hustle and bustle all around, cops either ending their weeks or prepping for a busy night, the young folks out there on the streets getting wild, the adults getting sloppy, mean, or downright gross.

"Daniel, you in there?" Snapped his fingers in front of the drunk's face.

He lifted his chin. Slackjawed.

"Daniel? You fucked us, didn't you? You fucked us good."

"No sir. No I did not." Slow and slurred.

"But you did, because what you told us was a lie, wasn't it? A set-up."

"Wait, what…I didn't…It wasn't me."

"It was."

Daniel was nowhere close to sober, but Hosea recited the story the stepsister gave. She was there to meet her much younger boy-toy, one her babydaddy didn't know about. The boy-toy claimed he didn't know *anyone* named Charles, ever, and confirmed this was a secret booty call. They were going to get in his car and have themselves a party.

Daniel grinned. "A party."

"Where are your girls? You lost them?"

He waved it off, eyes turned to the floor. "Their grandma's."

"You should call her. Tell her they need to stay for a while. You might be staying with us for a few days. A guest of Hotel County Jail."

"I didn't do nothing. I told you what they said to tell you."

"What who said to tell me?"

A big grin. "You can't trip me up that easy-speasy, hon."

Tara handed back his the coffee cup. "Drink some coffee."

He did, sort of. It splashed on his cheek. She took the cup away.

"Daniel, no one is tripping up anyone. Tell me what happened. The truth."

"You        were        supposed        to…Church's Chicken…Pascagoula."

"And we did. And it was wrong. You fucked us, remember?"

He sat back in his chair. "I don't want to do this anymore."

Hosea leaned closer. "*You fucked us!*"

Tara hissed through her teeth, "Hosea!"

Didn't stop him. He was thinking of Charles taking his sister, almost killing her. "Where was the real meeting? Why did you guys do this decoy shit?"

Daniel tried to shake himself out of the fog. "You turn left, she goes right. Listen, I'm sorry. But my old lady, my girls, what can I do? I need a place to live, man."

Hosea slapped the shit out of him.

"Hosea!" Tara leapt off the desk, rounded the chair and spread her arms. "No!"

He pushed her to the side and grabbed Daniel by the shirt, dragged him out of the chair and across the office floor. The man was barely able to walk. Stumbling. His knees went out from under him.

"Get up!"

Tara followed, shouting at Hosea the whole way, all the scattered cops staring after them.

"He's going in the tank! And he's not coming out, I don't care, for a long fucking time."

He wrestled Daniel to his feet, kept going.

"Jesus, Hosea, stop!"

"Don't you get it?" Still dragging Daniel towards the holding tank. "Hours wasted! People wasted! Aiding and abetting! This piece of trash! Charles is on a fucking killing spree, and this guy fucked us."

From across the room, Lydia was heading to cut him off, calling his name. She caught up and grabbed Hosea by the wrist, stood in front of him. "Enough."

Hosea tried to break free, but Lydia had a strong grip and about three inches of height and thirty pounds of muscle on him. Chest to chest. "Let him go."

"Don't get in my way!"

Tara caught up, pulled Daniel from Hosea's grip. "We'll let him dry up, take him home, and pick up the mother. She doesn't know we have him yet, does she?"

"It was a wild goose chase."

"So what? We'll get them. You know we will."

"I don't know a goddamned thing!"

The Captain stood outside his office door and shouted, "Hosea! Get over here."

Hosea turned. A tall lieutenant stood next to Sarasota. Both staring him down. He backed off from Daniel, palms out. Lydia and Tara staring too. He walked across the floor, hands in his pockets. Didn't look at the Captain as he passed by him into the small office.

Ten minutes later, he was off the case for good and on his way home.

# CHAPTER 25

Sunday School at a Pentecostal church would surprise you. Sometimes a raucous worship service with never-ending Southern Gospel music. Other times a pleasant Bible lesson to make everyone feel better about themselves. Or a fire-and-brimstone sermon to bring the congregation to their knees, weeping and wailing, praying for mercy.

This one started out lively in spite of everyone knowing about the murder, Rodney's gruesome deed, and Rachel's close call. The church was probably packed because of it, everyone spreading rumors on the phone all night before. The music was closer to R&B than Southern Gospel. The church had a few black families, and Brother Marcel was the keyboard player. The Hammond B-3 organ had been sitting empty since Sister Watkins "retired." Truth was she couldn't keep up with the rest of the band anymore. Synths, drums, bass, a guitar player, off to one side of the platform, one step lower than the pulpit stage. On the other side, three singers, all women with their long hair pinned up – the pastor's requirement – harmonizing. The song: *This is the day that the Lord has made, I will rejoice and be glad in it.* Over and over.

Hand clapping. Whooping and hollering. Raised hands praising, some crying. Pastor Elgin led it on, shaking the shekere he'd brought back from Africa. He walked from one side of the stage to the other, urging more shouting, more clapping, more more more!

*He has made me glad! He has made me glad! I will rejoice, for he has made me glad!*

Both Glen and Hosea had told him it was okay to take the morning off, let Glen handle everything, since the stress of these ordeals was showing on his face and in his walk – a hand to his lower back, wincing. But he wouldn't hear of it. In fact, he pulled the sermon back from Glen, told him he'd been inspired. Glen would never admit it, but it pissed him off. He'd worked hard on the message, stayed up too late, got up too early to finish it. Now it would remain undelivered, at least for now. Another night, when the congregation was smaller, full of the die-hards instead of those in need of soul salvation, all of them sleepy after a full day of work.

But this morning, Glen stood and clapped in front of his appointed chair on the platform, not singing along as he usually did. Dad was making it *rain* Holy Ghost. Amping the crowd *come on come on come on*! He stepped down among the pews while the worship music segued into *Got that Holy Ghost and fire, shut up in my bones!* He'd pick someone, whisper to them, then move on as they cried or rejoiced, leapt or fainted, or burst into unknown tongues.

On and on it went, longer than usual. Sunday mornings were typically much more organized, needing to fit in between ten and noon. Had to also think about the Sunday School kids in the building next door, who came into the sanctuary near the end of the adult service, carrying pictures they'd colored or drawn, or the older kids turning the lessons they'd been given into paper airplanes, or notes they'd pass to each other along the back pews. But on this day, the worship stretched to a half hour, then forty-five minutes, before Dad took his place behind the podium and signaled the musicians to play low and soft in the background as he welcomed the regulars, the guests, and remembered those who were too ill to be there.

Hosea sat in his usual spot, on the far back next-to-last row with his arms stretched across the back of the pew, remembering his days of sitting with the teens, getting in trouble for the exact same stuff the kids did now – passing notes and whispering to each other, seeing who could get who to laugh out loud. It had gotten them moved to a section on the first three rows where Dad could keep a closer eye on them. Hosea smiled. The "youth section" never lasted more than a few months before everyone crept back to their old spots. Some of those friends from the old days were still here, though they never talked much anymore. Married, kids, divorced, remarried. A handful of them had moved away years ago. Hosea forgot the names.

The new sanctuary – after the last bad hurricane – was built with growth in mind, ambitious. There were more empty pews waiting for hungry souls, meaning there was more space between Hosea and the rest of the congregation, only a few stragglers, scoffers, and walk-ins separating them. Rachel was there today, sitting with their Aunt Eileen, about five rows back on the far left, drained of color and sleep. She had been mobbed during the part when Dad asked people to shake some hands or kiss some cheeks with people around them. All those old ladies said they were praying for her. They treated her like a celebrity. Or a zoo animal.

Glen never strayed from his chair on the platform, one seat away from where he'd most wanted to be. He'd been trying to find reasons to get up there next to his dad since he started learning to play the bass, hoping the Pastor would let him take over from Brother Dixon, an old stalwart better suited to a country beat than what these youngsters wanted to play. Eventually, that's exactly what happened. Glen had been scooting closer to the pulpit ever since.

Dawn Hollingsworth was one of the singers, in a white dress with a repeating yellow and blue floral print running down it. She was tall and thin with a prominent nose Hosea found endearing. Freckles, dishwater hair, and a goofy smile. The little imperfections made her prettier to his eyes. But she had been raised in church and followed all the social rules to a T – what they called living the "holiness" lifestyle. Since they weren't officially dating, she wouldn't sit with him during the services. Very old-fashioned. Why put up with it, then? Well, who knows.

He wore his tan-and-brown windowpane sports coat with a white shirt, brown slacks, and a blue patterned Zegna tie. He was angry to be off the case, itching to know if they'd made any headway overnight. Still, at least he could take some time to help Rachel and the kids get through it, but he wasn't much of a shoulder to cry on.

God knows what he would've done to Daniel if they hadn't stopped him – the man was stone-cold drunk, defenseless. Not a fair fight. Tara had called him at home later to tell him about the interview with Meredith. Oh yeah, they'd faked out the cops and were proud of it. Wouldn't tell where Charles had met them or what he was driving and wearing until they started throwing "months in jail" at her – six, then eight, then twelve.

"Opened her right up. We know how much Charles is worth to her now."

He planned to sit through Sunday School, have lunch with his family at Shoney's, then try to make up some lost sleep with a good long nap, followed by some TV. *The Simpsons.* He'd deal with his dad tomorrow about skipping Sunday night service. Dawn wouldn't like it either, so there was her scolding call to look forward to. But no need to tell them up front what he was going to do.

While Dad was getting the congregation to turn to First Kings, about Elijah and Jezebel, Glen was distracted, eyes on the exit into the vestibule. Hosea turned his head, saw one of the ushers gesturing at him. Talk about bad timing. Glen tried to ease off with as little disruption as possible, stepping down from the platform on the right side, walking the long aisle past Hosea without a glance, and out.

A lot of eyes followed.

But Hosea went back to the Bible he'd had since he was eighteen, scribbled, doodled, highlighted, cover tearing apart, and all those questions he'd written in the margins, still there, still valid. It was called a "study bible," full of all kinds of maps and context and extras, but he pretty much only opened it once or twice a week anymore. Much less than this crowd, but probably a lot more than the people he arrested.

Dad talked about the "spirit of iniquity" squeezing many

people in its grip. He strutted and fretted his way across the stage meaning everything he said. A spirit can bind us, each of us. Name the problem, there was a spirit for it. Drinking? Violence? Drugs? Of course. But also gossip, worldly music, and improper thoughts. Jealousy, a filthy tongue, and being too embarrassed to witness. The spirit would break its hold if only the children of God would *rebuke* it. But how many people are willing to do so?

"You get comfortable in its embrace. You tell yourself, 'There's no need to take an extra step. There's no need to witness to my neighbors. There's no need to carry forth our message to strangers.'"

Dad was in great form. After months of depression, he was seeing the light at the end of the tunnel. Or maybe his sermon was a cry for help.

Didn't matter, because Hosea wasn't going to see the rest of it. Someone gripped the back of the pew, one hand on either side of him. Glen leaned towards his ear and said, "You need to come outside. Right now."

"What?"

Glen was already stalking back towards the vestibule. Red-faced.

Hosea slid out of the pew and followed.

They were waiting in the parking lot. Tara, Broussard, Lydia, and a handful of uniformed cops. Several cruisers. They were talking to one of the ushers, who stood as if standing guard, arms crossed.

Hosea and Glen walked over and stood beside him.

Hosea asked, "What's up with this?"

Tara handed over a piece of paper. A search warrant. "I should be talking to your dad about this."

Hosea read it over. They wanted to search the entire search property for Rodney and Charles. Parsonage included.

"Seriously? On Sunday morning?"

"Time's a-wasting."

"But…why?"

"You had to realize this was coming."

"On Sunday morning? The middle of service?"

She looked embarrassed, but only Hosea could tell. She put her hands on her hips and sighed. "It's got to be done. We brought it over as soon as we got the signature. If you ask me, we should've done it sooner."

Glen paced a few steps behind Hosea. "An outrage! How dare you! This is sacred time. I've got a whole congregation in there—"

"Reverend, please."

"—Government overreach! This is what happens when you take God out of public life. No respect at all."

Tara turned to Hosea. "You going to explain it to him?"

"Aw, he knows. Your timing sucks."

"Listen, my momma's in church right now, too. I can't stop thinking about how mad she'd be if I was doing this to her."

He nodded towards her holster. "Especially packing heat."

Glen was still muttering and mumbling. "The Bible said. *Just* like the Bible said. The end is near"

The usher, still standing firm and crossing his arms, was dying to go in and tell everyone, tell them what was going on. Talk about your spirit of gossip.

Hosea pulled Tara aside. "Can you wait until noon? A little after?"

"Hosea—"

"I mean, think about it. Our whole congregation."

She cocked her hip and stabbed a finger towards the church. "If one of these guys is in there, and they get away because *you* told me to come back in an hour, I tell you what."

"Do you seriously think they're here?"

Tara blinked, stood down. "I don't know what I think. But it's got to be done. Church or no church."

He nodded. Of course it had to be done. This place meant a lot to Rodney before. Makes sense he'd come here. Who would hide him? Glen? Dad? Or would he have sneaked in on his own, none the wiser?

"How about this? Ring our guys around the buildings, keep an eye out, but get rid of some of the cruisers for awhile. Come back at twelve-thirty, we'll do the search."

Tara nodded. "Twelve-fifteen, and *we'll* do the search. You're not on this case anymore, remember?"

It stung. "I'm still a cop."

"Not today. Today you're just another Elgin I've got to deal with." She turned on her heel and walked away without another word.

Hosea called after her, "Thanks, buddy."

The church was buzzing during the final prayer, word starting to spread about cops outside. Glen and Hosea tried to keep the milling about after service to a minimum, telling the people the church was needed for a private event. There were still some lingerers as twelve-fifteen rolled around, and Tara drove back into the parking lot with the other cops.

Broussard kept an eye on the Elgins in a couple of the back pews. Rachel's children were restless – Molly laid out on the pew beside her, fighting a nap, while Joshua ducked under the pews and crawled along, popping up, laughing at his grandpa, then ducking under. Glen couldn't stop pacing, Broussard telling him to sit every few minutes.

Dad was surprisingly sanguine about the whole thing. "They have a job to do, same as we do."

He'd handed over the keys to the offices, the Sunday School building, the guest apartment, the house, all of it. He made small talk with Broussard, found some common ground. Turned out they both enjoyed tennis, Southern Gospel quartets, and the Book of Revelation. Better than Hosea was doing. Broussard had been in his corner for years, but now Hosea couldn't help feeling betrayed.

The cops were thorough. It felt weird to sit in the sanctuary while they went over every inch. Under the pulpit, in the back rooms and Glen's office, the baptismal tank. Then it was on to the other building, then the parsonage. Tara came through occasionally and asked the pastor or Glen a question, flicked her eyes away from Hosea.

It took forever. It was nearly five o'clock when the cops

retreated, having found nothing. No sight of a man, no sight of evidence either Rodney or Charles had been there.

During the search, though, Hosea's heart had been in his throat. What if Rodney *was* here? What would that make Dad and Glen?

Tara braced Hosea in the vestibule. "I'm sorry."

"I understand."

"No, you're pissed." She lowered her voice. "You're pissed. I can tell."

He sighed, turned away. "No, really."

"We had to look. We need to talk to your family more, too."

"Why didn't you when I was still on the case?"

She stepped back, eyes shooting a death-ray. "Don't give me any guff."

"Guff? *Guff?*"

"Hey, we're in church. And you know why."

He did know. It would've happened anyway, but there were other things to get to first. Standard procedure. Just because he'd gotten himself benched didn't mean anything had changed about police business. Watching from the sidelines ripped at him. Sitting in a pew, his usual colleagues ignoring him, and him not bothering to lift his head for any of them either.

Until Lydia came over. "You grew up here?"

He nodded. "I know all the good hiding places, too."

She grinned, not sure how to take it. "I'll bet."

Tara thanked Hosea's dad, then Glen, who had become his normal dickish self once they didn't find Rodney or any proof that he'd been here. Hosea stood back, hands in his pockets, watching the cops pack up and go.

When they had, his father's shoulders slumped. He turned to each of his children in turn. "You know, I would never reject someone, if they needed help."

"Of course, Dad."

"Sure."

"But I wouldn't lie to the police either. I want you both to believe me."

Hosea willed himself to shut up. What he wanted to ask is *What about a lie of omission?* What if that person came to the church, asked for help, and Dad didn't call the cops right away? Was that the same thing as lying to the police?

Glen stepped over to Dad and rested his hands on his shoulders. But Pastor Elgin shrugged away from him, started towards the parsonage. He stopped long enough to say, "I can't do this tonight. Glen, you take the service. I…I can't."

He made his way across the lawn to his home, alone.

# CHAPTER 26

She hated to admit it, but secretly, Rachel was hoping they would find Rodney at the church. If only she knew he was okay. It would give her a big sense of relief.

Could she still love a monster? Would she turn him in if she knew where he was? Could she stay mad at him?

Yes, no, and maybe.

She could be mad he didn't come to her, didn't get in touch with her as soon as he'd gotten someplace safe. Why wouldn't he? The fight didn't count. No, that wasn't the reason. Of course he would call if he could.

Then, standing in the parking lot after the police left, Glen gave her a hug – weirdly un-Glen-like – and whispered to her, "He's safe. Trust me."

What? What did he say?

Rachel eased back, stared into his eyes for a moment. "Why would you say that?"

Glen smiled. Big teeth, big gums. "I just know. You don't have to worry."

"What are you saying?"

"I love you, sis. I'm watching out for you."

Then he walked away, back into the church. He had a service to prepare for.

She turned on her heel, passed Hosea, and pushed through the doors. She caught up with Glen at the door of his office.

"Don't give me any bull. What do you mean he's safe?"

"I can't tell you." He looked around. "Keep it down. Nobody else needs to know."

"Why won't you say—"

"It's all going to be okay." His voice tremored. "I promise."

"Promise what? Divine intervention? If you've seen Rodney and won't tell me, I don't know. Jesus, Glen!"

"Watch it. The Lord's name—"

"He came to you for help." Rachel took a step back, covered her mouth with her fingers. "Oh my God."

Glen leaned in. "Quiet. Be quiet. Trust me. He's safe."

"Does…does he want to see me?"

"I don't know."

Rachel groaned and pummeled Glen on the chest with both fists. "No! No! No! I need to see him, Glen! It's not fair."

He grabbed her wrists, gently. In his soothing baritone, "Stop this. When the time is right. But it's not yet."

"Has he asked about me?"

Glen grinned. "Of course. But we can't talk about this. There's nothing to say. He's safe. Trust me."

Rachel pulled her wrists free. "Fuck you, Glen. I said it, right here in church. Fuck your self-righteous bullshit. This, this, this *act* of yours. This is my husband we're talking about!"

Around the corner, someone cleared his throat. They both turned. Hosea, standing near the back pews, hands in his pockets. He didn't say another word, watching.

Rachel glared at Glen one more time, then stormed out past Hosea as if he wasn't there.

Hosea took his time, a snail's pace, while Glen stood frozen. The lights out in the church, the only illumination from early evening sun through the windows.

Yep, took his time. He'd heard enough. Glen wasn't going anywhere.

When they were face-to-face, Hosea said, "Tell me where he is."

"What?"

"I heard you guys."

"I don't think you heard right."

"Nope, pretty sure. Let's not kid each other."

Glen didn't blink. Stared Hosea down, jaw tight. "I thought they threw you off the case, anyway."

"You want to talk now, or should I take you down to an interview room at the station?"

Hosea reached out, took Glen by the crook of his elbow, but the preacher yanked it away. "I've got a sermon."

"I don't care."

"Do it, then. Arrest me."

"Glen..." But nothing else came.

Glen walked over to his office door, put the key in the lock, twisted the knob. "Church starts at six. You know where I'll be."

He stepped inside, closed the door quietly.

Hosea stood there for several more minutes, digesting it. Glen knew where Rodney was. He fucking *knew*.

Glen's voice floated from behind the office door. Praying. Loud prayers for inspiration, for courage, for guidance. More worried about his sermon tonight than about going to jail. Guess he wasn't planning on pulling a runner, then.

Hosea pulled the cell phone from his pocket, called Tara, and told her to meet him at the church after service.

Glen's voice, louder now, "—to give the glory to *you*, Lord, and not myself! Help me to be humble!"

Hosea drifted over to the front pew, a place he'd avoided for years, and sat down. He'd definitely be staying for the service.

The sermon had been, as Hosea expected, a big act. No real emotion, no matter how much the congregation shouted and shook. It was all a performance. A practiced rhythm. Their dad could do the same exact thing, but make it feel honest. He knew how to twist and provoke the crowd, make them feel joy, then regret, then bring it on home with forgiveness. But Glen, ham-fisted, forced the amens and the hand claps and the shouting.

Once the sermon was done and the altar call complete – no one was saved – Hosea waited for the crowd to disperse before bringing in Tara and a couple of uniforms to apply the pressure.

Glen, sweating, his tie loosened, kept up a friendly face. Shook hands. "Too bad you weren't here for the whole thing."

"Reverend Elgin, Hosea says – "

"Please, Tara, no need to be formal. Glen is fine."

"Hosea says you might have more information regarding the whereabouts of Rodney Goodfellow."

"Did he? I think there's been some misinterpretation."

Tara flicked her eyes at Hosea, who gave a little shake of his head.

"Do you have time for some questions?"

"You mean here? Now?" He spread his hands, looked around the church as if it was a marvel. "I wouldn't want to degrade the house of God."

"Your home, then? The parsonage?"

"My dad isn't feeling well."

He agreed to come along to the station.

Hosea wasn't supposed to come along, but it would take every demon in Hell to keep him away.

Glen kept stoic in the interview room, waiting for Tara to come back and question him. The asshole even brought his Bible along, pretending to read it while waiting. Hosea could tell he was pretending as he watched through the glass. He wasn't supposed to be there.

Tara stopped by the observation room, a relic. Everything these days was recorded. The observation room was now a place where they kept copier paper and the bikes they used for sting operations. Still, there was a speaker and two-way glass, which made Hosea feel closer. Watching on a square TV monitor wasn't the same.

"What do you think he knows?" Tara asked.

"I think he helped Rodney, and I think he hid him out on the water somewhere."

"What? On an island? In a boat?"

"No, no, he *borrowed* a boat to take Rodney to an island, or somewhere up in the creeks or bayou. I don't know where. The pieces fit, though."

"I know they've searched the water some already. But, Jesus, there's a lot of it."

"We need some sort of clue as to where. Trip him up talking about the boat."

Tara nodded, started for the door. Stopped. "If you're right about this, you know Glen will—"

"I know it. Fuck, don't I know it."

Glen stated his name. His address. His occupation.

He talked about his family connection to Rodney Goodfellow.

He talked about his whereabouts on the night and early morning of the murder.

And then he started deflecting. Preaching. Taking control.

"I know you all are doing some good work. I know my brother is doing his best to make up for his mistakes as a minister."

*Bastard.*

"But to do good but not accept the truth of the Gospels, well, it's an empty well. You need to understand the foundations of what is good and evil, *why* God set it up the way He did."

Tara sat back in her chair. "The Garden of Eden? The Bad Apple?"

"The Bible never said it was an apple. I believe it is a special fruit on that particular tree in the Garden, never to grow again."

"I don't need to know the history of all religion in order to know a person killing another person is a bad thing."

"Not all religion, no. I'm not talking about religions. I'm talking about Jesus. I'm talking about the Holy Ghost."

His engine was winding up. Glen had taken a wide stance in his chair, as if he was about to leap up and pace the interrogation room like it was his pulpit. Hosea eased closer to the glass, wishing he could have a go at his brother.

"Glen, please." Tara leaned on her elbows. "Did you in any way aid Rodney Goodfellow on the night of June eighth, or any subsequent day or night this past week?"

"I prayed for him. Is praying for someone allowed in our country anymore? Regardless of what he's accused of, he's still my brother-in-law, *and* my brother in Christ. So I prayed for him, and I continue to do so."

Broussard, sitting beside Tara, looked exasperated to Hosea, but was doing a good job of hiding it – pursing his lips, nodding now and then. Definitely the good cop. Tara wasn't as good at hiding her feelings.

"You're saying you haven't had contact with him?"

Silence.

"Glen?"

Glen was staring straight at her, stupid grin on his face.

"Did you hear me, Glen?"

He let out a long breath. "He called me."

"Okay, tell me about the conversation."

"I can't."

"Can't, or won't?"

He put his hand on the Bible. "As a Man of God, I can't tell you. He spoke to me in confidence. I cannot betray him."

Hosea held his breath for a moment. Shit.

Tara looked past Glen's shoulder at the mirror. *We got him.*

Hosea wanted to go in there, raging. The fucker, after all that had happened with Rachel and Charles Lott, he'd known all this time. He'd *helped*.

Tara continued. "I don't know, Glen. I mean, technically, you're not his actual pastor. You might be a minister, but your Dad would have the privilege, not you."

Hosea winced. Not quite sure she was right.

Glen sat up straight in his chair, crossed his arms and said, "Lawyer, please."

# CHAPTER 27

Charles Lott.

Infamous.

Untouchable.

Now he was responsible for most of his family ending up at the police station. How dare they arrest his own *mother*. And his step-aunt. And Daniel.

He had to give it to Daniel, though. He played his part to a T. Charles owed him an apology. No, that was too much. Let's say a beer.

And now he had traded the Pontiac for an eighties' Taurus with a different colored rear door and worn spots where the primer showed through. No a/c, rolling with the windows down. No stereo, either. If he'd known, he wouldn't have taken it.

Late summer sunset. Darker here in the pinewoods than it would be on the beach. Shadows, tall trees, hills and valleys.

Where was Rodney?

Someone must've be protecting him if the cops hadn't got him yet. Ain't none of their mutual friends had any idea. Not a word. A man couldn't just disappear, *poof*, in smoke. Charles was betting it had to do with his church.

That church. The wife's father and brother, leaders over there. Her other brother, the cop. Not just a cop, a *detective*. Wonder if he was covering up for Rodney.

But him and his black bitch partner, they were working on finding *Charles* pretty hard, but what about Rodney?

It all circled back.

This fucking car. Sweating his ass off.

Bored.

After a while, Charles had to take a leak. Kept his eyes open for a convenience store where he could top off the tank, get some relief, and grab a Dew and spicy jerky. Had to navigate himself out of the country and back to the Interstate. Next exit, a Circle K. He pulled in. Kinda busy at the pumps but he managed to find an open one.

Jesus, gas was expensive. Over a dollar a gallon? What was it? Gold? Lucky his mom had slipped him more cash.

Into the store. Chin up at the guy behind the counter. Hispanic, of course. Nine out of ten stores, the counter jockey is either Hispanic or Arab, taking over the whole country eventually. They wouldn't be content with convenience stores. Wanting more, more, more. Charles swelled with anger, thought if he didn't have a mission to complete, he'd beat the living shit out of this one behind the counter for shits and giggles. Make him and his whole race think twice. Motherfucker.

First, a trip to the bathroom. Two urinals and a stall. He took the taller urinal and did his business. With nobody else in there, he pulled some crystal from his pocket and took a couple bumps to keep him feeling fresh. Back into the store. He picked up his favorite, Jack Links Sweet & Hot Beef Steak, grabbed a liter of Dew.

Was he getting some funny looks? What, was he on a *Wanted* poster?

Smile at the silly people. Give them a smile and move on.

The spic behind the counter asked for ID. Jesus. "For jerky and Dew?"

"Policy."

*Bullshit.*

"Here's my ID." He pointed to his face. "I look like a kid to you?"

The spic, quietly. "I have to see your ID."

"And I told you no, bitch."

The man sighed down at his cash register before ringing up the soda, the jerky, the gas. Told Charles the total. Thirteen and change.

Charles pulled out a hundred, slammed it down.

The spic didn't take it.

"What?"

"I don't know if I have change. We don't take hundreds."

"All I got." He tapped it. "Come on."

The spic reached for it. Grabbed a corner. Charles flattened his palm on it, pinned it down. "Give me some, um, some Marlboros. For my mom. Or do you want ID for that, too?"

He let go of the hundred and the spic lifted it from the counter. Held it in midair, stared at Charles.

"You're him, aren't you?"

Charles lost the smile. Who was he dealing with? Three people waiting behind him, all sick of his bullshit. More people wandering the aisles. Kids and their fat moms.

Turned back to the Big Boss Counter Boy. "Him who?"

"Please, go. I don't want any trouble."

"I asked you a question." He snatched the hundred back. "Him who?"

He could tell the spic was shaking now. Pissed. Scared. Didn't matter, it was all the same to Charles. He got a glimpse of the people behind him in the fish eye mirror. The woman at the end of the line set her Diet Sprite on top of a rack full of cupcakes and walked out.

Charles couldn't help but smile. He picked up a packet of Skittles from the candy display in front of the counter, laid it down. "Him who?"

The spic backed up into a wall of cigarettes, mini-booze bottles and porn mags. Wobbly. "I saw you on the news."

A big gorilla of a white man, white-haired but body-builder strong, swaggered away from the hot dog roller, stepped up behind Charles and clamped a gorilla hand on the back of his neck. "What did you say? This guy was on the news?"

The spic nodded, relaxed a little. "He killed a man. They're searching for him."

The clamp tightened. "Buddy, you call the police and I'll hold this boy here for you." The other gorilla hand wrapped itself around Charles' right arm.

But he still had his left free.

He grabbed the plastic bottle of Dew top first, swung toward the gorilla and smashed it into the side of his face hard enough to explode. Blood and fizz. The gorilla staggered back and fell to the ground while Charles said to the spic, "I'm not him."

He walked out, head high, everyone staring. Now he had to truck it out of here, high speed. He would have to dump this car, but it sucked anyway. He was going to find Rodney and, sing it one more time, *go out in a blaze of glory!*

Too bad. This was kinda fun.

CHAPTER 28

Dark as pitch, Rodney's grandma would say.

Yes, it was.

Hot. Stifling.

But he was safe. He could *sleep*, for the first time in God knew how many hours. His body demanded it, but it was a fitful sleep. He was afraid of the dreams awaiting him. The severed head of Burt. The murderous smile of Charles. Rachel, in danger, pale with terror because he wasn't there to protect her. And now…Dad.

Glen told him what had happened at his dad's house. How Vincent had died protecting Rachel. How close she had come to being killed. It froze his blood.

Charles Lott had killed his father. Kidnapped his wife. And Rodney was helpless.

He woke up shouting, had to clamp down quickly, hoping no one heard.

Trembling.

Rodney imagined what would've happened if Dad hadn't had his rifle. If Rachel hadn't known how to use it. If their *kids* had been there, for Christ's sake.

Glen had asked if he wanted to see Rachel.

Like this? Who would want him like this? He shook his head, tight-lipped.

But it was the only thing he wanted in the whole world. Rachel, Molly, Joshua. Rachel, Molly, Joshua. Rachel, Molly, Joshua.

Squatting together in this tight space, Glen sweating more than Rodney had ever seen him outside of a Sunday night service, the preacher said, "We can't do this forever. You've got to turn yourself in."

"I know, I know."

"Seriously, I'm only doing this for your *soul*. Make sure your soul is ready to face what comes next, but you're running out of time. If you don't soon—"

"I said I know!" Trying to keep calm. He owed Glen a lot, but not this bullshit lecture all the time. "Please, you promised."

"I know I promised, but—"

"You can't take it back, *preacher*."

Glen sighed and nodded. "Jesus has infinite mercy. But people? Well…"

"That some kind of threat?"

"Let's pray."

Rodney closed his eyes, went through the motions, but where he'd usually feel brightness and warmth, there was only the cold dark.

Glen left him, and it had now been many hours.

No matter what Rodney did, no matter how hard he pleaded with the almighty Lord above, all he heard was the buzzing of electrical lines below him and the sound of his own heartbeat.

He was on his own.

When Rodney had tapped on Glen's window that night, he thought he would be begging. Then Glen came out to meet him, and the first thing Rodney said was, "Enough. I've had it out there!"

No more sniveling.

"What are you thinking? Someone could have seen you! Could've followed you."

"Did you hear me? I've had enough. I'm *done* with the water. Take me someplace dry, or I swear – "

"I've risked all sorts of trouble for you."

"I swear I'll take you to jail with me. Now find me a place to stay."

That's what Glen did.

Rodney was woken by the echo of the organ, the muffled beat of the drums. The deep thrum of the bass.

It was Sunday.

He felt out of place. The air was thick and itchy, all the insulation up here. He'd found an opening where a board had gone missing, letting in fresh air. Better when he could put his face right next to it and inhale. He wished he could fall asleep with his nose there, but the room wasn't designed for it. The opening was in a far, tight corner, a beam of light his only clock.

Flat on his back in the dark, Rodney remembered Sunday morning services when he'd been a front-pew man. The beautiful, driving gospel music from the band had sent him jumping, shouting, spinning. He'd clap his hands so much they stung after the songs were over. But it didn't matter then because the *spirit* – the Holy Ghost – wove its way inside and let them know it was all going to be alright.

He couldn't feel a goddamned thing anymore except fear and pain.

And anger.

Rodney followed along with the service, making a movie of it in his mind. He wondered if it was Glen preaching today, or the Pastor. He wondered if Rachel was there today, this close to him without knowing. He wondered if Molly and Joshua were below him in one of the Sunday School rooms, coloring pictures of the apostles, or cutting angels from construction paper. A little glue, a little glitter. He wished he could somehow see into those classrooms.

This had been "the old church," as the long-timers remembered. An old Baptist church had left it when they relocated across town before Elgin took over, built back in the fifties. It used to be everything – sanctuary, Sunday School, fellowship hall – until the last big hurricane pummeled it, flooded it, ripped off most of the roof.

Not only did they rebuild "the old church," but they made some adjustments. Took out the sanctuary, added more classrooms, a meeting room, and a larger fellowship hall. Next door, they built the new church, a new sanctuary, nicer offices for the pastor and his son, a better prayer room, a better sound system.

Glen moved Rodney to a space in the original attic of the old church, which used to be easily accessible for storage. After the storm, which had blown everything in it away, there was no need for the space anymore. An empty area at the peak of the roof very few people knew about.

Glen had led him through a maze – starting in the kitchen, climbing onto the stove in order to access a ceiling tile, leading to a series of wooden planks built a few inches above the drop ceiling, which they walked across carefully, hunched over, until they had to crawl on their backs to get inside the hiding place. Rodney realized Glen knew this church inside and out. He'd mentioned how he and Rachel and Hosea used to play hide and seek in the church, and they'd gotten good at it. Now, way past the age of playing games anymore, Glen had still found a way back to one of his best spots after the renovations.

Through a hole in the old attic floor. Glen turned on a flashlight. The attic was split into three parts. Glen showed Rodney where he'd pulled the nails from a sheet of plywood, and if Rodney was careful, he could hide underneath without falling through. Glen showed him how to balance on two beams and pull the wood back over himself.

"Wow."

"Am I right?"

"Glen, why did you do this? What is this place?"

The preacher climbed out of the hole and replaced the plywood. He sat cross-legged on top of it. "I have never stopped looking for places to hide in this church. Because one day, it's not going to be just *me* who needs it. It's going to be the whole church. If we don't hide, the world will come after us."

"I thought we were pre-Tribulation people." He'd been told – by both Glen and the Pastor and many other men of God – the Pentecostals would be taken away from this Earth in the blink of an eye during the Rapture, while the "unsaved" remains of humanity would face seven years of horror before the end of time.

Glen grinned. "That doesn't mean we won't suffer in the End Times. There has to be a testing of our faith, which is why it's important for you to get your soul right." The preacher – Rodney's brother-in-law – reached across and gripped Rodney's arm. "You are probably going to end up in prison. It's not going to be good. But like Peter and Paul before any of us, take *God* inside with you. Understand?"

Rodney's eyes watered up. "I've tried. I've tried. There's nothing there. He's not listening to me."

"I didn't say it would be easy. If I were in your shoes, I would sure as heck keep trying. Otherwise, God's a liar. But we know He's not."

*Do we?*

Rodney wiped tears on his arm. The last thing he needed was Glen sermonizing.

But in the dark, unable to hear the words of the preacher, only following along with the rhythms and the applause, what he would've given to listen to the service below.

Once the noise faded, Rodney ate some of the snacks Glen had left him. He moved to the small opening, tried to breathe as much fresh air as he could before his back began to hurt. He toweled the sweat off – a simple, threadbare towel Glen had left with him, something he would have taken for granted before…you know.

Was he really going to turn himself in? He couldn't imagine it.

Rodney made up his mind. Let Glen do what he had to do, but Rodney wasn't going anywhere unless they dragged him out of here kicking and screaming.

Sorry, Jesus.


Noise beneath him. Lots of people walking through. He could make out voices clearly. Police.

A man said, "What about the attic?"

"There's no way up there."

A woman's voice: "They said it's been blocked off. After the hurricane."

Another voice interrupting: "All clear in the classrooms."

"Shit."

"But what about the attic?"

"See if you can figure it out," the woman said.

"Are we sure? What about the opening over the oven in the kitchen?"

"Might as well."

Rodney crept across the floorboards, barefoot, trying hard not to squeak or set off groaning wood. He eased the plywood sheet from its hole, slid it to the side. He eased into the space below, covered himself, splinters scratching his nose, his stomach, and his knees. An earthy smell. He turned his head and tried to control his breathing.

The muscle cramps began soon after. It took everything he had in him and more to stay still.

But no one came. The voices below eventually faded away. He slid the plywood off him and crawled out, flopping onto his back. The aches ran through his back and legs. He felt empty, an animal operating on instinct. Survival.

If Rodney had been smart, he would've taken off after Charles shot the dealer. Should've gone straight to the police. What the hell was he thinking? He didn't *know* Charles was going to kill the man. Why did he stay? Why?

Would Rodney have cut up the girlfriend? Could he have looked into her eyes while sawing off her head the way he couldn't with Burt's?

His stomach roiled. He clenched. Glen hadn't given him a bathroom option, which was going to be a problem soon enough. Could he sneak down to the men's room without being detected? Or shit in the farthest corner of the attic and hope the smell drifted another way? There was no other option, not like he had in the bayou.

Then, down below, footsteps. Light and hollow. He thought he was imagining them at first, but when he put his ear to the attic floor, they were definitely real.

Likely a church member, picking up a casserole dish left behind. Or Glen, coming to bring him news or a bite to eat.

Not Glen. Glen's footsteps were solid, loud.

Other sounds. Someone fiddling with the drop-down roof? Someone struggling to climb into the attic?

Rodney rolled back into his hole, slid the wood over himself, tried to control his breathing. Through his nose, nice and easy.

He tracked the movement. Someone definitely coming.

What about the woman cop from earlier? She had sounded suspicious. Or, worse, maybe Glen had stabbed him in the back and told the cops how to get up here and drag him out.

But why come alone?

Rodney prepared himself. He could take whoever it was. Give himself time to escape.

*Would you kill her?*

He squeezed his eyes shut. Gritted his teeth.

Would he? Could he? It would only make things worse for him.

But he would have another chance to be free.

The sounds, closer still. Through the hole at the far side of the attic.

Closer still.

Those hollow footsteps, coming straight for him.

Rodney braced himself.

Someone lifted the wood panel, slid it aside, leaving him helpless. A flashlight blinding him, darkness all around it.

Then a gasp.

Rodney was ready to pounce.

A very familiar voice: "You're here."

"Rachel."

The flashlight turned around. Even bathed in shadows, he would know his wife's face anywhere.

She didn't look happy to see him.

His cry stuck in his throat, and he turned his face away.

# CHAPTER 29

Tara and Broussard went to call the lawyer Glen wanted, someone who used to attend the church before trying his hand at local politics. That left Glen alone to hum hymns and pretend to read his Bible some more. Probably flipping through the "begats."

Hosea stayed in the observation room, fists balled, nose almost touching the glass. Fogging it up. Did Glen know he was watching? He fucking well hoped so.

If Rodney wasn't in the church, Hosea thought it still shouldn't be too hard to think like his brother, figure this out on his own. After all, Glen had borrowed a boat, but he couldn't have known those waters too well. Where would he have gone? Maybe the boat itself was the hiding place? But that was too risky, too easy.

What if there were other church members in on it? What if Rodney was hiding at someone's house? How deep did it go?

Glen had barely mentioned the situation at all in his sermon. Hosea sat right there on the front pew and watched, stone-cold silent the entire time. Not standing for the songs or the prayers. He sat and stared at his brother. His lying, cheating brother.

Of course he was.

He'd cheated and lied as a kid to get what he wanted, but still convinced Dad it was Hosea in the wrong. Candy theft, throwing rocks at the African kids, ripping pages out of the hymnals to make paper airplanes, copying off kids in school. Glen had no conscience back then. Why would Hosea believe he had one now?

A couple of taps on the door. Hosea's dad walked in, one hand resting on his stomach, shrinking in his suit before

Hosea's eyes.

"They said you were in here."

"How?"

"One of the patrol cars. They gave me a ride."

"I would've."

"It's okay. I understand."

The pastor closed the door, stood beside one son and watched his other son. They passed a few minutes before Hosea couldn't handle it anymore.

"Swear you had nothing to do with this."

Dad let out a deep breath and seemed to shrink farther. "I don't know what you mean."

"Dad…"

"Listen to me. If Rodney *had* come to me, I would've given him a place to hide, some food to eat, and some words of wisdom."

"You'd break the law."

"I'd follow Jesus."

Hosea turned to his dad. "He'd let a dangerous criminal –"

"Your brother-in-law."

"Whatever."

"As far as God is concerned, he is my son as much as you and Glen are!"

"You don't believe that."

"Have you sunk so low?" Pastor Elgin reached for Hosea, both hands, rubbing his upper arms. "Have you forgotten what it means to *love* the way Jesus does?"

"This is about murder. This is about good versus evil."

"Good is about forgiving."

Hosea backed away. "Jesus, Dad, that's what you tell a child. You and Glen, seriously, both of you have lost your minds."

He left the room, needed a minute to breath. Wished he had a cold six-pack of beer right about then. Nothing special, a good old Bud Light, and down it in front of his Dad as if it was water. The holier-than-thou bastard. He'd raised his kids to believe there was a giant pair of invisible eyes on the horizon always leering, waiting for the slightest mistake. But then he goes and tries to justify *this* bullshit.

Poor Glen. Glen the innocent. Glen the martyr.

Some commotion as a few uniforms and a couple of other detectives rounded the corner, talking to each other while radio handsets squawked on shoulders. These detectives, in JC Penney suits and ties, were from farther along the Coast, older and more experienced than Hosea. They were the ones who would be doing the questioning.

Porter Broussard and Tara were with them, as was the Captain, glowering at Hosea.

"Why are you here?"

"He's my brother."

The Captain got in his face. "You are not assigned to this case. You are only a family member."

Hosea fought to keep his cool. "Sir. This is ridiculous, and you know it."

Pastor Elgin opened the observation room door and stepped out, closed the door behind him without a word.

"And your dad, too? Is this a reunion? Do you all want to share a cell with him?"

Broussard reached for the Captain's arm. "Let's calm down a second."

"I want them out of here, Sergeant. We have some help over from Pascagoula."

The detectives nodded towards Hosea, sheepish.

One of the detectives, gray-haired in a navy sports coat and khaki pants, "We're here to help. This is still Detective Killebrew's case, but we know you guys are short staffed."

The man looked at his partner – also getting up there into retirement age, but with spiky brown hair and huffed cheeks to go along with his beer belly. Sunglasses on the back of his neck. Some cop telepathy passed between them, and the one with sunglasses cleared his throat.

"Listen, I think you'll agree it's not a good idea, you watching us question him."

Hosea blinked. He should've already guessed what would

happen. Of course they didn't want him around.

"You won't even know I'm there."

The Captain huffed. "Absolutely not."

The gray-haired detective sighed. "I understand, I really do, but you've got to understand where we're coming from."

"I do."

"What are you doing here? Did you talk to him?"

"No, no, just...watching."

"Your dad shouldn't be back here."

Broussard stepped forward. "My call."

"Well, it was a bad one."

"You want to say that again – "

Hosea said, "Whoa, whoa, whoa," and spread his arms between the two. Tempers were on a hair trigger. "Hit pause, folks. I get it. I'm sorry about all this."

Everyone eased back.

The one with sunglasses crossed his arms. "If you and your dad could wait at your desk – "

"Okay, okay."

"No," the Captain said. "Go home, take your dad. You need to get your head straight, mister. Let us do what we've got to do here."

"Good lord, you're an asshole." Hosea said it without thinking.

The Captain lifted his finger. "I'll let your insolence go, but one more time…"

The Pascagoula cops worked to avoid his eyes. Tara turned her face towards the ground. No respect. Hosea placed his hand on his dad's back as they walked back down the hall, out into the parking lot.

It was a quiet ride back to the house. Not one word. There had been fewer and fewer words as the years went on, but were they down to nothing?

In the driveway, the Pastor climbed out. Not even thanks for the ride, which was unusual. His dad had never missed a moment to be formally insincere.

174

Hosea got out of the car, too, and said over the roof, "Are you giving me the silent treatment?"

The Pastor started to speak. He couldn't get a word out. "Uh. Um."

"Seriously, you weren't involved in all this?"

"Hosea—"

"Because I can keep your name out of it. I swear. I can help Glen catch a break. But you've both got to start being real with me."

"Haven't you done enough already?" Dad's voice like ice.

"I've done my job. I'm trying to *help* here."

"Stop helping."

"Dad, come on—"

His dad held up a hand, closed his eyes. "I have nothing else to say. Good night, son."

He walked into the garage and through the door to the kitchen, leaving Hosea in the driveway watching the overhead door creep down, wondering how long it would be before his dad would talk to him this time. The pastor would never cut him off completely, but their relationship had changed since Hosea's fall from grace and joining the police. Dad could certainly stretch out a grudge much longer than he used to.

What was to stop Hosea from going in right now? Interrogating his own father?

But he couldn't bring himself to do it. His dad already looked defeated by the world – of course, he'd called it *demonic forces* – and Hosea couldn't bear to add to the weight.

Instead, he closed his car door and walked across the yard to the church parking lot, hands in his pockets, taking in both buildings, giving the place a look. Did the search party miss something? Anything?

Glen's car was in its usual spot since he'd been carried off in a police cruiser. He wondered what was going on back in the interrogation room. He wondered if the detectives would keep him updated on what Glen told them. Probably not. Tara would, though.

When he and Glen and Rachel were kids, they played hide

and seek in the church, all around the church, the entire property. He thought he knew every nook and cranny. He'd given the search party a pretty good idea of the layout. And still, nothing. Was his memory faulty? It had been a long time, after all.

Hosea was sixteen when they were caught by a nosy church member who thought it was some sort of sacrilege. She screamed at them. She warned them the Rapture was coming soon, and they needed to repent right then and there because "there will be no place to hide when they come to implant the Mark of the Beast in you!"

Hosea grinned. That ol' Mark of the Beast, which was meant to allow people to buy and sell things once the Tribulation times started. It would also mark the billions of lost souls who followed the Antichrist, who would be some sort of politician. The President, or an Arab strongman, or the leader of the UN. What it actually was was up for debate, as time went by. It had first been described by preachers as a tattooed "666" on the forehead. Later, once technology advanced, it became a bar code, and now the latest rumor was a microchip implant. There was no salvation possible for a person once they carried that mark.

He remembered this mean, bellowing, beehive-wearing old woman forcing them to their knees for a loud prayer session where she laid her hands upon the tops of their heads and spoke in tongues. Glen and Hosea went along with it, playing the game they learned from watching the adults. But Rachel, much younger, was scared out of mind. Crying, screaming, begging the Lord to let her go to Heaven.

What an awful thing to do to a kid. But those people didn't care, the holier-than-thous. They thought they had God on speed-dial and were keen on his every word. Love only went so far, but fear worked better, though they would never admit it. All his life, Hosea had heard about the Rapture, coming *soon, soon, soon.* And now with the year two-thousand fast approaching, there was endless talk of End Times, Antichrist, seven years of Tribulation, Armageddon, demons, and a God who'd had enough bullshit from humanity.

Enough.

He'd preached it himself, too, while wishing deep inside it was all phony. He'd preached about the Second Coming of the Lord over and over, while hoping it wouldn't happen in his lifetime, if at all. Because no matter how much he had prayed, preached, tongue-talked, felt the fire of the Holy Ghost make him run and jump and holler, Hosea still thought it all sounded too good to be true. This small denomination of people who claimed to do things exactly the way God wanted, interpreted the Bible exactly how it was supposed to be regardless of what anyone else said, and who claimed to live the sort of "holy" life as prescribed by the teachings of the church – they were the only ones, out of all the people everywhere on Earth, many who had no idea about Jesus or salvation, who were going to be saved? That was all?

Once logic got involved, and this foundation for his faith flittered away, everything else crumbled down around Hosea.

He hated himself for it. He wanted more than anything to believe *something*, other than what his job showed him every day: people being terrible to each other.

Like cheating. Like stealing. Like assault. Like murder.

Like ratting on his own brother. Terrible.

He could never see himself liking Glen, but he had to admit, his brother did what he did out of real love. Hosea could've never done that.

He put his hands on his hips and wondered…

…wasn't it Glen who always won hide and seek?

# CHAPTER 30

All his life, Glen had heard about the apostles being thrown in jail for preaching in the name of Jesus. Their only "crime" was preaching the wrong message. But it was Jesus the authorities were afraid of. His followers threatened to upturn their entire way of life.

Into the cells they went – Peter, Silas, Paul.

Once, there was a bit of an earthquake, the locks opened, and *voila*. God broke them out on his own.

Other times, Paul had to suffer in chains for a long time, but he stayed faithful.

Glen, sitting in a cold and bare interrogation room at the Moss Point police station, sipping hazelnut coffee from a small cup, waiting for the arrival of his lawyer, decided to emulate the Apostle Paul.

Every once in a while, the new detectives and Tara would talk, not exactly questioning Glen, but trying to draw him into the conversation. They tried football (Glen didn't follow it) and politics (it all led back to End Times), which got them nowhere. They went straight at it, asking about his whereabouts the past few days, questions about his friendship with Rodney, some mild ribbing about how they didn't want to drop Glen into a cell and lose the key. Glen smiled at them. "Thank you, Jesus!"

"Right, right, listen—"

"It doesn't matter where you put me. A cell or a hole in the ground, I'm still going to give Jesus the glory." He threw his hands up in the air, closed his eyes and started laughing. "Glory!"

But he was really thinking about the look on Hosea's face

as his own flesh-and-blood stalked down the aisle like the devil himself as Tara made the arrest. Glen had never thought he would understand what Jesus felt when Judas met him in the garden, kissed him on the cheek, and marked him for death. But now it was clear.

He'd already said too much, talking about the phone call. He shouldn't have. But it was one mistake. He promised the Lord he wouldn't falter in the future.

The detectives let him get the preaching out of his system. He'd already tried to convert them several times. He wanted to get up and dance around, but the detectives put an end to that quickly. "Sit in the chair, you can do all the shouting you want."

The gray-headed detective told his partner, "My aunt went to a Pentecostal church. Had the beehive hair and everything."

"Did you ever go?"

"No, my mom was dead-set against that sort of thing. We were Presbyterian."

"Were you now?"

"I don't remember much of it. Do you go to church?"

"First Baptist. Every Sunday, except when there's a game I want to see. Or fishing. You, Tara? A church goer?"

She grinned. "I might dress up a bit for Easter, go with my grandma. I'd rather sleep in on Sundays. But these Pentecostals? I've been there once or twice. They're nuts."

Glen laughed. "We sure are, praise Jesus."

He concentrated on his breath. His heart was beating faster. His legs were restless. It was all a test. *Isn't it, Lord? Are you testing me? What's it going to take to please you?*

The gray-haired detective said, "Glen, we're trying to help you. You're not a suspect here."

A knock on the door. The partner answered. In walked a man with slicked black hair and a navy suit, wide tie. His smile said he was too young to be wearing that, but the lines around his eyes said he was much older. He shook hands all around, introduced himself as, "McCool. David McCool."

Glen's attorney.

"Now if you'll excuse me for a minute or two, I'll need to speak to my client alone, please."

The gray-haired detective rose slowly from his seat. "Absolutely. Let him preach to you for awhile. We'll be right outside."

They headed towards the door, Tara lagging behind, trying to send a message with her frown. But Glen kept on smiling like a goon. He didn't care.

As soon as the detectives left, Glen gripped the lawyer by his forearms across the table and said, "Let's pray."

"Wait, now, wait. First, tell me if you're doing alright. Are they treating you good?"

"Let's *pray*." The reality of it all was starting to set in. He didn't want to be the Apostle Paul in chains after all. He didn't want to let his light shine among the imprisoned. "Please."

"I'm here as your lawyer."

"You can be my lawyer later. But right now, I need to pray."

David McCool sighed, nodded, and they started in together. Each prayed his own prayer, thundering, joyful, hoping for the presence of God to fall upon them.

Glen shouted, "Praise be to Jesus! Glorygloryglory!" He lapsed into tongues, as David McCool did too. Together they asked the lord to set Glen free, to punish the unrighteous, and reward the servant of God.

All the while, Glen thought, *Why me? Why did Rodney come to me? Why not my dad? Why not Rachel?*

He couldn't give Rodney up. He'd made a promise. He couldn't give him up now.

But he wanted to. He wanted to.

*Lord, please let this cup pass from me.*

Didn't he tell Rodney it was only temporary? Wasn't he supposed to turn himself in anyway?

*Please let this cup pass from me.*

It felt as if someone was pouring warm oil on top of his head and it flowed down all around him, coating him with a blessing.

He stood up, stumbled, and then fell to the floor, shivering.

Humbled.

The officer at the door opened the door. "What's going on?"

David McCool assured him, "He's praying, is all. This is how we do it."

The officer turned to Glen, shivering on the floor. "He's having a fit!" He spoke into his radio, "Medical needed at interrogation."

He sounded far away. There was a ringing in Glen's ears.

David McCool shoved the guard. "No, he's fine. Leave him alone."

"Sir, don't touch me."

"If you'd *listen*—"

"Sir, this is your last warning."

"Are you threatening me? You'd dare do that?"

Then a rough couple of grunts and moans, and David McCool was down, face being shoved into the floor, face turned towards Glen's.

Tara's voice rose from the hall. "The hell, man? What are you doing?"

*Please let this cup pass from me.*

Some cops with a medical kit were next, kneeling beside Glen, asking him how he was.

Glen was still shaking. The ringing kept on and on.

David McCool had been handcuffed, and his lip was smeared with blood. The officer was lifting him from the floor. He looked at Glen. "Don't say a word until I get back. Not one word. No preaching, no small talk, no nothing."

A nod at David McCool. "Okay."

Thinking, *I won't fail you, Lord.*

CHAPTER 31

Hosea left his suitcoat hanging over the back of the last pew and went to work. He tried to remember his best hiding spots. Rachel's best spots – but she'd been much smaller than her brothers, so those wouldn't fit a grown man. The few places he'd been able to find Glen. He'd been amazing at it, waiting until Hosea and Rachel were completely exasperated, on their last nerves, then pop out of hiding, laughing at them.

Glen was almost never "it."

The church was dark, but he was used to it. They'd played in the dark so no one would know.

They were too old to play once the new church was built, but Hosea had still wondered, if they *were* playing, where would he hide?

The search party had to have missed someplace. Glen was too good for them.

Hosea checked back beneath the baptismal pool, where there was a tight but surely possibly crawl space place in case they needed to run new wires or mics or speakers, or if they needed to fix a leak. Seemed damned uncomfortable now, but doable. He'd fit beneath the one they had in the old church when he was younger and thinner. He stuck his head and shoulders in, a tight squeeze. Utter darkness. He dug out his pocket flashlight, clicked it on. Nothing down there but discarded hymnals, yellowed stacks of paper, wires, pipes and dust. It billowed out as he pulled away, left him coughing and blinking. Great, now he had dirt all over his shirt. He brushed it off and got up.

He searched the new sanctuary top to bottom. He broke into his dad and Glen's offices. He crawled through the daycare room, the sound room, and both bathrooms. He checked every possible inch of the evangelist's quarters.

And then he moved on to the second building, the one he knew best – the sanctuary, fellowship hall, and Sunday School classrooms all under one roof. It had a homespun quality to it, the decorations mirroring what the old ladies of the church had in their kitchens. Lots of angels and white-guy Jesus. Lots of posters with scripture scrolled on top of sunsets, beach scenes, nighttime over a lake. It smelled like potpourri when it wasn't smelling like the back of someone's closet.

Hosea shone the flashlight down the hall right inside the doorway. It was narrow, more noticeable now than ever before. There were terribly-crayoned Bible scenes hanging outside each classroom except for the teens. They stopped letting them color around eighth grade because the pictures were getting too bloody.

He turned on the lights.

The fluorescents buzzed and splashed the place with their harsh light – nicks on the wall, paint rubbed off, industrial carpet dirty.

Hosea went through each classroom. Nothing. He checked to see if the carpet might have been pulled up. Maybe there was a hidden door.

Nothing.

The fellowship hall. Nothing.

The old sanctuary, now mostly used for storage. Nothing.

He checked his watch. He'd been at it for over an hour.

His shirt had sweat through and was filthy with cobwebs, dust and crud. His hair, a mess. He wondered what Dawn Hollingsworth would think seeing him filthy this way. The thought of her pained him a little. It wasn't going to work out after all. He wasn't sure he could ever step foot in this church again.

There was a catch in his breath. He rubbed his hands absently on his thighs as he swallowed hard. It felt like his own personal rapture, as if watching his brother, his dad, his sister, his church, all disappearing in a flash.

*He* should be the one feeling that escape. *He* should be glad to put them behind him and move on.

Instead, he was the one being left behind.

The tears came, and he did his damnedest to stop them at the source, but soon they ran down his face, his chin, to the floor.

Rodney was nowhere to be found.

Hosea tossed his head back, his neck cramping. He stared at the ceiling.

In the old days, the attic had been a primo hiding spot. After the last hurricane, though, it had been shut off somehow.

Or that's what he'd been told.

*Glen, you son of a bitch.*

Where would he have hidden the entrance?

Down the hallway, a glance in each classroom. He didn't see any ways to climb up there. Back into the fellowship hall. Through to the kitchen.

It hadn't been used recently except for making coffee, and the scorched odor hung in the air. The refrigerator and oven were fairly new, since the old ones had been ruined in the flooding. They'd put in a drop ceiling, too, made up of beige tiles. He could barely reach them standing on tiptoes. He climbed onto the stove, balanced himself, and stood up. He lifted the tile right above him, and slammed into a board.

There was only enough room to stick his head in. He grabbed his flashlight and held it up, shone it between the boards at the ceiling tiles. No one in there. A nearly impossible squeeze.

Until he rotated back to the start, the tile right next to the one he'd lifted. It was out of place, didn't quite fit. Hosea lifted it from its spot and pushed it aside. There was wood above that one, too.

No, this had to be the way. It had to be.

Hosea pushed his hand against the board. It wouldn't budge. More pressure. Still nothing. It was solid. He felt all the way around and across, poking and prodding. But there was nothing.

*Damn it!*

The stretching was getting to him. He eased back, breathing hard. There was no way up there. It ended here. Of course the search party had already done this exact thing he was doing, to no avail.

He was about to jump down from the oven when he decided to give it one more go, for the sake of saying he did it. He removed a third tile, hitting wood immediately, and moved it out of the way.

A solid wood beam.

And a ring bolt right in the middle of it.

A single bolt, for no reason at all.

Hosea touched it. Tried to move it. It was tough, but it started to rotate. He wished he had some pliers right about then. But he kept loosening it, bit by bit, bit by bit, bit by bit.

Until it released, and a large plank of wood fell into the top of the tiles. The hole had been cut large, so anyone lifting a few of the tiles wouldn't be able to find the edges. Very sneaky.

It was heavy, but Hosea was able to shift the wood off to the side to see a wider opening above, and an old water pipe that hadn't been used for years. Glen had screwed the bolt into the pipe. Hosea reached up, grabbed the pipe by both hands, stretching high on his toes, and started to pull himself up. He strained at first, his feet leaving the stove and flailing. Hanging in midair. He tried to keep a grip but fell, bashed his ass on the edge of the stove and rolled off onto the floor.

On his back, writhing, Hosea looked at the hole in the ceiling and thought he should give up, call Tara, and let them know what he'd found. Get a team back down here to check it out. Tell Glen they'd discovered his hiding place.

But then he thought, *Rodney is up there right now.*

He had to have heard Hosea's fumbling around.

How the hell did they get through? It took all he could to hang on.

Obvious. A ladder.

So where was a ladder?

Another search around the old sanctuary, and there it was, by the far wall behind some sheetrock that had never been used when rebuilding. A folding metal stepladder about six feet tall.

No wonder Glen was the master at hide and seek. He planned several moves ahead. It was never about fun for him. He had to win. He had to humiliate his siblings. Probably explained the preaching, too. First in a kid's game, first in Heaven.

Hosea carried the ladder back to the kitchen, wondering how someone could hide it after climbing into the attic. There had to be someone on the ground. It was easy enough to drop down onto the stove on the way out, but once you were in, someone had to help with the ladder.

And who else was around here all the time except their dad?

He set the ladder under the hole and climbed up, holding onto the pipe the last few steps as he squeezed into a cramped space, dark and hot. The flashlight showed him nothing except some boards covering the top of the drop ceiling, and barely enough room for Hosea on his knees. But he crawled onward, trying to be as quiet as possible. Sweat pouring. Arms and legs shaking. The flashlight beam slashed to and fro as he moved his hands one over the other along the wooden beam.

It wasn't the old wide-open attic he remembered. Here, everything was sectioned off. It felt bigger back then because he was smaller. There had also been a built in pull-down ladder out in the main hallway, long gone. Up ahead, more wooden planks turned him to the left, leading him to a hole in the wall. A very small hole. He crouched further onto his stomach and shone the light. It went through to somewhere, but he didn't know what was waiting for him

He could fit if he turned onto his back and pushed himself through with his legs. It was hard going, his shoulders snug, the rough wood around him threatening to rip his shirt, his pants, his skin. He couldn't tell how long the tunnel was, and as he pulled his legs all the way into the hole, he had to rely on the rest of his body rocking back and forth to help get him through.

Just when he thought he would get stuck tight enough he couldn't wiggle his way out, end up dying in this place – irony – there was an opening above him.

Hosea sat up and quickly twisted as far as he could, slashing his flashlight all around.

"Rodney? Buddy? You up here?"

He climbed out of the tunnel, recognizing now the old attic, steep-arched, dusty, the skeleton of the church with its braces and beams. Barely any light, but enough so someone accustomed to it might be able to see. Like Rodney.

"It's over, man. Come on out and we'll get you some help. We can talk this out."

Quiet.

Nowhere to hide up here, Hosea thought, until his flashlight caught the piece of plywood lying in the middle of the floor. He crouched and duck-walked his way over to it. He pushed it out of the way. There was a space there. Just enough space for a man to hide.

Hosea swept the flashlight, slower this time.

Some towels, some fast food bags, some plastic grocery bags.

And then there was the smell. A man who hadn't bathed in days. A man covered in shit and fear.

Rodney had been here, yes he had.

But he was gone now.

Hosea's legs weakened. He sat and covered his face with his hands.

CHAPTER 32

The drive was quiet. For one, Rodney was hunched down on the floorboards in the backseat of Rachel's car. For another, she'd told him to shut up his blubbering back in the church attic.

It had been a hard climb and she was soaked with sweat and dirt, but once Glen told her how to get into the attic, she was determined to get Rodney out of there before someone found him. The police had come close. Then Hosea had to get Glen arrested. One less person to help them now.

Why do this? Why protect Rodney? Why not let him face the consequences?

*No*, she thought. *Tonight's not the night for those questions.*

Several miles north, she pulled into the driveway of this dark, small house in the woods. She parked behind a twenty-year-old Buick LeSabre in pristine condition. Must not have been driven in years.

"We're here." She reached behind her and gave Rodney a whap. "Get out."

The gardens in the front of the house under two windows with white shutters had grown wild – weeds and wildflowers. The yellow vinyl siding needed a good wash. The nearest neighbor was across the street, but set far back from the road. When these homes had been built, the owners were chasing a dream of privacy. They were fleeing what the Coast had become in their minds – "urban." Code word for too black, too Vietnamese, too much sin and vice with the casinos. So they moved up here and spaced out their homes and pretended it was 1950 forever.

Rachel had been here many times with her mother, and a

few times since then, too. Not lately, though, and she regretted it.

She waited until Rodney climbed out of the backseat before leading him around the carport to a waist high chain-link fence. There was a "Beware of Dog" sign on the gate, but there hadn't been a dog in this yard for a decade or more.

There was a cracked concrete patio around back, and the bricks around yet another flower garden were still in place. Rachel knelt beside a marked brick, picked it up, and was relieved to find the key underneath.

She unlocked the back door and stepped inside, waved Rodney in after her. The lights were off. Rachel flicked on the one for the dining room, open to both the small kitchen and the living room. She closed the door.

The house was decorated exactly how most Southern country church women did it – lots of blue and white, lots of ducks and bunnies, lots of "Home is Where Jesus Is" type pictures on the walls, along with photos of children, grandchildren, old black and whites from the owner's childhood days, her "courting days" with her long dead husband.

Rodney stood still. "Where are we? How did you know about that key?"

"They put Sister Triplett into an assisted living apartment a few weeks ago. Her kids don't live on the Coast anymore, and they haven't gotten around to dealing with her place yet."

She crossed her arms. There was a chill inside, and the place held the mustiness Rachel had always associated with an old lady's house. Sister Triplett had been close to Rachel's mom, and they had visited this home together many times in the past. Rachel had continued to visit after Mom passed, but then in recent years, not as much because…Rodney.

He nodded, head tipped towards the floor. "Thank you. Thank you for coming to get me."

"Don't."

"I've missed you so much. I'm sorry, sweetie." He started for her, his arms outstretched.

"I said don't. I don't know what I'm doing. We need to talk."

"Okay, okay." He stopped. "Believe me, if I could take it all back, I would."

Quiet for a long moment. Then Rachel said, "Your friend found me, you know. Threatened me."

A long ashamed silence. Then, "Yeah. Glen told me."

"He broke into our house. He forced me to go looking for you. He was going to kill me."

He came closer. "I should've been there. I'm sorry."

"Did you hear? He would've killed me. He's insane. He could have killed you, too."

"Oh God."

"He…killed your dad."

The pain on his face, more boy than man. "I know."

"He shot him, Rodney. He shot your dad. I thought he was your *friend*."

Rodney was numb to the world, his eyebrows scrunched. Nothing she said made sense. "All I can say is I'm sorry."

Rachel backed off. "Stop it, stop apologizing. I don't want to hear another apology."

He came closer still.

She held out a stiff palm. "Go take a shower."

So he did.

At least Glen had given Rodney a change of clothes, but still the stink sloughed off him – blood, dead fish, and hot garbage. She sat on the edge of the couch cushion, holding herself tightly with her crossed arms on her legs. The shower squeaked to life as Rodney turned the spigots. She took a deep breath but nothing could help release the tightness in her stomach.

She'd asked herself on the drive over why she was doing this. The only answer she could come up with was *He's still my husband*. That was worth a lot. More than romance, more than fights, more than the kids. She'd been taught in church all her life the man was the head of the household and made the final decisions. She'd watched the dynamic of the subservient wife and the bullheaded ass of a husband over and over. It wasn't what she wanted in her own life, and she fought hard any time Rodney pulled some macho crap.

But what was a wife supposed to do? Let them haul away the man in a police car? Abandon him?

Rachel didn't realize how much time had passed before Rodney turned the shower off. She checked a clock on the wall. It had been twenty minutes. She hadn't moved a muscle.

Rodney stepped into the room, t-shirt sticking to his chest, an old towel looped around his neck. He stopped. Their eyes met. He eased across the room to a chair opposite the couch and sat down. He looked broken. Rachel wondered about evil spirits – could she gaze into his eyes and tell if a spirit had taken over in there? Because right then, there was nothing sinister, but something else about them made her uneasy. Like the photo she'd shown around at the bars. Funny how eyes could freak you out.

Rodney started, "I know, I can't take back what I've done. I'm sorry."

"Stop."

"Okay, no apologizing. Listen, I didn't kill anyone. I'm not a killer. I need you to understand."

"You're worse than a killer."

"Wait a second—"

"You chopped a man to pieces! How could you?"

"I don't know, I don't know! It happened so fast."

"Fast?"

"So fast."

She stood up. "You left, you went to the store, you got your tools. You could've stopped at any time."

"I was scared, alright?"

"And there was a *girl*, too? Was she your next slab of meat?"

"Stop it and let me answer!"

"Really? You have an answer for all of this? Wait, don't tell me. It's all the devil, right? Big ol' Satan whispering in your ear? None of it was your fault."

Rodney leapt up, and for the briefest second, Rachel

thought he might hit her for the first time in their years together. She steeled herself for it. But nothing came.

"I've never hurt anyone in my life."

"You sold drugs."

"You smoked it."

"Don't you even –"

"You're not perfect either. We all make mistakes!"

"You *chopped* a *man* to *pieces*, Rodney!"

"He was already dead!"

She turned her back on him and walked around the couch, ran her hand along the top of it. "You have to turn yourself in."

"I know. I'm…not ready yet." He lifted his face to hers. "What, what about the, um, what about the kids?"

"They're safe."

"He didn't hurt them? Tell me he didn't—"

"They weren't there. I made sure of it. You need to understand, Rodney." Rachel was beyond tears. "This is over. I'm giving you one chance for us to say what we need to each other, but then we're taking you in."

Nothing. He breathed through his lips.

"Where were you? When I could've died, where were you? Hiding in the church attic."

"If you'd let me—"

"When Charles Lott murdered your dad, where were you? Where were you?"

"You kicked me out!"

Rachel felt heat in her face. "You want to blame this on me? *You* want to make *me* feel guilty right now? Are you kidding me?"

"You kicked me out. If you hadn't done that, I wouldn't have been at his house."

"How dare you. That's low. That's the lowest."

There was a long pause. Rodney hunched his shoulders. "I don't know what to do."

She forced out a hard breath and paced behind the couch, arms crossed tight. "You'll never see your children again.

Ever. There's no excuse in the world you can make to change my mind."

"Baby, please."

"No, not going to happen."

"But they're *mine*, too. My children."

"Yeah, I know. That's something they are going to have to live with. But I tell you, this is the end. Of all of it."

She didn't know why it had taken so long for her to come to terms with it. She had expected Rodney to be, well, less *awful* somehow. He had made this all about him and his feelings. His fears. His wants. She couldn't have him weighing her down.

He slumped, mouth hung open. Rachel stepped over to the phone mounted on the kitchen wall covered in floral-striped wallpaper. A custard yellow push button with a wildly long springy cord. She picked it up and started to dial Hosea's cell phone number, if she could remember it. The first try, it rang a few times then stopped. She pressed the lever down and tried once more.

Then the numbers were in shadow. Rodney stood over her shoulder. He grabbed her wrist way too tightly to keep her from dialing. She dropped the handset. It hit the floor, cracked.

"Rodney! You're hurting me!"

"*Shh*. My turn to talk."

# CHAPTER 33

After Hosea put everything back the way it was before he'd found the way into the attic, he stepped out the doors of the church into the night. Still stifling hot, but better than the cramped, unforgiving space he'd been in. A breeze, at least.

The suit, ruined. There was no doubt. Some of these stains were too deep to ever come out. Mighty expensive. It would be long time before he could afford another one.

He stared across the lot at the parsonage, a light on in the front window. Thought about how his dad told him he hadn't known about Glen and Rodney's plans. How could Dad have been oblivious? How could he have been blind to what was going on? He *must've* known.

Hosea wondered if he should walk over, lay it all out. Try to pry a few revelations loose.

Right under his nose. They'd helped the man and the evidence was right under Hosea's nose and he didn't want to believe it. Glen, maybe, but Dad? It wasn't like Dad to lie, to omit, to break the law. In Africa, he'd confronted false prophets, fake evangelists, local beliefs, witchcraft, and stayed true to what he believed. Never lied to the people there, even though it would've helped build his church much faster, promising what he couldn't deliver.

It had never been this close to home before, either, Hosea guessed. A lie of love didn't count, did it?

Hosea's next step should've been to call the police, tell them what he found, and get them out here for a more thorough search of the attic. They would definitely take his father down to the station, put him in a different room from Glen, and spend the rest of the night breaking him down.

They would have taken the church apart, pew by pew.

So he didn't call, not quite yet. He would wait until Glen was ready to talk, let Tara and the other detectives do what they did best. Leave the pastor out of it.

He got a weird vibe someone was watching him. Probably Dad from the front window. Both of them wondering who should make the first move.

*Or*, he smiled, *God himself.*

Sure.

He pulled his cell phone from his pocket. Dialed Tara.

She answered, "He won't crack. All he's doing is preaching at us."

"Sounds like my brother."

"How are you?"

Hosea looked up at the night sky, mostly cloudy, a few of the planets bright enough to cut through the haze. "You know, I'm good. I am."

"At least one of us is."

"Has Glen convinced you to give up your Sunday mornings yet?"

"You guys can do whatever you want with your Holy Ghost. I'm good."

"Amen."

"Did you know the Lord loves justice? Your boy is throwing Bible verses left and right. He says, um, let me get it right: a brother is born for adversity."

"I don't remember that one."

"And, and, get this, if your brother sins against you, you have to go work it out with him alone. See what he's doing?"

Hosea knew exactly what she was talking about. Dad would pit them against each other over the dinner table, a "Bible-off." Who could recite the most relevant scripture about whatever subject he threw out there. Glen's mind was a steel trap. He had whole chapters in his head. A show off.

"Tara, do you think you can get hold of a Bible?"

A laugh. "In Mississippi? Hell, there's got to be one around here somewhere. Probably a dozen. Why?"

"Use it. He gives you verses about how he's right, give him some showing he's wrong. Stuff about respecting authority. Stuff about lies."

"I don't know where to find any. I can barely name a commandment."

"Get the Captain, he can help. I mean, it's worth a shot."

Tara hummed a few notes. Quiet. Then, "Why not?"

"Yeah. Why not?"

He pressed the off button and slid the phone back into his pocket. Started across the lot to his car, figuring on driving home, taking care of Pecan, who had probably peed on the floor by now. Then getting out of this suit, taking a shower. Nothing to do now but wait for Glen to talk.

He stopped. What kind of plan was that? He turned towards the parsonage, the light in the window. It didn't matter if he and his dad were arguing, Hosea still needed to be here for him until this thing was over.

The pull of his shower and his dog was strong. But he shook it off and turned towards the walkway up to the door.

Off to his left. A monster. Moving fast.

Hosea turned in time to see the man rushing him. The snarl on his face. Charles Lott.

Down they went, Charles' arms wrapped tight around Hosea, knocking the air out of him as they hit the ground.

Charles let go with his arms, straddling Hosea, and held a gun in his face.

"I hear you've been looking for me?"

# CHAPTER 34

Rodney's grip on Rachel's wrist was the hardest he'd ever held her.

The pain shot up her arm. She cringed.

He dragged her from the phone in the kitchen to the living room, forced her to sit beside him on the couch, knee to knee. He let go of her wrist but interlaced their fingers, squeezed.

"Rodney, stop."

"Babe, let me have my say. I've heard you out. Now listen to me."

"You're hurting me."

"I'm not hurting you. I would never hurt you."

She blinked at him, trying to avoid his steady gaze. His glasses were scratched and filthy. He'd washed the rest of him, but there was still dirt in the creases of his face. This was a shadow of the man she'd married.

"Rodney. My hand hurts."

His grip lightened and she felt her fingers throbbing.

"What do you want to tell me?"

He couldn't keep his head still. "You see, you see…"

"Yes?"

"I've been wrong about all of this. I can't turn myself in now. They won't understand. I want a second chance. Me and you, baby, yeah, we can get the kids, go start over somewhere else. I'm sure I can find a good job. A better job. No one has to know. We can leave tonight."

"Oh, really? That's what you were thinking hiding in the attic? Because it seemed to me you were leaving us behind."

"At first, to protect you." He leaned towards Rachel, causing her to tuck her chin. "Everything's changed."

It was going off the rails. "You need to turn yourself in."

Rodney gave her hand another squeeze. "I can't. I said I could, but I can't. I won't make it. Please, you and the kids, we can make it work. You're strong. Stronger than any woman I know."

He wasn't going to take no for an answer, and Rachel thought she should have played nice. Should have tamped down her anger, keep him on her side.

"Let's talk about it." The whole time, she thought of how to keep her children out of his reach. She absolutely was not going to let them near Rodney. "How are we going to do it?"

"I can get us some fake IDs. I can get a job, you can get a job. We'll be across the country, no one would ever find us."

"Let's think. Where would we go?"

He furrowed his brow, as if she was speaking in tongues. "Where?"

"Yes, sweetie, where would we go?"

Then he bolted upright, still holding onto her hand. She jerked away. It stung.

"Momma!" Rodney glared down at his wife. "He killed Daddy, but what about Momma? Who's watching Momma! We need to go see her."

"Rodney, please. I bet there are a hundred cops at her place."

"I've got to see her, though. We can't leave until I see her."

"You can't."

"Don't tell me what I can't do! I got the life sucked out of me by fuckers telling me what to do all the time, wanting me to be holy. Ain't a damn one of you holier than me. Not a damn one. If all y'all were in the same situation, you'd've have cut up the son of a bitch, too. I'm sorry to have done it, but, but…"

He exhausted himself. Never was a man of too many words. He put his hands on his hips and wandered around the living room, then stopped, rushed to the front window, and parted the blinds. "Shit!"

"What?"

Rachel could see it now. The headlights bathed the walls of

the living room and then faded away. The gravel crunched as the car made its way up the long drive. Who would that be? Sister Triplett's kids weren't coming until next week, they'd told her. She got up and eased up to the window beside Rodney.

It was a County Sheriff's car.

Rodney hissed at her, "You called the cops"

"I didn't."

"You did. You called nine one one."

"I swear, I did *not*." She backed off. "I swear."

"Then why are they here?"

"There were some following me earlier today. Maybe the car has been flagged, maybe they got lucky."

The headlights outside switched off. Car doors opened, and two uniformed deputies stepped out.

Rodney recoiled from the window and fell to the floor. He scrambled up.

"Get rid of them."

"What?"

"Get rid of them. Act like nothing's wrong." He started for the hallway leading to the bedrooms. "I swear, if you tell them, I swear…get rid of them."

He disappeared. She heard him rustling around somewhere in the back of the house.

She peered through the blinds. The deputies had their flashlights out, examining Rachel's car. Speaking into their radios. They must be checking the plate.

If they were, game over. Done. She could tell them Rodney was here and end this. They wouldn't be too hard on her. This was her husband, after all. Anyone would understand.

The deputies lumbered up the walkway to the front porch as if they didn't have a care in the world. Rachel heard one of them laugh.

It would be easy. Open the door and tell them he was here.

Do it. Jesus would approve.

One of the deputies knocked on the storm door with the butt of his flashlight. *Tap, tap, tap* on the glass.

She went to the door, opened it, and widened her eyes, pretending. One was pretty young, the other in his forties. "Oh, wow, hello."

They spoke through the storm door. "Ma'am, how are you tonight?"

"Fine, just fine. Something wrong?"

"We had a call from your neighbor," he pointed across the street way back there. "She said people are not supposed to be here."

"I don't know about that." *Tell them.*

"Are you the owner?"

"No, not the owner. She was moved to assisted living."

"Are you her daughter? A relative?"

"No." *Tell them.*

The deputies glanced at each other. The baby-faced one reached for the door handle. "You mind if we come inside?"

He pressed the lever, but the door was locked.

Rachel stared at the lever. The cop tried it a few time, but it held fast.

"Ma'am?"

She blinked. Stepped over to the door, unlocked it. Pushed it open for the deputies. "Of course, sorry. Sorry. You surprised me, is all. No one's called the last few times I was here."

The deputies stepped inside, their radios chirping at low volumes. Looking all around, as they do. Flashlights beaming across the floor and walls.

"Any reason it's dark in here?"

She'd forgotten to turn on the living room overheads. Silly. "No, I've only been here a couple of minutes. I've been on the phone with my brother."

The older deputy said, "Now, who are you?"

Rachel sweetened up, clasped her hands in front of her. "Yes, yes, I'm Eloise." First name that popped into her head.

"Eloise?"

"Yes." They had checked her car tags. Crap.

"Do you have any ID on you?"

"Darn it, I don't have my purse on me tonight. I came right after church. See, I go to the same church as the lady who lived here. We're going to help move some of her things, put the rest in storage. Tonight, I'm here to gather her some clothes, some other things she needs."

"Okay."

"I don't know if the person who called you knew what was going on. I don't think they knew each other well."

"Sounded like she did."

"I've known Sister Triplett most of my life, and I've never heard her mention it."

The young deputy, thumbs hooked on top of his belt. "Is this your car."

*TELL THEM.*

"No, I borrowed it from my cousin, Rachel. Mine is a disaster. I need to get a new one."

The knot in her stomach tightened. She wondered if Rodney was still in the house or long gone through a window. She somehow hoped he was here. Why? It didn't make any sense.

The older deputy turned off his flashlight. "Do you mind if we take a look around?"

"Must you?"

"Do you mind?"

Rachel laid her hand flat on her chest. "Well, it's not my house. I guess if you don't touch her things—"

"A quick look. Promise to keep our hands to ourselves."

What was the harm? They'd either find him or they wouldn't. They would take her, too. An accessory. She was in it now. Spinning lies for a man she loved and loathed equally right then. She nodded. "Sure, okay."

Rachel sat on the edge of the couch cushions while they ambled around the small house. She couldn't watch. Kitchen cabinets squeaked open, then closed. Closet doors opened and closed. The shower curtain, pulled back. She listened and waited for it to happen. For them to find Rodney, pathetic, crouched in a closet under an old lady's dresses.

The longest minutes of her life. Longer than the two nights she slept alone after kicking Rodney out. Longer than watching Rodney's dad gunned down, with her as the next target. Nothing compared to this.

Until they were done.

Both deputies walked back into the living room, murmured to each other, then headed for the door. "Ma'am, thanks for your help. I think you should talk to the neighbor over there if you're going to be here more often."

Rachel stood. Stayed still. "Thank you. I'm sorry for the misunderstanding.

Where was Rodney? Why hadn't they found him?

The knot tightened more and more. She was going to be sick.

Still one more chance to tell them. This was it.

She said, "Deputies…"

They turned back to her.

"Good night. Thanks for watching out for us."

They nodded and headed outside. She closed the door, then watched through the blinds as they climbed into their car, sat there for a few more minutes. She wondered if they were really calling it all in. Suspicious activity. Requesting back-up. Could they tell she was watching them?

Then they turned on their headlights and reversed out of the drive, and off into the night.

From behind Rachel, "We've got to go."

It made her catch her breath. She'd guessed Rodney was already gone when the deputies came up empty. When she turned to him, he was halfway across the room, but coming closer.

"How did they miss you?"

"I don't know."

"But they looked –"

"Never mind. We've got to go, I said."

She didn't move. "Where can we go?"

"Let's get the kids."

"No, Rodney, I told you."

"We have to. We have to stay together." Closer still.

"We can't. If you want to run away and start over somewhere, fine, but the kids need to stay. *I* need to stay. They need me."

"You don't see it yet. We need to leave together, one big happy family. We can fix this." Closer still. His familiar scent now turned sour to Rachel. He was right in front of her. Nowhere to look except his eyes. Rodney took her by the shoulders, pulled her towards him. Her lips to his lips. "I think this may be God's plan."

He kissed her.

She let him, afraid of what he'd do if she said no. Rachel had kissed Rodney thousands of times, tens of thousands, but this time he was a different person. His hands felt heavy, made of concrete. His tongue moved over and around her lips, and she imagined it as a slug.

She coughed. Nearly choking. She broke away, pushed him back. She leaned over and let her spit trail onto the carpet. Hands on her knees.

Why hadn't she told the cops? She'd lost her last chance.

"Are you okay?"

Rachel couldn't speak.

"It's going to be fine. It will be." He rubbed his hand over her back. "Try to breathe through your nose."

Her voice returned. Weak. "Please, tell me where you were. With the cops, where were you?"

"Invisible. I'm the invisible man."

She straightened up. There he was, touching her, coddling her. How she wished he really was the invisible man.

No, he was right there, and he wanted her to take him to his kids. Their kids. No, her kids, the ones she raised. The ones who depended on her more than they ever had their father. Going to get them was a bad idea. Real bad.

But there was nowhere left to go. She needed to stall.

Hardest words she'd ever said. "We'll go get the kids."

CHAPTER 35

After another hour of keeping Glen waiting, Captain Sarasota and Tara walked back into the interrogation room. The Captain closed the door and stayed beside it. Tara asked to take one of the detective's seats at the table. In her hands was a cheap Bible, the kind you find in hotels or Walmart. It was tagged all over with multicolored Post-it markers.

Glen had grown quieter as the time passed, letting David McCool do most of the talking for him. It was mostly legal roundabout, McCool trying to uncover what the cops already knew, and the cops trying to convince both he and Glen they knew the whole story without telling them. Trying to find a middle ground for a deal.

Every time a break seemed within reach, Glen would make some pronouncement. "My loyalty is to the Lord," or "Draw nigh to me in my time of need!"

The gray-haired detective gave up his chair, and Tara sat. She opened the Bible, flipped to one of the Post-its, and read, "'Obey them that have rule over you, and submit yourselves, for they watch over your souls.'"

Glen grinned. "Are you saying the police have rule over me? They watch out for my soul? I think not. 'We ought to obey God rather than men.'"

Tara met his eyes for a second before flipping more pages. "'Render to Caesar the things that are Caesar's, and to God the things that are God's.'"

"Oh, come on. He's talking about taxes, not about whatever *this* is. Unlawful imprisonment. What are my charges anyway? Can anyone tell me?"

Over Tara's shoulder, the detective sighed and said, "We've

already told you."

Tara turned her head and shushed him. Turned back to the Bible and flipped more pages. "'Remove from me the way of lying, and grant me thy law graciously.'"

McCool leaned forward. "What is this? What are you doing?"

Glen reached for his lawyer's arm, gripped it. "No, no. Wait a minute." Then to Tara. "You're calling me a liar?"

She didn't speak. Back to the Bible. "'Lying lips are an abomination to the Lord, but they that deal truly are His delight.'"

The smugness dropped. Glen swallowed hard, lips parted. "Job. 'To him that is afflicted, pity should be shown from his friends.'"

McCool's eyes went wide. "Wait a minute—"

Tara flipped pages. Read to herself. Flipped again, spoke up while David McCool was still protesting, half out of his seat.

"Now, why are you doing—"

She found her verse, stabbed it with her finger. "'If we say that we have not sinned—'"

"Don't say it."

"'—we make him a liar, and his word is not in us.'"

David McCool pushed his chair back. "Captain? Seriously?"

Captain Sarasota just raised his eyebrows.

Glen nodded. "'A friend loveth at all times, and a brother is born for adversity.'"

"'A true witness delivereth souls, but a deceitful witness speaketh lies.'"

"'He that loveth his brother abideth in the light.'"

"'A false witness shall not go unpunished, and he that speaketh lies—'"

Glen stood, planted his hands on the table. "'All thy commandments are faithful! They persecute me wrongly. Help thou me.'"

Tara didn't lift her head, flipped more pages. "'They have taught their tongue to speak lies, and weary themselves to commit iniquity.'"

"I haven't lied to you once!"

Tara glanced up for a second. Then back to her pages.

David McCool stomped around, hands on his hips. "This is an outrage. This is intimidation."

Glen stared a hole through Tara. "'And I heard a loud voice saying in Heaven, is come salvation, and strength, and the Kingdom of our God, and the power of our Christ.'" Louder. "'For the accuser of our brethren is cast down, which accused them before God day and night.'"

Tara let the moment ride.

David McCool said, "Are we done now? You can't use any of this, you know."

Tara ignored him, turned back to the Bible. Flipped. "'All liars shall have their part in the lake which burneth with fire and brimstone.'"

"Detective, look at me."

She did. Wanted to tell him to sit down. Wanted to tell him to cut the drama. But she kept her cool.

"I'm no liar."

"Okay, Glen. I guess you're the preacher. You know what a lie is and what it isn't. I'm sorry I doubted you."

He stepped away from the table. Slid his palms together. Sweaty. Turned to the back of the room and looked into the two-way mirror.

David McCool started on about how this was illegal and they should release Glen right then and there. The Captain told him he would have his chance in front of a judge. But Tara kept her eyes on Glen. His reflection, downcast. He stood very still.

Tara got up and went to him. Hand on his shoulder while the Captain and McCool shouted at each other:

"This is a travesty! I'll get this thrown out!"

"We're trying to *save lives*, counselor. We don't have time."

Tara said to Glen, "If you tell us the truth, you'll go free, you know. We don't want to bother with taking you to trial. Seriously."

"I keep thinking God is telling me what to do. God wants me to save souls, God must be leading me. And now I don't know. Maybe it was me leading me all along."

"It's normal to have doubts."

"You know how many times I've preached to *not* doubt God?"

"But it happens, right?"

"I don't think I'm the right person to answer right now. If I tell you what I know, can I call my Dad?"

"Sure, sure." Tara felt relief for the first time since this started. It wasn't the end, but she finally caught glimpse of the finish line. She turned to the others, all bickering now. "Listen up!"

Glen came back to the table and sat down. "Rodney called me, four in the morning, and told me what had happened. I mean, not all of it. Hosea had to fill in the rest later. But still, I knew Rodney had messed up badly, and I needed to find him someplace safe until we could settle his soul. I didn't want him going to jail without some peace. Some forgiveness."

He told them all in a flat monotone different from his preaching voice. No longer bombastic, exaggerated, a performance. This was any other guy spilling his guts. Resigned to his fate.

He borrowed the boat, hid Rodney in the duck blind. But Rodney got scared, made his way back to the church. "I put him in the attic."

Tara said, "There wasn't any way into the attic. It's been closed off since the hurricane."

"Well, there's a way. I fixed it myself. One day soon, the church is going to need a place to hide when the persecution starts."

The Pascagoula detectives rolled their eyes. Tara ignored them.

"You'll tell us how to get up there?"

Glen nodded. "I will."

They all perked up. The Captain said, "Let's get some

people over there pronto."

"But he's probably not there anymore."

All heads turned back towards Glen. "What do you mean?"

"I told my sister where to find him. I told her to get him out."

Tara sat on the table, leaned closer to Glen. "Where would she go?"

A sad grin crawled onto his face. His last little bit of rebellion. "I have no idea."

# CHAPTER 36

Charles Lott bashed the gun barrel into the side of Hosea's face twice. It bit into the skin, ripped it. Hosea didn't know if he'd cracked his eye socket. All he knew was *pain*. He flailed with his arms and legs, but the bastard had pinned him down, slapped his arms out of the way like they were gnats.

Frisked him one-handed, the gun an inch from Hosea's nose. Found the clip-on holster on his belt, empty.

"Where's your gun, man?"

"My gun?"

"Yes! Your fucking gun, where is it?"

More frisking. Hosea pulled his arms close, trying to cover his face.

"Where is it?"

"I don't have it! I swear I don't have it."

"Well, where is it?"

"I didn't, I swear, I didn't bring it!"

Another bash across the face. The pain seeped all the way through his skull.

"Liar." Charles hopped off Hosea, kept his pistol trained on him. "Is it in the car? This is your car, right?"

Hosea held his hands above him, flinching. "Please. I can help you. Let me help you."

"Look at you down there, can't even help yourself." Charles tried the passenger door. Unlocked. He opened the glove compartment with his free hand, still keeping the gun on Hosea.

Hosea felt the fear rise.

"Yeah, there we go." Charles rose from the car, a pistol in each hand. Hosea's in his left. So stupid, leaving his pistol in an unlocked car.

Never been a problem before. Never been that sort of town.

Charles admired the piece, tossed his own on the ground. "I was starting to get freaked, man. Out of bullets. But this one, you're ready to party."

He checked the clip, slammed it back home. He racked the slide. Held it sideways above Hosea.

"So, you found Rodney yet?"

Hosea shook his head.

"I *said*, have you found Rodney yet? I expect an answer."

"N-no. No, we haven't found him."

"Is he in the church? I bet he's in the church. I bet you're helping hide him."

"I'm not, we're not."

"Yeah, you're going to get him to flip on me. I know how it works."

"I swear! He's not here! I don't know where he is!"

Charles, muscles popping, shoulders hunched, stalked in a circle. Wound tight.

Hosea thought he was about to die by his own gun.

Thinking, *a miracle would be nice.*

Thinking, *it's either Hell or nothing.*

Whispering to a Lord he had turned his back on: "Sorry."

Charles turned back to him. "You're going to help me. We're going to find the motherfucker."

"Listen, I can help you. We don't know where he is, but we can work with you on this."

A laugh. "You kidding? Man, I'm going out in a blaze of glory! Like Bon Jovi? *Young Guns*? Dude. But I'm taking some motherfuckers with me. You understand? I've got shit to do."

A voice behind Hosea's head: "Son?"

*No.*

"Son, are you out here? Were you shouting?"

Charles lifted the gun.

Hosea craned his neck, looked behind him. Dad stood on the walkway, slacks and white dress shirt, in his socks.

"Dad, go back inside! Lock the doors!"

"What's going on out here?"

"Dad, run! Go inside, call nine one one!"

Instead, the pastor stepped closer. "Who is this? Who are you, young man?"

Charles still hadn't fired. Hosea sat up. "Wait, wait, wait, don't. I'll find Rodney. We'll go find him. I think my brother knows where he is. I can call him. Just, please."

Charles glanced down. Teeth grinding.

"Dad, don't come any closer. Go inside. Now."

Pastor Elgin kept on down the walkway, slowly. "Young man, what's your name?"

"Stop right there." Charles was shaking. Wavering.

Was he scared of preachers? A chink in his armor?

The pastor stopped, his hands spread wide. "I'm not going to hurt you. You're not going to hurt me. I'm going to pray, though. I'm going to pray for you right now."

"Dad, please—"

"Quiet, Son."

"Dad."

His dad glanced down at him. His face was peaceful. He remembered the times when Dad was solid as a rock in the face of danger, back in Africa, here in Mississippi, warlords, criminals, drug dealers, con men, all of them had tried to destroy his ministry. But Dad faced them all down.

"In the name of Jesus is how we're going to pray. Nothing can hurt you when you pray in his name. I promise no one will hurt you. Let me come to you, let me lay my hands on you."

"Stay away from me."

"Dad, please."

He kept coming. He stepped around Hosea and eased his hand up, reaching to place it on Charles' head. Walking right past the gun barrel. Charles didn't move a muscle.

Dad placed his palm flat on top of Charles' head and shouted, "*Jesus!*"

Charles yanked back from the preacher, shot the preacher

*One two three four* through his chest. Hosea knew what the hollowpoints in his pistol could do to a body. He watched four explosions exit his father's back.

Hosea screamed.

His dad stayed standing for a moment longer. He staggered. Turned to Hosea with wide, frightened eyes. He opened his mouth.

"Jesus?"

He fell to the ground.

Sirens in the distance. Charles turned the gun back to Hosea. "Get up. We've got shit to do."

Hosea got to his knees, crawled to his dad's side. Those wide eyes, frozen. Gone. He placed a hand on his dad's cheek and lifted his face. Was there any clue there in his eyes? Had he made it to his reward? Was he dancing around the throne?

Hosea said to his father, "You…you…" Finished it in his head: *idiot*.

No, that wasn't fair. Dad was a better man than Hosea would ever be.

Charles grabbed Hosea by the arm and tried slapping him across the face with the gun again. He missed. Charles dragged him to the passenger door and shoved him in. "Move over! Drive, you drive! Let's go!"

Hosea aimed the key for the ignition and missed a few times until Charles pushed the gun into his temple and shouted, "Now or die!"

The key slid in. Hosea cranked up. He pulled the car out of the driveway and back onto the streets.

In the rearview, his dad lay in the grass.

Through the windshield, it was dark.

Hosea wondered if he would live to see daylight.

# CHAPTER 37

Rodney rummaged through the drawers in Sister Triplett's kitchen until he found a chef's knife, a back-up plan. He didn't want to stab his wife – Jesus, that was the last thing he wanted to do – but she wouldn't listen! She was ruining everything. Ruining their love, ruining their family. Ruining his escape.

Rachel sat in the living room, quiet, while he went through the kitchen. When he'd first seen her standing over him in the church attic, he thought it would be a happy reunion. He thought she'd come to save him.

Now he wasn't sure what the point was. At least she hadn't ratted him out to the deputies who dropped by.

She would get it soon, though. She would understand.

For better or worse, in sickness and in health.

It was *right there* in the vows.

It would take time, but they would overcome this. They had to.

Once they got in the car, Rodney hid under the blanket in back. Rachel was taking a long time to get wherever it was they were headed. Lots of turning in circles.

He was starving and his stomach was beginning to cramp. Back at the old woman's house, he'd scoured the shelves and the fridge desperate for any leftover food. The fridge was cleaned out, and most of the cabinets, but he did find some stale Chex and choked down a handful before they left.

It wasn't enough. The hunger, the paranoia, the fear, his aching back and arms and legs were near their breaking point, all of it making this harder.

*Keep it together, keep it together.*

Rachel didn't tell him where they were going, but if he had

to guess, he'd say Eileen and Joel's house. That woman was a godsend while Rachel worked, offering to take care of the kids and refusing to accept one dollar for it.

"How much farther?"

"Can you let me drive? It's not far."

"Seems pretty far."

"I need to stop for gas."

"Are you serious?"

"It'll be fine. You stay low and I'll hurry up. There's a station not far."

Her voice was all wrong. He rose from the floorboard, eyes over the top of the center console. He checked the gauge.

Half a tank.

"You've got plenty of gas."

"You think so?"

"Plenty. We'll get more after we get the kids."

"I need to pee."

"Bullshit." He let out a rattling breath. "I can't believe I trusted you. Why did you bother getting me out of the attic if all you wanted to do was fuck me over?"

"Please, don't talk like that." Her hands slid to nine and three. He watched her struggle to slide them higher.

His arm snaked over the seat, the blade held tight, until the tip was touching the thin skin of her throat. He felt her swallow. He fought hard to steady his hand.

"You won't kill me," she said. "In Jesus' name, in Jesus' name, in Jesus' name—"

"Quit it. I'm sorry about this."

"In Jesus' name!"

"Stop it! *Listen* for once tonight."

She was already off to the races. "I call on the power of Jesus to rebuke the spirits of evil that afflict my husband now! I call on you to *bind* evil spirits!"

Evil? She thought he was evil?

He'd made a terrible mistake. He chopped a human being to pieces. He had placed his wife and children in mortal danger thanks to Charles Lott. He had turned away from everything the Church had taught him, and for what? What had it gotten him?

His own wife thought he was *evil*.

Fuck.

Rodney lifted the knife and ran the edge down Rachel's cheek, pricked the skin. The blood trickled down, dropping onto her shirt, her skirt. She stopped praying.

"Don't use Jesus against me. We're in this together. Think about it." His mouth on the tip of her ear now. "Remember our wedding?"

"Uh huh." Blood splashing in big drops.

"People said it would never work out between us, but we did it. We overcame. We can do it someplace new. Where are the kids, Rachel?"

She pursed her lips. "No. You can't see the kids. I will die first."

"They're at your aunt's house, aren't they?"

"Don't."

"Of course they are. You thought I wouldn't know? Here's what we're going to do." Rodney speaking softly now. "You're going to drive to your aunt's house. We're going to get our kids. We'll get this taken care of, bandage you up, and then we can get on the road."

"I can't. I won't."

He moved the knife down and pressed the blade against her neck. It was easier this time. "You can. You will. Because if you don't, then I'll have to leave you by the side of the road. I'll still go get the kids. But they need you. They need us both."

"You, you're crazy. You're insane."

He kissed her cheek, the bloody one. "If I'm crazy, it's all over you. It's all going to make sense soon. You'll see."

Rodney made Rachel drive past Eileen's house a couple of times, searching all around for cops lying in wait. He didn't want an ambush. It was a typical small-town subdivision, with clean streets and large enough yards, ranch style houses with attached garages, and the same gray mailbox on a pole at the end of every driveway. Plenty of streetlights to make it safe for the kids to walk home. The cars in the driveways or on the curb were nothing fancy – Hondas, Chevrolets, pick-up trucks, none of them brand new. Sunday night, no one on the streets except a couple of skateboarding teenagers, everyone tucked inside.

Rodney was sweating, even with the A/C. On fire.

He didn't see anyone in front of Eileen's place, hadn't noticed any people sitting in their cars, an obvious giveaway. They couldn't outsmart Rodney.

"We're going to do this quickly. Pull into the driveway. We get out, go to the front door, and get the kids. Go on and knock like everything's the same as it ever was."

She pulled into the driveway.

She opened the door. Rodney opened his. They got out together. He got right up close, the knife held low on her back. She was shaking.

"Lord, please, I beg you."

"Shut up. I said I'm sorry. Now walk."

She took small steps, wobbly, as if she might fall over. She put her hand on the car to help her along. Rodney was right there with her, threatening to pierce her kidney at the first sign of trouble.

*Would you do it? Can you do it? Remember how hard you fought to win her over?*

"Lord, *Lord*, Lord Jesus." Crying now.

"Ask her to send out the kids. Tell her you're taking them home. No tears." He stepped to the far side of the door against the front wall. "Play it cool."

Rachel kneaded her fingers together, looked at her toes.

"Come on!" Like a cat hissing.

She pressed the doorbell and waited.

Another few minutes was all it would take.

Rodney could feel Eileen, big woman that she was, shaking the house as she walked to the door. The deadbolt snapped back. The door opened.

"Girl, I was starting to wonder where you were. Don't

make me worry."

"Yeah." Eyes flicking back and forth.

*Don't do it. Don't give it away.*

"Come on in. We'll – " Then she cut herself off. "What happened to your face?"

Rachel let out a banshee wail and shouted, "He's here! He's here!"

She flung herself into the house. Rodney wheeled around as Eileen slammed the door, but he gave it a kick before she could close it all the way. Another kick to swing it wide open. Rachel was on her hands and knees, scurrying. Eileen used her bulk to block the door, screaming at him.

"Out, Satan, get out of my house! Get out!"

Goddamn it! So close! So *so* close!

Rodney grit his teeth. He stabbed Eileen in the stomach, ripped the blade to the side. He shouldered her away from the door. He heard his kids inside yelling for Mommy while Rachel told them, "Get to the bathroom, lock the door! Go, right now!"

Eileen toppled to the floor, her head clipping a glass end-table on the way down, the sound a sickening thud. The glass exploded.

Rodney got a glimpse of Joel, still a brick wall at age sixty, running from the kitchen. Rodney reached down and wrapped up Rachel around her waist, pulled her to her feet, and held the now blood-slicked knife across Rachel's chest.

"Stop, I swear, stop right there! I'll do it!"

Joel stopped in the middle of the living room, hands up, fingers wide. "You don't want to do this. Please, son, think about it."

From behind Joel, Molly and Joshua peeked around the corner.

Joel shouted, "Eileen, honey? Eileen? You alright? Talk to me honey, please."

Eileen didn't move, didn't say a word. Blood soaked her dress, pooled under her head.

Rachel wailed, fought, but Rodney held her tight.

Almost out of breath. He sucked in enough air to say, "Hey kids. It's Daddy."

# CHAPTER 38

Dad's eyes. Nothing there.

It had terrified Hosea. He drove without thinking. Charles Lott held the gun on him but didn't tell him much else except to turn on the police scanner. Quiet between them as the radio traffic squawked.

Hosea knew those voices. He was friends with these people.

All the worse when he heard Tara's voice: "Oh God, no." And call for an ambulance to his dad's address.

"Be advised, suspects may be in the church."

Glen must've broken.

Tara, her voice choking up. "We have a fatality. Multiple gunshots."

Hosea should've told her about the attic right away. So arrogant. If he'd told her, his dad would still be alive and he wouldn't be driving to his execution.

"Whoa boy, we got out of there just in time. I thought you said he wasn't in the church."

Hosea's throat was dry. He could barely talk. "He's not."

"What'd you say?"

"I said he's not."

"Better not be." The kid was lit up, Hosea knew. Sweaty, hyper, electric.

Passing under streetlights down on the bayou road. Light, then dark, then light, then dark.

Hosea's cell phone rang.

Freaked Charles the fuck out. "Shit, man!"

"It's my phone."

"Who's calling you?"

He guessed Tara, demanding he get his ass back to the church.

Charles Lott waved the gun around Hosea's face and said, "Get it out. See who it is."

"I can't. I'm driving."

"Get your fucking phone out, I said!"

Hosea took his left hand off the wheel and dug in his pocket, twisted the phone free from the fabric.

"Answer it. Be cool."

Hosea pressed the on button but it was too late. "They hung up."

"Who was it?"

"I don't know. I don't know this number."

"Call it back, then. Come on."

He was still having trouble one-handing the thing, but he called the number. Got a dial tone. "Nothing."

Charles Lott snatched the phone away. "I want to get one of these."

"You can't have one where you're going." Hosea couldn't help himself.

"I guess you're right. No cell phones in Hell. But I guess it's the same for you. None in Heaven either."

"You think I'm going to Heaven?"

"You're the preacher. You're the cop, being a Boy Scout."

"It's not as easy as you think."

Charles laughed. "You're probably safe."

"There's still a chance for you, too. It doesn't have to end badly."

The gun barrel poked Hosea hard in his ear.

"Too late, preacher. I sold my soul. Shit, I *gave* my soul away. It's been a blast."

The scanner bled more info: Dad's body, waiting for the ME. The church attic being empty.

All Hosea's fault.

Charles picked a spot along the water and told Hosea to park. It was near a spot on the bayou they called "The Point," some old concrete slabs and other huge rocks where high school kids went to hang out and drink on weekend nights, or where fishermen came for catfish. At night they'd switch to spearfishing.

Charles wasn't doing this off in the woods somewhere hidden. He was doing it in a place where people would find the body. He *wanted* Hosea to be found quickly.

As soon as Hosea threw the car into park, he opened the door and puked all over the ground. Sour. Charles Lott laughed some more, reached over and grabbed Hosea by the shirt and dragged him back inside.

"Be careful, man. Don't get any in the car. I've still got to drive this thing."

Spit dripped from Hosea's lips. His insides shriveled.

"Aw, cheer up, man. I hear it doesn't hurt. It's real fast. I'm giving you a nice exit. Could be worse."

Hosea gripped the wheel. Rested his forehead on it. "Please."

A prayer to the wrong god.

Charles pulled the gun back, let the barrel point towards the roof. "I've got an idea. You don't know where Rodney is, I understand. But how about your sister?"

"No."

"I almost had her, you know. Fuck, she almost had *me*. I'm telling you, we're talking inches. I owe her one."

"No, leave her alone."

Charles held up the cell phone. "Why don't you call her up, find out where she is, and take me to her? Then you and me'll be good."

Hosea took the phone, but shook his head slowly. His cries were stuck in his throat.

"Come on, it's a good trade. I owe her a lot more pain than I do you."

"Never. Go on, kill me now."

Charles slapped the gun barrel upside Hosea's forehead. "You're making it worse, man. I'm talking some serious fucking agony. Get out, nice and slow, and don't think of running."

Hosea unbuckled his seat belt. He wondered where Rachel was, and if she was with Rodney. Was she okay? Were the kids okay? There was no way this creep was going to get anywhere near them. He couldn't stop shaking. Willed himself to, though. Charles Lott opened his door, too. They both climbed out together, Charles keeping the gun leveled on Hosea the entire time.

Hosea's life didn't flash before his eyes. He thought about Pecan at home. He hoped Rachel would take her in for him. The kids loved her.

Charles closed his door. "Back here. Come on."

They were on a jut of land in the woods overlooking the bayou, the dirt beneath eroding away over the years. Pine trees. The smell of brackish water and dead fish. Hosea had grown up with the smell. It meant "home." The night was so dark he couldn't see a reflection of the moon off the water, but he heard it lapping.

He thought about Dad. He thought about Mom. He thought about Mom's parrot. *My boy's home!*

What was about to happen? Would he wake up in Heaven? Hell?

Or not wake up at all?

Charles moved in behind him, grabbed him by the shoulder and pushed him ahead.

Hosea thought about Glen. How he wished things between them weren't this damaged. And about Rachel, hoping she would be able to find her own way once Rodney was in jail.

"Here's good," Charles said. He let go of Hosea and brought the gun up and it was going to go down right now this fast—

Hosea's cell phone rang. It was a snap of the fingers, dragging Hosea out of his own eulogy. Hosea dropped to the ground right before the gun went off.

*Boom.*

He spun and leapt at Charles, trying to pin his arms. Tackled him. But Charles had his gun arm free. They rolled in the dirt and the pine needles.

*Boom.*

Off into the night.

Charles slammed the butt of the gun on Hosea's skull *one, two, three* times before Hosea had to let go. He swiped and pawed for the gun arm, got hold of it, trying to hold it up and away with both hands.

*Boom.*

Charles was much stronger. He wasn't afraid. He was jacked to the gills.

He kicked Hosea square in the balls.

Hosea dropped. He screamed. He watched the gun swing towards him and—

# CHAPTER 39

Tara stood over her partner's dead father, the entire church parking lot a sea of strobing blues and reds.

She'd met him several times before. He seemed a nice enough man, if a bit stiff. But she didn't doubt he was trying to do some good in the world.

Now the pastor stared at nothing.

She set her jaw.

Her colleagues in uniform had gone through the church one more time, Glen's instructions leading them to a place in the attic where Rodney Goodfellow had supposedly been hiding. A waste. His DNA wasn't much help tonight.

But what happened here out on the lawn? Was *this* Rodney Goodfellow's work? Based on what she'd learned about the man, Tara had a hard time believing that. She also had a hard time believing this was completely unrelated, either. This was too small a town for such a coincidence.

And where the hell was Hosea? She'd tried the radio, got nothing. She had to borrow the church phone to call Hosea's cell phone, got nothing. Had he gone home, turned it off? Last she'd seen him, he was with his dad. Could he have –

Ridiculous. She raised her hands to both sides of her head and gave it a squeeze.

Where was Charles Lott?

Lydia Hunter walked over to Tara, a radio in her hand. "This is for you."

Tara took the radio. "Yes?"

"Detective, this is Louis here with Fabrice."

"I hear you." Tara had sent them to stake out the aunt's residence, where the Goodfellow children were staying. They had taken up a spot in the house right across the street, watching through the front window. "What's up?"

"He's here. I think he's already killed a woman. Get over here now! We're going in!"

Holy shit.

Tara handed the radio back to Lydia. "You, grab Porter, let's go!"

Then she shouted to all the uniforms and suits milling around, "Listen up! We've got one."

# CHAPTER 40

Burning.

Piercing.

But Hosea was still breathing.

The bullet had sheared off the side of his face, destroyed his ear, hurt like he'd never been hurt before.

*Move!*

Jerked his head to the right before the next bullet

And the third.

Hosea launched himself at Charles' knees and locked them up, sent him tumbling. Charles kept hold of his gun and came around fast. Hosea climbed over him and got his hands around it.

*Boom.*

Two fingers turned to pulp.

The adrenaline kept Hosea alive, kept him fighting in spite of the pain.

Too bad the meth in Charles Lott kept him fighting harder. Stronger than Hosea.

Charles tried to buck Hosea off. Hosea tried to pin down Charles with his legs. His damaged hand was still wrapped around the gun but slipping as the blood flowed. He reached over with his other hand, grabbed Charles' wrist, and fought like hell to hold on.

How long could he do it? In the end, Charles Lott would still have the gun, still have the advantage. There would be no escape.

Charles curled his free hand into a fist and began pummeling Hosea in the guts. Goddamn, it hurt. Made Hosea sick. He retched, emptied stomach acid all over Charles Lott.

Didn't faze the bastard one bit.

He twisted the gun out of Hosea's grip, bucked him off. Charles got up on his knees, held out the gun.

When four more arms reached out from behind and grabbed Charles, pulled him straight up into the air.

Two fishermen, must've been heading out to the Point for some fishing. They'd dropped their stuff and run over, wrapped up Charles while he struggled.

One of the men was fat, with thick powerful arms. The other was an average guy, strong enough but nothing special. Even two on one, Charles was giving them a hell of a time. He stood his ground, even as they were trying to wrench the gun away from him. He let out a yowl. Only a few seconds away from breaking free.

Hosea searched around him. A big branch to hit Charles with? No, didn't see one. In the car? A tire iron? Could he get it in time?

Hosea turned to where the fishermen had dropped their gear. There it was.

*Spearfishing.*

Speargun.

He'd never used one before. He'd seen a few people do it, though.

He staggered over to the gear, picked up the gun. It was long and thin, unwieldy. He tried to understand it.

Charles pushed the smaller man off of him and kicked at the fat man still gripping his arms.

It was a big rubber band. Hosea braced the gun between his knees and tried to pull back the rubber. The gun kept flopping up and down. Hosea kept trying, down two fingers, blood. Come on, pull the band, *pull it*. Pull harder. Don't let it defeat you.

He strained. The pain was white hot.

Charles wrestled his arms back from the big fisherman. Kicked him away and casually shot him.

*Boom, boom.*

He tried to get his bearings. Found Hosea. Lifted his gun. The rubber stretched but not enough, not enough, not enough.

But then it caught.

*Boom.*

The bullet tore through Hosea's jacket, his shirt, exploding into his ribcage.

The shock of it.

Hosea felt his breath leave his body. He fell onto his side. The speargun clattered on the ground in front of him.

Charles stalked onward, still holding out the pistol.

*The speargun.*

It was the only move he had. He grabbed it

Only to have the other fisherman lift it out of his hands, take aim, and send a spear through Charles Lott's throat.

It didn't seem to have an effect at first. It passed right through, still connected to the wire on the gun.

Charles fired again and again, missing, missing, until he was out of bullets.

Hosea watched as the blood began to run down Charles' neck, flow from his mouth. Charles grabbed the wire coming out of his neck by both hands, pulled hard, but the fisherman held on tight. Charles began to hack and cough. Dropped to one knee. More blood. More hacking. He threw the empty gun towards Hosea and the fisherman. It bounced off the ground, then stayed put.

Charles Lott keeled over face first into the dirt.

The fisherman kept watching, mesmerized, until he was sure the maniac was going to stay down. Then he ran over to his friend, shouting, "Darren! Darren! Oh, god, Darren!"

"Shit, man." Charles had shot Darren in the gut but he was still moving.

Hosea, wheezing, sure his lung was shredded, sure he was bleeding to death and there was no way to stop it, dug his cell phone from his pocket. He was shaking too bad to hold it still. His other hand was too damaged to dial.

He took in as much breath as he could and tried to shout, "Hey!"

The fisherman looked up.

Hosea waved the phone in the air. "Nine. One. One. Nine. One. One."

Then his vision collapsed, a tunnel. A pinpoint of dim light appeared, growing larger as the real world faded. He'd heard it many times from many people who'd nearly met their maker – the light. There was always a light. A good sign? A feeling of floating, numbness. The light brighter still.

Then the light blinked out and all was dark.

# CHAPTER 41

"You're not going to hurt her, Rodney." Joel backed away slowly. "No one else needs to get hurt."

But Rachel, knife edge sharp on her neck, didn't believe that anymore. The Rodney she'd known and loved was gone, leaving a mess of evil spirits wrapped in Rodney's skin.

She wanted to call out to her children to run as far away as possible, out the back door. Find the nearest neighbor, call the police.

Why didn't she turn him in when she had the chance? Why did she let him get this close to her children?

Eileen hadn't moved for several minutes now. Not a sound. The blood had spread and soaked into the carpet.

Molly and Joshua stared wide-eyed, deer in the headlights. Daddy had never hurt Mommy. Daddy loved Mommy. None of this made any sense.

The blade tightened. Rachel was scared to breath, to swallow.

"You don't know what I'll do, Joel. You have no idea. I'm taking my family out of here, and you're never going to hear from us as long as you live."

"Let's talk about this."

"There's no talking to do. I'm sorry about Eileen, but…shit." Then, back to his Daddy voice. "Come on, guys. Molly, sweetie. Josh, buddy. Come on out here. It's going to be okay. I promise you. Daddy keeps his promises, right?"

"No, no, no." A croak from the bottom of Rachel's soul. "Joel, don't let him."

Joel said, "Stay where you are, kids."

Rodney took Rachel's hair, looped as much of it around his fist as he could and yanked back, causing her to shout. Her throat was even more exposed, several thin red lines where the knife had already skipped and slit.

"Tell them, Rachel, tell them to come to you."

*No. No more.*

"See, guys, Mommy is fine. Come see your mom. Right, baby?"

She closed her eyes. "No, don't come any closer. Do you hear me? You need to go with Uncle Joel."

"Rachel – "

To her God: "I'm ready to meet you, Lord. I'm ready to meet you if you'll protect my children."

"Tell them!"

"I won't! I won't do it! Jesus, help me! Joel, save them, please."

"Calm down," Joel, still steady, still soft. "Everyone calm down."

"I'm not going to calm down. I don't want to hurt anyone, I swear." Rodney was barely keeping it together. "I didn't want any of this. It was a mistake, see? It was all a mistake. Give me a second chance. I can make everything right this time."

"Sure, I'm sure you can. But we need to talk about it first. Just talk."

Rachel shook her head. "Let him kill me. I don't care about me. Save my babies."

She saw in her uncle's eyes how this was hurting him. There were no other options. They were out of time. No one even knew they were here.

"Joel. My babies, please."

Rodney's voice took on a strangled quality. "Kids, come on out, we're going on a trip. Might even go to Six Flags. Don't you want to go to Six Flags?"

Joel kept his eyes on Rachel.

Rachel wanted Joel to let her die rather than let Rodney near those kids. It took seeing their frightened eyes to know it was the right thing to do. She'd been scared before. That's how she ended up coming here, Rodney's threats. Pure fear.

But now, seeing them in the flesh, Molly and Joshua, the people she loved more than her own life, she didn't care what happened to her. Hopefully, she wasn't too late.

Joel took a couple of steps back towards the hallway.

"Wait, Joel, I'm warning you."

A couple more. "Kids, go into my room. Right now."

Rodney pushed Rachel forward, covered half the distance to Joel. "Listen to me!"

The blade definitely slicing her skin now.

Once the kids had shuffled down the hall, Joel turned and ran.

Rodney let Rachel go and ran after him.

Rachel fell to the floor. Screaming now, "*Leave them alone! You don't touch them!*"

"Don't move!" A voice from the open door. A police officer, pistol out, crouched. His partner right behind. Two young men in uniform, one black, one white. "Where is he? Where is he?" They moved into the living room. The white cop knelt, still alert, and checked on Eileen. He shouted back to his partner. "We need an ambulance!"

She was still alive.

Rachel pointed wildly towards the back of the house. "He's back there! My babies! He's got my babies!"

But she was cut off when Rodney came around the corner with a shotgun and unloaded on the black cop first, nearly point blank, then another shot at the white cop, who screamed. Rachel turned. The cop's gun arm had been reduced to raw ground sausage. He struggled to grab his pistol with the other arm and return fire, but Rodney had a bead on him.

Rachel had never seen what a twelve-gauge shotgun could do to a human head before. She'd seen bucks her uncle had brought home, but to watch the gun bark as the cop lost his face, as pieces of his skull and brains splattered across the entryway…

In all of the shouting and gunshots, they had missed the sirens. Here they came, wailing, out of sync. Rachel glanced outside the door as a whole squadron of police cars jumped the curb into the yard. Behind them on the street, more cop cars, an ambulance, and a Fire Rescue truck.

She shivered, mouth agape, turned back to Rodney, standing there with the shotgun slung over his shoulder, staring down at the first cop he'd killed.

Rachel scrambled to her feet and ran past Rodney. He reached out to grab her, but she slipped past, ran into the bedroom. She slammed the door and locked it, knowing it wouldn't stop him for long.

"Mommy!"

The kids, under the bed, wailing. Rachel ran over to them, got down on her knees, and held their hands.

"Stay under that bed. Don't come out until I say so."

Joel was lying face down beside his bed. His back a lake of blood from too many wounds to count. Rodney had left the knife dead center.

She covered her mouth with both hands. The kids had watched their father murder their great uncle. His dead eyes staring at them.

In Joel's closet, behind all the clothes and shoes, his guns. One was a thirty-aught-six like the one she'd tried to take out Charles Lott with, Rodney's dad's gun. But she had no time to take it from its bag, find the box of bullets, load it, and threaten her husband with it. She was no good with a handgun unless she was very close.

How close was very close?

She was shaken from her thoughts by the first kick at the door from Rodney. A loud *crack*. Another kick. More cracking.

*Very close.*

Rodney kicked harder and faster.

Splintering. The kids screamed for Mommy.

The handguns.

All of them in their cases, pristine.

She knew her uncle, though. A big heart, but a manly man. Old-fashioned.

Rachel scrambled over Joel's body as Rodney unloaded a shotgun shell into the door, shearing off the lock. Pulped wood flying, stinging Rachel's skin.

Joel's bedside table.

She opened the drawer.

A Glock nine, and of course the man had kept it loaded, even with kids in the house.

Rodney at the door, wide open now. "Rachel!"

She lifted the gun from the drawer, turned and fired.

The shots surprised her. She knew how to shoot rifles, but this didn't feel the same. The jump of the pistol in her hand, the empty shells flying back at her. She squinted. A hard blink for each shot.

*Keep squeezing, whatever you do.*

She didn't stop firing until the magazine was empty.

A burnt smell in the air. She opened her eyes. Gaping holes in the walls.

But Rodney was gone. He must've gotten out of the room. Rachel didn't know if she'd even hit him one time.

She was out of bullets.

Then, from right outside the door. "I thought you loved me, Rachel. Now watch what I'm going to have to do."

He stepped back into the room, nice and easy, staring his wife down with eyes she'd only seen in bad dreams. The shotgun in his right hand, slung low.

Molly and Joshua, loudly crying now.

Rachel started to say "In Jesus' name," but it got stuck in her throat.

Rodney eased the shotgun up to his shoulder.

# CHAPTER 42

This was the point of no return.

Rodney, breathing heavily, holding the shotgun up, ready to kill his own wife and kids.

It had all started with a murder he didn't commit.

Trying to get rid of the evidence, help out a friend.

If not for the girl.

If not for these fucking Elgins, all of them.

If he'd only stayed in the duck blind.

If he'd stayed at his dad's house rather than crash on Charles' couch.

He could play "if" all night.

If he'd never met Rachel.

If he'd never heard about Pentecost.

If he'd never felt the Holy Ghost down deep inside.

Now he had killed Rachel's aunt, her uncle, and two police officers.

It wasn't supposed to be this way.

Rachel had shrunk into the farthest corner. She slid to the ground. Her face resigned to her fate.

The kids, whimpering, calling for their mom.

Rodney took another step closer.

Yeah, there were sirens and more cops. Yeah, the whole street was flooded with the filth. Which was why he needed to do this now. Her. The kids. Himself. A proper ending.

It felt as if it wasn't even him holding the shotgun. Not his finger on the trigger. No, it was one of those spirits the pastor had gone on and on about. A demonic spirit. Pure evil, exactly as Rachel had said. Pushing and pushing and pushing, taking over the first chance it got.

They can only possess you if you want them to. You have to *invite* them in. You have to be open to it. Nothing so formal as saying, "I want you to possess me." Lots of little invitations, quiet, harmless, easy.

That's the only explanation for the man about to murder the woman he loved.

"I love you," he said.

Rachel lifted her face. Eyes open. "I don't believe you."

"I don't care."

All there was left to do was squeeze the trigger.

*Squeeze the —*

# CHAPTER 43

Lydia jumped the curb and the others did the same. She'd barely put it in park before Tara was out the door, shouting at Louis and Fabrice, the uniformed officers she'd posted across the street, already charging the front door of Eileen's house, not waiting on backup, not following the rules for a proper hostage negotiation.

There would be Hell to pay if this went worse than it already had.

She barely had time to register the neighbors who had already gathered on the front lawn in the half-a-minute the cops had been here. Older folks, an older neighborhood. Peaceful, she guessed, most of the time.

Before Tara could tell them to move, Fabrice's voice over the radio, "We need an ambulance!"

Followed by the first shotgun blast.

Tara ducked beside the car, right behind Lydia. She worked up a glimpse of the front door. There was Fabrice, on his knees, aiming his pistol towards someone –

Second shotgun blast.

Fabrice collapsed, screamed, scrambled.

Third shotgun blast.

Fabrice lost his head.

Broussard shouted over the car, "Jesus! What's going on in there?"

They all braced for another shot, but it didn't come. Lydia shouted into her radio, "Officer down! Officer down! Louis? How about you? Louis?"

Nothing.

SWAT wasn't on the scene yet. No one else was going in.

Tara and Lydia crouched, moved around the car to where Broussard had taken cover behind his car door.

Tara shouted over the sirens. "We don't have a clue who's in there."

"It would be huge fucking surprise if it's not one of them." He pointed to the driveway at an older Honda. "That's Rachel Goodfellow's car. She's here."

"Shit. The kids!"

Broussard tossed up his hands. "I don't want to think about it."

They peered into the open door of the house, where Eileen's body – Fabrice had said she needed an ambulance, hopefully not dead – was clearly visible past what was left of the young uniformed officer, one of the best in his class last year. This was supposed to be a babysitting gig, not open combat. Jesus, what were they thinking?

Her head snapped around when the muffled sound of another shotgun blast bled through the walls. A handgun next. A whole damn clip.

Fuck it. No more of this.

"Lydia, with me." Tara pulled her gun and started for the house before Broussard could stop her. But when she glanced back, he was following along, waving for another group of cops to close in.

In the door.

Sweep the room. Clear.

Lydia went left. Tara right. Broussard was behind her.

The hallway, leading to the bedrooms.

The door at the end. Splintered, hanging off its hinges.

Kids, banshee wails. But still alive.

Oh God.

Tara eased down the hall, careful now. Slow steps. Slow breathing.

A sliver of a man's back.

Another step.

The man began to lift his shotgun, aiming it at, what, the far corner?

Tara heard him say, "I love you."

Another voice, from the corner. Rachel? "I don't believe

you."

Tara extended her arms. Center mass.

The butcher said, "I don't care."

"Police! Drop it!"

Rodney spun, the shotgun spitting out fire, but into the window on the dresser. The glass exploded, flying into Tara's hair, her face, her eyes.

She and Broussard fired *One two three four five six seven eight nine*

Rodney, eyes black, let out a roar on his way down. Tara tripped trying to get out of his way, and Broussard caught her.

Over the ringing in her ears, she heard the kids crying. Molly and Joshua scuttled out from under the bed and ran to their mom, fell into her arms. Rachel wrapped them up and closed her eyes and began shouting in a language Tara didn't know.

Dropped her eyes to Rodney. She couldn't explain it, but she was suddenly cold. She could see her breath for a moment. Ran one hand up her arm. Goosebumps.

She blinked glass dust from her eyes, and turned to Rachel, rocking her children back and forth, still speaking in tongues.

Tara thought, *A 'thank you' would've been nice.*

Once outside, the car holding her up, Tara caught her breath. A sea of police cruisers and ambulances, as if every one of them on the entire coast was here, lights spinning. Seizure-inducing. She rubbed the back of her hand under her nose, but couldn't shake the smell of blood and cordite.

The EMTs gave Rachel's aunt CPR all the way from front door to back of the ambulance, shouting as if it might keep her soul inside her body long enough to get her to surgery.

Louis and Fabrice and the uncle were well past shouting. All gone.

Tara glanced at a second ambulance where Rachel sat, blank, a child on each side hugged tightly under her wings. One day Tara would have to ask her what she was thinking, bringing Rodney here. How close he came to killing their children.

They'd tagged Charles Lott as the killer all this time. Rodney had no history of violence. But a few days on the run was all it took to unleash the beast. What she felt back there, the cold, reminded her Dante's final circle of Hell was not fire, but ice. It was as if the gateway opened beneath Rodney as he fell, and kept on falling.

Tara didn't believe in such crap. She and Broussard had cut out the man's lights. Nothing spiritual about it. She hoped he hurt like a motherfucker before dying.

On the edge of her vision, Captain Sarasota approached Rachel, reached out, touched her arm, and leaned closer. Tara imagined him saying, "You're safe now. We have everything under control."

But whatever he'd said led her to a low moan, rising in volume and pitch until she threw her head back and screamed at the moon. No, he must've told her something awful.

Right, Tara thought. She hadn't been told about her dad yet, either.

Where the hell was Hosea? He should've been here by now. Maybe Tara needed one of those cell phones after all. She couldn't very well go tromping back into the house, the crime scene, to call him, could she?

The Captain stepped away from Rachel, Lydia taking over as grief counselor for the moment, and started towards Tara. This was it. She took some steady breaths to calm her nerves. He was going to read her the riot act for disobeying procedure. For putting more lives at risk than necessary. For being a goddamned fool.

She bet Broussard would simply get a "good job" and a pat on the back.

Not the time, she thought. Tamp it down.

Standing before her, the Captain, his face ashen, told her in the softest voice, "Um, there's been a nine one one call."

Tara blinked. "Yeah?"

"It's Hosea."

# CHAPTER 44

Dying was strange. Your wildest dreams swirling with your recent memories. It was confusing. People you knew turned into different people you knew, on and on. Places changed often. Time was pointless. Nothing felt right to the touch. It was neither Heaven nor Hell. It was chaos.

Until the voices began to make some sort of sense. His own breath was amplified. He felt a heart beating inside of him.

Hosea opened his eyes.

He was aware of the oxygen tube, the IVs in his arms, the hospital bed. A very dry mouth.

Not dead after all.

He turned his head – not far. Too much pain. Took in the machines at his bedside, the black and silent TV on the wall. More bandages on his chest and stomach, more around what used to be his hand. His brother Glen sat in a bedside chair, reading the local paper.

"Glen."

The preacher lifted his chin, grinned. "They told me you'd be coming around soon. Glad I waited. How do you feel?"

"I don't know." Hard to speak, out of practice. "How long?"

Glen turned away. "Almost a week. It's better than we hoped. You fought hard."

"I just laid here."

"Then the Lord fought hard for you. Lots of prayers, I'm saying."

Two minutes out a coma, and Hosea was already tired of Glen. Nothing had changed, apparently.

"Charles Lott? We got him, right?"

"You did, yeah, you did. He's passed on."

Good.

"And Rodney?"

"Seriously, let's slow down. I'll get the nurse and give Rachel a call. I took over from her. She's been here so much for both you and Eileen. Hasn't gone back to work since."

"Eileen?"

Glen pushed himself from the chair with a little grunt. He was dressed immaculately as usual – a full navy blue suit and patterned tie, a check print shirt. Probably all Perry Ellis. He slid his hands into his pockets and turned towards the windows. Outside, some dark-gray thunderclouds gave an electric quality to the air. Must be afternoon, when the storms brewed down south in the summer.

Glen explained what happened: Rodney forcing Rachel to take him to the kids at Eileen and Joel's house. Him nearly killing Eileen, stabbing Joel to death, coming within a hair of shooting Rachel and the kids if not for Tara and Broussard taking him out.

Hosea felt sick to his stomach.

"You helped Rodney hide. I found how you got into the attic."

"Do you want me to get you some juice? Ice chips?"

"Why didn't you turn him in?"

"I need to tell you about Dad."

"I watched him die, Glen." Hosea felt weak. "I watched Charles kill him, and then he tried to kill me. I thought he'd gone and done it, too."

Glen stepped over to the foot of the bed. "I'm sorry."

"What for?"

"I knew you were getting close to finding Rodney, so I told Rachel how to get to him. I told her to take him somewhere else. I had no idea he was...I thought I was doing God's will. Thought Rodney could still be redeemed. I wanted him to make amends with the Lord before turning himself in. I guess I was wrong. I got it all wrong."

"Yeah, you did,"

Glen nodded absently. Sniffed. "I almost lost you. I almost lost Rachel."

"But you gained the church." Hosea couldn't help himself. "No fair."

"All yours now."

"I'm trying to, you know, apologize here. I'm trying to make things better between us."

"Okay."

"Okay?"

Hosea let out a breath, already exhausted. "Ice chips."

The doctor went over the injuries. Rachel stood in the corner while he did. It was a long list.

GSW to the face, ear. They could do a little plastic surgery, build him a new ear, one he might not hear out of, but at least it would hold his sunglasses up. Skin grafts to his face. Eventually, it would heal close to normal.

GSW to the torso. Broken ribs, deflated lung, other organ damage. He would never have full lung capacity. Still, he was very lucky the bullet didn't do as much damage as it should've.

In the corner, Rachel said, "A miracle."

Sure, Hosea thought. Waste a miracle on me, Lord.

The list continued.

His hand. They'd only been able to save his thumb and his pinkie finger.

Plus, he had caught an infection after one of his surgeries, and was still on antibiotics to fight it. He would still need to stay in the hospital for weeks.

When they left, Rachel drifted over to his bedside. Took his good hand in hers.

"Hey."

She'd aged a lot these past few months. Thinner, too. There was a fresh streak of white in her hair. The jewelry was gone, the make-up was gone. She was dressed modestly in a blouse and long denim skirt. It told Hosea everything he needed to know how this had affected her. As the old hymn went, *Taking shelter in the arms of God.*

243

"How are you doing?"

Hosea cleared his throat. "Better."

"It was touch and go. You have no idea how many people were praying for you."

"Appreciate it. Tell them I said thanks."

"I hope soon you can tell them yourself."

At least she was sincere. The weight of the deaths showed on her. Glen treated mourning as any other ritual. It was more important how he appeared to be doing it than actually doing it.

Still, Hosea had no idea what was going on in the deepest part of Glen's mind. No one could. It was possible that late into the night, alone in bed, he was tortured for what he'd done. But if that was the case, it never surfaced.

Hosea said, "How about you? How are you and the kids?"

Rachel crossed her arms, hugged herself. "Some days are better than others. We need a new place to stay. Or, you know, *want* one. I can't live in that house, not anymore. Too many bad spirits hanging around."

"You can get rid of those, can't you?"

"I'd rather have a clean start."

Rachel had been picking at her cuticles, now red and puffy. She couldn't stand still, constantly swaying or tapping or silently moving her lips to a song only she could hear. Whatever it took to keep the memories away.

"You can stay at my place while I'm here. I have the pullout bed for the kids." Thinking of home reminded him. "Where's Pecan?"

A smile. "She's with me. I can tell she misses you."

"Thank you."

"Where's your key?" She stepped towards the closet. "In your things?"

It took Tara a little longer to come by once he'd woken up. Seeing her partner in the coma had overwhelmed her. They should have been working together the whole time, then this wouldn't have happened. The Captain had made a mistake splitting them up.

She stepped into the room full of energy, wearing her boating clothes again. Shorts and sandals and a thin shirt.

"Any excuse to get out of a day's work, Hosea?"

"Do you think I'd be caught dead dressed like this?"

It was obvious his appearance bothered her – the scars, the stitches, the bandages, the hand – but she darted her eyes away often, fighting to remember the handsome devil he'd been before. For a white boy, anyway.

Tara sat in the bedside chair and pulled it closer. "Tell me. When you were with Charles Lott, did you think he was, I don't know, *evil?* Real evil?"

"What do you mean?"

"Were you cold around him?"

"I don't remember." He didn't, but he knew what she was getting at. "Rodney?"

"The moment he died, it was weird. I got goosebumps. I saw my own breath. It was June, for fuck's sake."

"Maybe they had the A/C on."

She sat back. "Hey, don't play with me. Not after I've seen what you folks believe. I was mighty skeptical before, but now, I'm saying it was weird. His eyes, I'd swear, those weren't people eyes. Snake eyes, cat eyes. Creepy."

They let the moment ride. A swell of silence.

Hosea leaned on his elbow, faced Tara. "As long as I've known Rodney I got a bad vibe off of him, but it was the same way we get bad vibes off people all the time at work. Or in everyday life. I thought he was smarmy, full of himself, and probably hiding a lot of his past, but I can't say I felt he was evil when I knew him."

"Mm hm." Tara pursed her lips. Then said, "Weird."

"If you're saying he was possessed, I mean. We do evil. The only way to tell is by our actions Don't you think any one of us can be evil if it comes down to it? Depending on the situation?"

"Hey now, speak for yourself."

"I mean, in order to survive. Is that evil, or is it only

human?"

Tara laughed nervously. "You're getting a little deep for me. I don't mind the dancing and shouting, but good Lord, Hosea."

Later, on her way out the door, she said, "When are you coming back to work? I kind of like being on my own, car all to myself. I pick the radio station, I pick my own lunch."

Hosea tried to smile but it hurt. It would hurt for a long time. "Spoiled rotten."

"Please come back to us."

But the look on her face told them both she understood: Hosea wasn't coming back. He was done being a cop.

# CHAPTER 45

Sunday morning.

Glen had already been pastor for a few months when Hosea hobbled back into church. Still getting used to his hand. His face was a bag of broken glass. He walked with a cane, easily winded.

Hosea took his usual seat on the next-to-last row, hoping to keep out of sight, but most of the congregation came back to shake his good hand and wish him well, tell him how it was all a miracle and they had been praying for him, as if they wanted credit for it. No, he wasn't being fair to them. Good intentions go a long way. Hosea kept a grin on his face, treated each and every one of them like a dear friend as Glen called the song leader and choir up to the platform to begin the service.

*Victory in Jesus, my Savior forever.*
*He sought me, and He bought me, with His redeeming blood.*

Blood. Always about the blood. Hosea had had enough with blood. While the rest of the people stood and clapped their hands and sang along, Hosea sat down after the first verse and watched the congregation. It would never feel the same to him, obviously. His dad wasn't on the pulpit in his high-backed mint-green upholstered chair. Every inch of the place had been searched and prodded by his police colleagues. An invasion, like in wartime. A sacred place losing its mystery. Its dignity. Hosea wondered if Glen felt the same.

Nobody else did, it seemed. The harmony was joyful, boisterous. After having mourned for so long, they were beginning to bloom.

The songs changed up every couple of verses, even though they were all in the same key.

*I've got that Holy Ghost and fire, shut up in my bones!*

The autumn sun filtered through the green glass windows. The pews, while not full, sat a good many people, more than Hosea had remembered from the last years of his dad's tenure here. Glen had been out working the streets, hunting for new converts and trying to bring some on-the-fence members back into the fold.

Look at him up there. Senatorial, almost. Back straight, a bounce in his step. In one hand he held their father's shekere, shaking it in time to the music while singing a line, then shouting to the crowd, "Come on, louder! This is your salvation you're singing about!"

As if he'd never hidden Rodney Goodfellow from the law. As if he'd never made any mistakes.

Among those standing at the front of the platform, losing themselves in worship more than the people in the pews, was Rachel. Molly and Joshua had been sent to their Sunday School classes, which allowed their mom to kick off her shoes and leap in place, waving her hands up and down, up and down. Eyes shut tight, her voice lost amongst the choir.

Rachel had refused therapy, instead hoping to deal with her emotions by embracing the church. It meant, more than anyone else, Glen was her confessor, her guide, her shepherd. Hosea didn't know how long this phase would last, but he guessed not forever. With the trauma they'd shared, there was no cure-all, no matter what the Pentecostals had to say about it.

Eileen was standing right beside Rachel, clapping her hands, swaying. She had lost a lot of weight while recovering from the wounds to her intestines and the blood loss. She wore one of her old dresses – some of the ladies in the church volunteered to take them in but it was still much too big for her new frame. Hosea had grown up thinking of her as a strong, imposing woman, someone he had to literally look up to for most of his life. Now smaller, weaker, lonely without

Joel, what could Hosea say? It was a profound change.

This sort of violence should not have touched them at all. They should have been left alone to enjoy their lives and never cross paths with Rodney Goodfellow. But the world didn't work the way we wished it would. Violence didn't punch up, but down.

Standing in the third row of the choir loft between two other women was Dawn Hollingsworth. She hadn't come to welcome him back. She refused to even glance at him. When Dawn came to see him in the hospital, holding his hand like a normal girlfriend might, Hosea pulled away. He gave her more of a cold shoulder than she deserved, but he didn't know how to tell her she wasn't in his thoughts while he fought with Charles. Lying on the ground, thinking this was the end for him, he didn't call her name. Lying in a coma for a week, he didn't dream about her. She never needed to know.

Besides, he was pretty monstrous now, with the face and all, and would be for a long time. A well-dressed monster, fine, but still. She deserved better. Sure, they'd *liked* each other, but that's all it had been. Time to let it go.

Hosea watched her sing. Kind eyes, cute nose, generous. None of this horror show he'd been living through had touched her, and it never would.

As the singing came to a close and the new assistant pastor, someone Glen hired away from a church in Mobile, stepped to the pulpit to deliver the announcements and prayer requests, Hosea set his sights on Glen.

Glen glared back.

No love lost between them, but Hosea remembered what Glen had said in the hospital: *I almost lost you. I almost lost Rachel.* Did he mean it? Did he *feel* it? Or was it a different kind of loss? A three-fingers-on-one-hand loss? A loss you had to live with, carry on, although it wasn't a hole in your heart?

They held the stare a long time.

Glen blinked when his assistant began asking the congregation for additional requests or testimony, went back to watching his flock.

Hosea took this as his cue to leave.

Outside, you wouldn't know it was nearly November. It was sunny, hot, and the trees were still mostly green. Hosea hated walking with the cane. It made him ache all over, his steps awkward.

He eventually made it to his car. He wished he could get rid of this car. All he could think about when he was driving was Charles Lott's gun, his dull voice, his threats. But Hosea couldn't afford a new one. He had quit his job. They would probably pay him a little disability at some point, but he would eventually have to find some sort of work.

But not here. Not in Mississippi.

He was no preacher. He was no longer a cop. He didn't know what he was.

Except a man searching for answers.

He opened his car door and eased his tired body inside. In the passenger seat was Pecan, curled up and sleeping. In the trunk, most of the essentials he would need to start over someplace new. He'd sneaked over to the apartment and packed while Rachel was out the night before, things she wouldn't notice were missing. Once he settled on a new town, he might come back and get the rest.

He wanted to be hundreds of miles away before telling his brother and sister he was leaving.

Hosea cranked the car. Pecan stirred, readjusted herself.

"Ready for this girl?"

Pecan farted.

If the Pentecostals were right and something truly terrible or wonderful was supposed to happen at the millennium, then he only had a few short years to find what he was looking for. But he lived with the hope Y2K would come and go like any any other day. Yawn.

Praise God.

*Fuck God.*

He shrugged.

Hosea didn't know where he would be sleeping that night,

but whatever city, town, barn, or ditch it may be, it was ahead of him, not in the rearview mirror.

He pulled out of the church parking lot, turned towards Highway 90, and was gone.

## THE END

About the author

Anthony Neil Smith is the author of numerous crime novels, including the Billy Lafitte series (including YELLOW MEDICINE and HOGDOGGIN'), award-winning ALL THE YOUNG WARRIORS, plus CASTLE DANGER: WOMAN ON ICE, WORM, THE CYCLIST, and more.

He is an English Professor at Southwest Minnesota State University.

He likes cheap red wine and Mexcian food.

Special thanks to:

Chris Black, our fearless leader and editor at Fahrenheit 13, who gets what I'm doing and then makes it better. Thanks for the support.

Chris McVeigh, the "Boss" at Fahrenheit Press, from whom I learn more every day. Especially "Don't feed the trolls."

Victor Gischler, much-needed confidant, who booked an AirB&B in Cleveland so we could have the Box of Wine Writers Conference (Version 2), where a big chunk of this book was written.

Sean Doolittle, much-needed confidant number two, who has kept my temperature down in these son-of-a-bastard cancel culture times we live in.

Brandy Smith, much-needed beloved wife, who makes every word I write worth it. But she still hates how all my books end.

**Know Me From Smoke by Matt Phillips**

Stella Radney, longtime lounge singer, still has a bullet lodged in her hip from the night when a rain of gunfire killed her husband. That was twenty years ago and it's a surprise when the unsolved murder is reopened after the district attorney discovers new evidence.

Royal Atkins is a convicted killer who just got out of prison on a legal technicality. At first, he's thinking he'll play it straight. Doesn't take long before that plan turns to smoke—was it ever really an option?

When Stella and Royal meet one night, they're drawn to each other. But Royal has a secret. How long before Stella discovers that the man she's falling for isn't who he seems?

*"A beautifully written, brutal & brilliant slice of hardboiled crime fiction. A Knockout."*

**Pure by Jo Perry**

Caught in a pincer movement between the sudden death of Evelyn (her favourite aunt) and the Corona virus, Ascher Lieb finds herself unexpectedly locked down in her aunt's retirement community with only Evelyn's grief-stricken dog Freddie for company.

As the world tumbles down into a pandemic shaped rabbit-hole Ascher is wracked with guilt that her aunt was buried without the Jewish burial rights of purification. In order to atone for this dereliction of familial duty, Ascher – in her own words 'a profane, unobservant, atheist Jew, frequent liar and grieving loser' –volunteers to become the newest member of Valley Haverim Chevra Kadisha, a Jewish burial society on-call twenty-four-seven during lockdown and performing Mitzvot at no cost to the bereaved.

What follows is a journey through the insanity of lockdown in Los Angeles as Ascher attempts to bring peace to a troubled soul, and perhaps in the end redemption for herself.

*"The mystery will get under your skin, for sure, but the humanity of this novel will resonate far beyond the page."*

## Turbulence by Paul Gadsby

Accidentally shooting a civilian during a bungled heist was bad enough, but when they upset the local criminal kingpin as a result of their ineptitude, newbie bank-robbers Birty & Cole figured the best thing to do was split town, and fast.

Smart plan - at least it was till everything went south, again.

An armed robbery is an unusual event which affects the lives of everyone touched by it and in this tour de force Paul Gadsby traces the lines of influence and connection that run through the lives of the people unwittingly caught up in Birty & Cole's heist.

The story is woven through the lives and perspectives of many characters - everyone from the bank staff and customers who witnessed the raid, to the journalists covering the case.

This remarkable novel from Brit-Noir legend Paul Gadsby ignores the usual crime fiction tropes of 'robbers on the run' and instead becomes a vivid study into cause & effect that will keep you gripped until the very last ripple fades away.

*"Gadsby has really come into his own with this book - the writing & the storytelling are simply superb."*

Made in United States
North Haven, CT
13 October 2021

10318333R00152